Joe Glick

About the Author

Don Robertson published eighteen books in his lifetime, including two others that featured Morris Bird III: *The Sum and Total
of Now* (1966) and *The Greatest Thing That Almost Happened*
(1970), which was made into a movie starring James Earl Jones
and Jimmie Walker. He is also the author of the highly acclaimed
novel *Praise the Human Season*. Robertson was born in 1929
and spent much of his life working at Cleveland newspapers.
Stephen King counts him as one of his greatest influences and
published Robertson's book *The Ideal, Genuine Man* in 1987.
Robertson died in 1999.

THE
GREATEST
THiNG
SiNCE
SLiCED
BREAD

THE
GREATEST
THING
SINCE
SLICED
BREAD

A Novel

DON ROBERTSON

HARPER

NEW YORK · LONDON · TORONTO · SYDNEY

HARPER

First published in 1965 by G. P. Putnam's Sons.

FIRST HARPER PAPERBACK PUBLISHED 2008.

Designed by Jamie Kerner

Library of Congress Cataloging-in-Publication Data is available upon request.

ISBN 978-0-06-145296-3

08 09 10 11 12   OV/RRD   10 9 8 7 6 5 4 3 2 1

For the late Josephine W. Robertson and Carl T. Robertson

I would rather sit on a pumpkin and have it all to myself,
than to be crowded on a velvet cushion.
If a man does not keep pace with his companions,
perhaps it is because he hears a different drummer.
Let him step to the music which he hears,
however measured or far away.

HENRY DAVID THOREAU

I propose to fight it out on this line if it takes all summer.

ULYSSES SIMPSON GRANT

If I ever said, in grief or pride,
I tired of honest things, I lied.

EDNA ST. VINCENT MILLAY

Life is just one damned thing after another.

FRANK WARD O'MALLEY

THE
GREATEST
THiNG
SiNCE
SLiCED
BREAD

The legless man was wise enough to understand that heroes can be found in the damnedest places. Which was why he didn't hesitate when he called the boy the greatest thing since sliced bread.

For the boy, though, the big thing wasn't his bravery. As far as he was concerned, too much fuss was made over it.

For the boy, the big thing happened before the explosion. It happened at the moment he saw his old buddy Stanley Chaloupka. The exact moment.

Why? Because it meant that the boy had accomplished what he had set out to do.

Which helped him come to terms with the things he felt badly about. Stupidities, for instance. Betrayals.

The explosion was just something that happened to happen.

Funny about that explosion. It really never should have happened to happen. Those gas tanks were the safest in the world. Everyone said so.

They were built in 1941 by the East Ohio Gas Co., supplier of natural heating gas to all of the great city of Cleveland and northeastern Ohio. There were four of them, and they were designed for the storage of natural gas in its liquefied state. Three of them were spherical. The fourth was tubular and about as large as the other three combined. Their capacity was 400,000 feet of liquefied gas, which was the equivalent of 240,000,000 feet of gas in its natural state. The gas company's publicists were proud of these new tanks, and photographs of them were run in all the newspapers.

A great deal of money was spent in assuring people there was no danger.

The campaign was successful. Those gas tanks were the safest in the world. Everyone said so.

But then one day the explosion happened to happen.

A lot of people were killed. The boy encountered the legless man. And the poor burnt lady. And the pretty Red Cross lady. And many other people.

When the day was finished, two things had happened to the boy.

First, and most important, he had accomplished—in seeing his old buddy Stanley Chaloupka—what he had set out to do.

Second, he had behaved in such a way that the legless man had called him, for whatever it was worth, the greatest thing since sliced bread.

THE YEAR WAS 1944, and the month was October, and Morris Bird III was nine years old, and he was in love with Veronica Lake. He also was in love with a girl named Suzanne Wysocki (her hair was also long and blond, and sometimes it fell over her left eye too), but his love for Veronica Lake was much stronger. Suzanne Wysocki was only eight, and he saw her just about every day. These things made a difference.

And anyway, sometimes Suzanne Wysocki was an awful pill.

HIS HOUSE WAS NEXTDOOR to Suzanne Wysocki's. Sometimes the two of them sat on her front steps and talked about things. Sometimes they talked about the war (her two brothers, Frank and Ralph, were with the Marines in the Pacific), and sometimes they talked about movies they had seen (her favorite star was Bette Davis), but most of the time—because of Suzanne Wysocki's solemnity—their conversations were serious and uncomfortable.

"You ever think of scary things?" she asked him one day.

"What kind of things?"

"Scary things, dumbhead. Like having babies."

"I'm not going to have any babies," said Morris Bird III.

Suzanne Wysocki made a fist. "Now be *serious.*"

Quickly he nodded. He didn't like it when people were angry with him. "All right," he said.

She opened the hand. "Good," she said. She looked at the hand and then she looked at the trees. "Uh, what I mean is—you know, being alone and having no one to run to, doing things on your own, growing up, getting married, having babies, getting old, dying—"

"Dying? Like Mr. Pisani?"

"Yes."

"I don't think much about *dying*."

"You should," said Suzanne.

"Why?"

"Because it's going to happen to you."

"Oh," said Morris Bird III. "Big deal."

"You know what my brother Frank used to say?"

"No."

"When I was little, sometimes I'd cry. You know. Over nothing. The way little kids do. If Frank was around, he'd come to me, and you know what he'd say? He'd grin at me and he'd say: Now now, honey, don't get so worked up. It's all going to be over soon enough. Just think, you're twenty-four hours closer to dying than you were at this time yesterday."

Morris Bird III looked down the street at an old Dodge with a B sticker. It was parked in front of the dying Mr. Pisani's house. He said nothing. There was nothing he knew to say. Not to something like *that*.

Suzanne finally spoke up. "Well?"

"So big deal," said Morris Bird III.

"God is supposed to take you. You believe that?"

"I don't know. I guess so."

"We're all His Lambs."

"Baa. Baa," said Morris Bird III.

Suzanne made a clucking noise. "You're not being *serious*."

Again Morris Bird III was silent. He wished he didn't love her. Then he would have been able to give her a good one. Preferably across the mouth. He looked at the sky and he saw a lot of nothing. The things he wanted to work in his mind were sleds and batting averages and leather caps that made you look like an aviator. So some day he would die. So big fat deal.

Suzanne stood up. "You *poop*," she said. She clomped into her house.

Morris Bird III said nothing. His love for Suzanne Wysocki was some love. If he'd known how to get rid of it, he wouldn't have wasted a second.

● ● ●

HIS LOVE FOR VERONICA LAKE was so much better it wasn't even funny. For one thing, he had seen Veronica Lake cry. He had never seen Suzanne Wysocki cry. Veronica Lake had revealed herself to him. Suzanne Wysocki had never revealed a thing—except, of course, her interest in babies and death and all that sort of beeswax.

He had a picture of Veronica Lake. He kept it hidden in the copy of *The Kid from Tompkinsville* that he had crooked from the Hough-Crawford branch library. This was a book about baseball, and its author, John R. Tunis, was Morris Bird III's favorite author in the whole world.

He had also crooked the picture. From Woolworth's. The price of the picture had been 15 cents. It had a thin cardboard frame. She was wearing a pale blue dress, and she was smiling, and written across her chest were the words: *Sincerely, Veronica Lake.*

Every night he kissed the picture, and did he ever hate Alan Ladd.

THE YEAR WAS 1944, and the month was October, and Morris Bird III was in the 4A at the Hough Elementary School. His teacher's name was Mrs. Dallas, and most of the time she smelled good. He probably loved her too, but he didn't want to admit it. He didn't think it was right to love too many people and thus spread yourself too thinly.

The name of the city was Cleveland, and there was a war being fought, and Cleveland was a busy and smoky place, what with all the War Plants. This was some war. It had to do with President Roosevelt. It had to do with blue stars and gold stars hanging in windows. It had to do with a place called Normandy and a general whose name was Eisenhower. It had to do with the filthy Nazis and the rotten little Japs. It had to do with gasoline rationing and the respect you had for people who rated C stickers on their windshields. These were very important people. As C sticker people, they were allowed to buy more gasoline than anyone. Next in line were the B sticker people, who were sort of in the middle. Last in line were the A sticker people. Almost everyone Morris Bird III knew was an A sticker person. There were three or four B sticker people on Morris Bird III's street, but there was just one C sticker person—Suzanne's father. This was because of Mr. Wysocki's job. He had a very important job. He was an auditor for the Internal Revenue.

Morris Bird III thought he understood something of what the war was all about, but he wasn't altogether sure.

THE NAME OF MORRIS BIRD III's street was Edmunds Avenue. It extended east from East 90th Street to Ansel Road, a distance of two blocks, or "squares," as his grandmother called them. The houses that lined Edmunds Avenue were made of wood and brick, and they were old. After a rain, they smelled good, especially if it was a spring or summer rain. This was very important to Morris Bird III, since he had a very sensitive nose. His grandmother called his nose his Smeller. He did not know why he had such a sensitive Smeller, but there it was, and you had to face facts.

Morris Bird III lived in one of the wooden houses that lined Edmunds Avenue. He lived with his father, whose name was Morris Bird II, and his mother, whose name was Alice Bird, and his sister, whose name was Sandra Bird (she was six), and his grandmother, whose name was Mrs. Elizabeth Jones.

His father was an announcer for Radio Station WCCC, which called itself The Voice of Cleveland & Northeastern Ohio. He had only one foot. One real foot. He had a wooden thing that served him as a second foot, but in Morris Bird III's mind it didn't really count for an awful lot. He had lost his real second foot in an automobile accident in 1927—or so Morris Bird III had been told by his grandmother. His father had never discussed it.

Morris Bird II was very tall. His face was narrow, and he always frowned when he spoke. Worked his lips too. He seldom laughed, but when he did his eyes vanished. When standing or walking, he leaned to the side that had the good foot. The best thing about him was his voice. It was immense and splendid, and it made Morris Bird III goosebumpy and short of breath.

Bing
Bang
BONG

went the chimes, and then came the voice of Morris Bird II, resonant and symphonic: *"This is WCCC, Cleveland, The Voice of Cleveland & Northeastern Ohio. The time is now 3:30 and 14 seconds. Please stay tuned for more Midday Reveries . . ."*

No matter how many times Morris Bird III heard his father's voice over the radio, he always sucked in his breath at the terrific sound of it. And naturally, whenever his father spoke to him, it was The Voice of Cleveland & Northeastern Ohio that he heard.

Which scared him. And made him very proud.

His mother, on the other hand, didn't have much of a voice at all. She was small and thin, and her voice sounded like new chalk on a blackboard. She collected china owls. People said she had more china owls than Mr. Carter had pills. There were even china owls in the bathroom.

What with the war and all, Morris Bird III's mother had a fulltime job these days. She was secretary to Mr. Thomas D. Beeler, office manager for the Cleveland Bolt & Screw Co., and sometimes she worked six days a week. She liked to say that she didn't know if the time and a half for Saturdays was worth all the effort and strain, but she always added quickly that now was the time for the making of money. You have to get it, she said, when the getting's good. This war won't last forever, and maybe when it's over there'll be a depression. If that happens, we'll be needing the Extra. It's always good to have the Extra.

SANDRA, MORRIS BIRD III'S sister, bawled a lot. But she was only six, and allowances had to be made. Or so he had been told.

AH, BUT THAT WASN'T fair. There were allowances he had to make for *himself*, weren't there? He was uncomfortable with his allowances. It wasn't much fun to know you weren't perfect. But what was he supposed to do? There wasn't much he *could* do—except make allowances.

In his nine years, he had done all sorts of bad and stupid things. If he'd not made the allowances, he'd have gone crazy. Not that the allowances did away with the pain of Conscience, but at least they helped him somewhere in the region of his mind. This was better than nothing.

The worst thing he had ever done had involved a great brutal loudmouthed boy named Logan MacMurray. He had betrayed Logan MacMurray because of a salami sandwich. It had happened long enough ago so that now he could make allowances for it—but the pain was still there. Sometimes it interfered with his breath. Sometimes at night in bed he was forced to make faces and bite his pillow.

MAYBE IT WOULDN'T HAVE been so awful if only Logan MacMurray had shouted No! No! I am innocent!

But Logan MacMurray had done no such thing. Logan MacMurray had only snarled. Logan MacMurray had simply stood his ground. Logan MacMurray had been very brave.

Morris Bird III often wondered what ever had become of old Logan MacMurray.

AS FOR STUPID THINGS, Morris Bird III was a champion. The worst of them had to do with the speedometer he'd once thought he had in his belly.

He got the idea when he was five. It wasn't until he was eight that he disabused himself of it.

The idea went like this:

Automobiles had speedometers that showed you (a) how fast they were going, and (b) how many miles they had traveled. It was the (b) part that worked itself into Morris Bird III's mind. Shortly after his fifth birthday, he got to believing that there was a large black

5

deep inside his belly. On his sixth birthday, he could have sworn he felt a small clicking sound as the

5

slid up and out of sight and was replaced by a

6

● ● ●

AND THEN THERE WAS the time—in 1940, when he was just five—he disgraced himself in Loew's Stillman Theater.

He and his mother had gone there one Saturday afternoon to see *Gone With the Wind*. About the time Atlanta was being burned, his stomach started to feel funny. He swallowed hard, burped a couple of times, but the funny feeling did not go away.

"Sh," said his mother, nudging him.

"Woop," said Morris Bird III. He tried to get up and run out of the auditorium, but then he was vomiting.

"You," said his mother. *"You."* She took his hand and led him up the aisle and into the lobby. He vomited just about all the way. Behind him, the flames made loud crackling noises as they ate up Atlanta. To either side of him, patrons drew in their breath and put their hands over their noses. "Ugh," said somebody, and naturally by that time Morris Bird III was weeping.

He fainted in the lobby. A little later he was in an ambulance, and he was holding his mother's hand, and she didn't say a word, and then a big blond man was smiling at him, and then a big black thing came down over his face. A big blond man and a big black thing: they both were scary, and Morris Bird III supposed he probably was going to die.

When he came out of it, the big blond man was grinning at him. "Ah," said the big blond man, "Morris old buddy, you hanging in there?"

"What?"

"Uh, how you feel?"

"Prickly . . . who're you?"

"Just a pal. A little while ago we took out your appendix."

"Huh?"

"Your appendix. Don't worry about it. It's very unimportant. You say you feel prickly?"

"Yes."

"Sort of goosebumpy, like when it's cold?"

"Yes."

"I did a very good job, if I do say so myself. On the appendix, I mean."

"Thank you."

"You're very kind."

Morris Bird III began to cry.

"Hey now, pal," said the big blond man.

"I . . . upchucked. Mamma said sh, but I upchucked. . . ."

"That doesn't matter. You couldn't help it."

"But she got mad. . . ."

"That was just because she was worried," said the big blond man. Gently he cuffed one of Morris Bird III's arms. His grin widened. "The important thing is that we got out the old appendix. You say you feel goosebumpy? Good. That's the way you ought to feel." He held out his right hand. "Morris old buddy, I'm Dr. McCluskey."

Morris Bird III shook hands with the doctor. He blinked, sucked the sniffles out of his nose.

"Your mother and father are here to see you," said Dr. McCluskey.

"Me?"

"Yes."

"But I upchucked."

Dr. McCluskey laughed, then went and fetched Morris Bird III's mother and father. The mother didn't say a word about the upchucking. It was a good three or four weeks before anyone again told him sh. Two of those weeks were spent in the hospital, and every evening Morris Bird III's father visited him and read him the funnies. It was good hearing the funnies read by someone who had such a splendid voice. Ordinarily, his father didn't read him the funnies. If he wanted the funnies read to him, he had to go next door to Mrs. Wysocki. But everything was different in the hospital. His mother was forever smiling, and his father even read him the baseball scores. (As for the funnies, his father didn't miss a one—not even Little Orphan Annie, where people had no eyeballs and were forever doing things that weren't funny and that Morris Bird III couldn't understand.) One day his mother brought him a little game that had to do with a clown and five little balls. They were under glass. The clown had holes in his hands, holes in his feet and a hole in his stomach. The object of the game was to get all the balls to roll into all the holes. It was very difficult. It made Morris Bird III frown and hold his breath and bite his tongue, and he was lucky if he got the five balls in the five holes once every two days. But it did help pass the time, and in that hospital there was more time than anything else. He never did get used to the smell. He wondered if maybe the smell was a punishment. The burning of Atlanta had been very exciting, and he should have been more considerate. He supposed his mother believed he'd upchucked deliberately. He worked these thoughts around his mind for all of the two weeks. He was in a ward full of children. He allowed them to play with his game of clown and holes and balls and his set of crayons and the Popeye coloring book his father had brought him. He told himself that maybe if he were nice to *them* he could start to make better the awful thing he had done to his mother. He never did see the rest of *Gone With the Wind*, and he was always uncomfortable at Clark Gable movies. He was unable to look the man straight in the eye.

IF *ONLY* LOGAN MACMURRAY had shouted No! No! I am innocent!

But Logan MacMurray had been too brave. Which meant that the salami sandwich cowardice was the worst thing Morris Bird III had ever allowed to have happen to himself. It made the speedometer and the upchucking seem like nothing. It made him bite his pillow. It made his insides feel like old stale oatmeal.

He knew of no way to get rid of the hurt.

The salami sandwich incident took place in October of 1942, when Morris Bird III was seven.

Logan MacMurray was in the 6A. He had been in the 6A for quite some time. He was fifteen years old, and he was enormous, and some of the real little kids thought he was a member of the janitorial staff.

The politest thing you could say about him was that he smoked cigarettes. He had been smoking them for a long time. His teeth weren't even yellow anymore; they were green. He was wider and heavier and taller than God. He had been attending the Hough Elementary School for nine years. His face was quite red, and he had his hair cut about once every six years, and he liked to disrupt games and break things. There were three boys who hung around with him. They all were in the *tenth grade* for crying out loud, but they were in great awe of Logan MacMurray, and he had taught them to call him their Imperial Master. No one was permitted to call him Logan.

The thing to do when you were around him was be inconspicuous.

The salami sandwich incident began with a young woman named June Weed. In October of 1942, Morris Bird III's mother had been working at the Cleveland Bolt & Screw Co. for about eight months. She'd hired this June Weed to take care of Sandra and feed Morris Bird III his lunch when he came home from school. June Weed worked Mondays through Saturdays, with Wednesday afternoons off. On those Wednesday afternoons, Sandra was taken next door to Mrs. Wysocki, and Morris Bird III ate at school. His lunch was prepared by June Weed, and it consisted of maybe a peanutbutter and jelly sandwich and an apple. Morris Bird III loved peanut butter, and if June Weed had only *stayed* with peanut butter, the entire salami sandwich incident could have been avoided. But she didn't, and because she didn't . . .

Oh well. No sense thinking about that. If the dog hadn't stopped to look at the scenery, he certainly would have caught the rabbit.

No, the thing was: on that one Wednesday afternoon in October of 1942, Morris Bird III's lunch contained no peanutbutter and jelly sandwich. Instead it contained this Thing.

Morris Bird III always ate his June Weed lunch in the schoolyard. On this particular warm Wednesday in October of 1942, he sat himself on a swing, whistled *Remember Pearl Harbor* through the openings between his teeth, and opened the paper bag that held the lunch.

There it was, staring up at him, this Thing.

He sniffed. He sniffed again. He caught the smell. *Uck.*

Remember Pearl Harbor petered out in a sort of sigh.

It lay thinly between two stale slices of rye bread. Spots and blobs of mayonnaise hung out. It smelled like bad breath. Specifically, it smelled like the breath of a boy named Alex Coffee. People said this Alex Coffee never brushed his teeth.

Sniffing, Morris Bird III separated the slices of rye bread. "P. U.," he said, grimacing.

It had white spots on it.

Morris Bird III shuddered. Anyone who thought he was about to eat *this* had another big fat think coming.

He slapped the two slices of bread back together. He stood up, holding the sandwich at arm's length. He walked back toward the school. He would go inside and drop the Thing into a wastebasket.

Then he saw dumb old Alex Coffee, and that was when the trouble began.

Dumb old Alex Coffee had one other outstanding characteristic besides his bad breath. It was his appetite. Everyone who knew him called him The Human Garbage Can. He was very fat, and every day he ate two lunches. He never was content with simply the lunch he received at home. He always had to stop first at the candystore across Hough Avenue from the school. No one had the slightest idea where he got the money for all the goodies he bought at the candystore (gumballs, candybars, peanuts—you name it and Alex Coffee ate it; wet of lip, sour of breath, he gobbled and slurped, all grinning and moist), but the money always was there. Maybe, for all anyone knew, he robbed banks.

Anyway, on that particular warm Wednesday in October of 1942, Alex Coffee was just emerging from the candystore when Morris Bird III saw him. Standing there in the schoolyard, the Thing held at arm's length, Morris Bird III stared out across Hough Avenue and saw Alex Coffee and allofasudden got a bright idea.

A bright *patriotic* idea at that.

"Hey, Coffee!" he yelled. His voice was shrill and carried well.

Alex Coffee hesitated. He was gnawing on what appeared to be a Hershey bar. He looked around.

"Over here! In the schoolyard!" hollered Morris Bird III, waving. He held up the Thing. He ran toward the street. "Come here for a second!"

Alex Coffee grinned, nodded.

Morris Bird III waved the Thing at him.

A wider grin from Alex Coffee. A more vigorous nod.

Morris Bird III's patriotic idea was simple. There was a war on. Meat was scarce. A good American didn't throw away sandwiches, no matter how stinky they were. A good American let someone else get some good out of it. But who in his right mind would eat this Thing? Only one person: Alex Coffee, otherwise known as The Human Garbage Can.

Alex Coffee crossed the street. They met on the sidewalk in front of the school.

"Here," said Morris Bird III, holding out the Thing.

"For me?" said Alex Coffee, gnawing.

"Uh huh."

"What kind is it?"

"I don't know."

"Give it here."

Morris Bird III gave Alex Coffee the Thing.

Alex Coffee sniffed. *"Uck,"* he said. He handed the Thing back to Morris Bird III.

"You don't want it?"

"You think I'm crazy?"

"It's free for nothing."

"Big deal," said Alex Coffee, gnawing. His breath came out chocolatey and warm.

Morris Bird III sighed. He looked around. "Well," he said, "I tried."

"Yeah," said Alex Coffee. "Thanks, but no thanks." Gnawing, he walked away.

Morris Bird III shrugged. "Fooey," he said. He tossed the Thing toward the gutter. Then he ran back into the schoolyard, where he became involved in some delicate baseball gum card negotiations with a boy named Melvin Minton. He finally traded a Johnny Welaj for a rare old Nino Bongiovanni.

THE NEXT DAY, THE ordeal of Morris Bird III began.

The principal of the Hough Elementary School, a Mrs. Clementine Ochs (pronounced Oaks, not Ox) called a special assembly in the gym. She made a speech.

The gist of the speech:

Honor is sacred. Confession is good for the soul. Vandalism is evil. Whoever it was who, in a fit of malicious devilishness, threw that *awful* sandwich against the side of Mrs. Ochs' parked car, smearing it with mayonnaise and making it absolutely *reek* of *salami* . . . well, perhaps the guilty party now felt remorse. Perhaps the guilty party had the courage to stand forward and purge himself. If this didn't happen, then there would be an investigation. A ceaseless and sur-passingly thorough investigation that eventually would be successful. No such horrible secret could be kept forever. Which meant that the guilty party might as well stand forward and save a lot of everyone's valuable time.

Morris Bird III made fists and jammed them in his eyes. He did not stand forward. Something with long scraggly teeth went to work chewing on his insides. He stood in the rear of that gym and kept back the tears and he figured it wouldn't be long before he died. But he never did stand forward.

MRS. OCHS WAS RUN down and killed by a streetcar in the summer of 1943, but Morris Bird III was unable to mourn her death. All it meant to him was that he wouldn't have to worry anymore about avoiding her eyes.

He had no real idea how he got through that first day—the day of Mrs. Ochs' speech. When he went home for lunch, he took just two bites of his hamburger sandwich. Then he lurched into the bathroom and threw up. June Weed ran in after him and asked him if maybe he was off his feed. He told her he supposed he was. She put him to bed. That was a Thursday. He stayed in bed the rest of the week. The following Monday, he still felt awful. His mother took him to a doctor. The doctor was a plump man with thinning hair, and his name was Sabath. He gave Morris Bird III a careful examination. He even took Morris Bird III's temperature—but in a place that made Morris Bird III blush. He smiled at Morris Bird III's discomfort, but Morris Bird III managed to keep from weeping. The thing with the long scraggly teeth was really doing a job on him, but he blinked the wetness out of his eyes, and no one noticed a thing. The doctor smiled at Morris Bird III's mother and told her there was nothing seriously wrong. He's just off his feed a bit, said the doctor, and he patted Morris Bird III on a shoulder. He wrote out a prescription, told Morris Bird III's mother to have it filled, assured her she had nothing to worry about. Two days later, Morris Bird III returned to school. As soon as he walked in the front door, he saw Mrs. Ochs. He lurched into the Boys' Toilet. He was sent home, and again his mother took him to Dr. Sabath. I can't understand it, said Dr. Sabath, writing out a stronger prescription. The following Wednesday, two weeks to the day after the salami sandwich incident, Morris Bird III again returned to school. This time he did not encounter Mrs. Ochs as soon as he entered the building, and he managed to last out the day. He hardly spoke to anyone, but no one noticed. After all, he *had* been sick. The name of his teacher that semester was Miss Miller. She had red hair and a big chest. At the end of the day, she came to him and asked him if anything was the matter. He made a low croaking sound deep in his throat, fought off a desire to make for the Boys' Toilet. He told her nothing was the matter. Oh, said Miss Miller, that's good. I was a little worried about you today. All you did was stare off into space. I thought perhaps you were still off your feed. No, no, said Morris Bird III, I'm fine. Good, said Miss Miller, and she told him to run along home. He was at the door when she called to him. Morris? she said. He turned. There something on your mind? she asked him. He could not look into her eyes, and so instead he stared at her big chest. No, he said, there's nothing on my mind. Nothing but, ha ha, my hair. Oh was that ever funny. But Miss Miller did laugh. Oh *you*, she said, get *on* with you. He ran out of the room. So Miss Miller was afraid he still was off his feed. Great. Big deal. *Off his feed*: if he never heard that phrase again as long as he lived, it would be too soon. That night, lying in bed, he got to thinking about fingerprints. He wondered if his fingerprints had been taken off the salami sandwich. *Could* fingerprints be taken off slices of rye bread? Oh fooey, he told himself, and after a time he went to sleep. The next morning the sheets were sticky, and he felt as though he hadn't slept at all. That day he spoke to more of his friends, and he managed to get the conversation around to the salami sandwich incident. They told him Mrs. Ochs' investigation was still very much the biggest thing that was happening at the Hough Elementary School. A number of children (including at least one *girl* for crying out loud, a big blonde named Henrietta Kelly who had a voice like old rocks and a build like Humphrey Bogart) had been called into Mrs. Ochs' office in the two weeks since the salami sandwich incident, but so far no one had confessed. Morris Bird III talked with several older acquaintances (sixthgraders most of them), and it was their opinion that Mrs. Ochs really had no clues. Later, when he was alone, he allowed himself to sigh. Fingerprints! For crying out loud how dumb could one person get! He didn't have anything to worry about. The people who had been called into Mrs. Ochs' office were all chronic troublemakers, and Morris Bird III had never been a troublemaker. Troublemaking was too much trouble. Henrietta Kelly and Logan MacMurray had been called into Mrs. Ochs' office a number of times each, and everyone supposed Mrs. Ochs suspected them more than she suspected anyone else, but what did she have to go on? She didn't have anything to go on, and everyone knew this, and just about everyone was delighted. No one particularly liked Mrs. Ochs. She called too many assemblies, gave too many speeches, just about bored a person half to death. Well, Henrietta Kelly and Logan MacMurray were a match for her, which pleased everyone. They were just as mean as she was. The knowledge that she had her hands full with them was very comforting. The only trouble was—that night Morris Bird III ran home and went into the bathroom and wept. He ran water in the washbasin so no one would hear. He hurt. He really and truly *hurt*. He was goosebumpy, and he shook. His head was full of thunder and lightning and marching feet and retribution. He wondered about Alex Coffee, otherwise known as the Human Garbage Can. Had dumb old Alex Coffee forgotten about the sandwich? Was anyone *that* dumb? *that* forgetful? Then again, maybe he was up to something. But what? Goosebumpy and shaking, Morris Bird III wept, swallowing most of the sound of it, keeping it hidden under the sound of the running water. He had seen Alex Coffee three times that day, but Alex had said not a word about the salami sandwich. He'd tried to avoid old Alex as much as possible, but three times that day he'd bumped into

Alex, and Alex had simply grinned, nodded, not saying so much as a howdydo. After the tears stopped, Morris Bird III sat on the toilet seat and wiped his eyes and looked up toward God or Whoever. He prayed for sleep. Good sleep. Thick sleep. Zzzzz, like in the funnies when people sawed wood. I'll do anything for some good sleep, he told God. Anything. You name it.

THE NEXT DAY MORRIS BIRD III didn't go outside for recess.

Instead he went to Mrs. Ochs' office. He didn't say anything to Miss Miller. His mouth was full of cotton, and his palms were pink and moist. He could smell himself, and the smell wasn't good.

He walked into the anteroom. The door to Mrs. Ochs' office was partly open. He could hear her talking with someone.

A thin blond woman sat at a desk in the anteroom. She asked him what he wanted. He told her he wanted to see Mrs. Ochs. The thin blond woman's name was Miss Kane. A pencil was in her hair. She asked him what he wanted to discuss with Mrs. Ochs.

"Something . . ." said Morris Bird III.

"Something like what?" said Miss Kane.

"Just something."

Miss Kane made an exasperated noise. It came from the roof of her mouth. "You'll have to do better than that."

Morris Bird III swallowed. "It's . . . it's real personal . . ."

Miss Kane sighed. It was a large sigh, and it made her lips flap. "Oh all *right*," she said. She pointed to a bench. "Sit down. You may see Mrs. Ochs when she's free."

Morris Bird III went to the bench and sat down. He stared at the floor. His stomach hurt, and so did his breath. He cleared his throat. Nothing happened. He looked at Miss Kane, but she was paying no attention to him. She was going through a pile of papers on her desk. She was humming something that sounded a little like *The Beer Barrel Polka*.

Then Morris Bird III recognized the voice of the person talking with Mrs. Ochs. It was Logan MacMurray. Himself.

Morris Bird III hugged himself.

The voices were too loud. Morris Bird III didn't want to hear them, but he couldn't help it.

Logan MacMurray was speaking. "I . . . I ain't going to say nothing."

"I wouldn't advise that," said the voice of Mrs. Ochs.

"Four times you've called me in here. Four times I've said nothing."

"Confession is good for the soul."

"I ain't done nothing."

"Oh yes you have," said the voice of Mrs. Ochs.

"Oh no I *haven't*," said the voice of Logan MacMurray, imitating the voice of Mrs. Ochs. Some other time it might have been funny.

"Don't you dare get flip with *me!*"

"Yes, Mrs. Ox."

"*Oaks!* My name is Oaks!"

"Oaks. Great. Oaks. Hot dog."

Silence. Something was digging at Morris Bird III's heart with dirty fingernails. Probably the thing with the long scraggly teeth. He glanced at the blond Miss Kane, but she was paying no attention to the voices that came from Mrs. Ochs' office. She was paying no attention to Morris Bird III either. He smiled at her, but she didn't see him. Then, from inside the office, accompanied by a cough, came the sound of Mrs. Ochs' voice. "I . . . isn't there any way to talk to you?" she said.

"You're talking to me now," said the voice of Logan MacMurray.

"*You!*"

"Now, now, Mrs. Oaks."

"If you didn't do it, *say* so!"

"That wouldn't do no good. You think I done it. What's the sense of me saying anything?"

"You *did* do it?"

"That's for me to know and you to find out," said the voice of Logan MacMurray.

"You *did* do it!"

"Suit yourself."

"Admit it!"

"No. I don't admit nothing."

"Then . . . then I take it you did do it." The voice of Mrs. Ochs was thin now, scratchy at the edges.

"You take it however you want to take it," said the voice of Logan MacMurray. "I ain't about to give you the satisfaction of knowing nothing. I'm just Logan MacMurray. No matter what I say, you're going to think I done it. So I ain't going to say nothing."

"You're expelled!"

"Huh?"

"Get out of here!"

"You throwing me out of school?"

"Yes! Now go away! Get out of this office!"

"Temper, temper."

"Coward! Filthy sneaking coward! Throwing a sandwich against the side of an automobile!"

"Don't call me no coward!"

"It's the truth! Get out!"

"Call me whatever you want to call me, only don't call me no coward!"

"Coward! Coward!"

Feet scraped. Then there was a falsetto sound that came from Logan MacMurray. Then Logan MacMurray spoke. He had lowered his voice. "Okay," he said, "if you want that I done it, I done it. Who needs this crappy school anyway?"

"Out. Just. Get. Out."

"Sure, Mrs. Ox. Sure."

And then Logan MacMurray came out of Mrs. Ochs' office. His lips were pulled back, and his mouth was all green. When he walked past Morris Bird III's bench, he kicked one of Morris Bird III's ankles. Morris Bird III made no sound. Logan MacMurray's mouth was in a grin, but it fooled no one. His eyes were too damp. Morris Bird III stared at him, and so did the blond Miss Kane. Inside the office, Mrs. Ochs was clearing her throat and coughing. Finally she managed to call for Miss Kane. As soon as Miss Kane went inside Mrs. Ochs' office, Morris Bird III scooted out of the anteroom as though he had been shot from a gun. He kept a good distance behind Logan MacMurray, who was lurching bonelessly down a hall.

• • •

A FEW MONTHS AFTER the salami sandwich incident, Logan MacMurray's family moved out of the neighborhood. He never was seen again.

If only Logan MacMurray had been likable. If he'd been likable, then people would have felt sorry for him. But no one felt sorry for him. He was a bully, a brute. Just about everyone at the Hough Elementary School was *delighted* when he was expelled. Which naturally made the pain of Morris Bird III that much worse. It took a long time going away, and it never did really go away for good. He wondered how he ever would be able to make it up. He tried to make allowances. A person had to make allowances. But allowances weren't enough.

He avoided dumb old Alex Coffee for months. Not that Alex Coffee ever said anything. He didn't. Not a word.

IT WASN'T UNTIL THE day the gas tanks blew up that Morris Bird III really was able to make his peace with the salami sandwich incident. In the meantime, a lot had happened. Two years was a long time. It was practically the next thing to forever.

As far as Morris Bird III was concerned, the biggest of all the things that happened in those two years was the arrival of his grandmother, Mrs. Elizabeth Jones. She came to live in the house on Edmunds Avenue on Thanksgiving Day 1943. Her husband, James N. Jones, retired, had died that summer. Morris Bird III had accompanied his parents to the funeral. (Sandra had been left with Mrs. Wysocki.) The funeral was held in a little southeastern Ohio town called Paradise Falls. Grandpa and Grandma had lived there a couple hundred years or so. Morris Bird III and his parents made the trip by train. They changed trains in Columbus, transferring from the New York Central to the Chesapeake & Ohio, and the smell of the Chesapeake & Ohio daycoach had been better. Deeper. Richer. Browner. The odor of the flowers in the funeral home had also been pleasant. Grandpa Jones had been very thin and white.

Morris Bird III had discussed the smell of the daycoaches with his grandmother. Goodness, she had said, you certainly must have a sensitive Smeller. This had pleased him. He loved his grandmother a whole lot.

A little later, Grandma sold her home in Paradise Falls and came to Edmunds Avenue. She came after receiving a hurried call from Morris Bird III's mother. This was because Morris Bird III's mother had had to fire June Weed. The official explanation was that June Weed had turned out to be Unreliable.

June Weed was a blonde, but she was fat, and her hair didn't fall over her eye the way Veronica Lake's did. She kept it what she called Permanents, and sometimes Morris Bird III's sensitive smeller detected a burnt odor to it. He didn't understand her the slightest bit.

Shortly after the beginning of the war, when Morris Bird III's mother decided to go to work and earn the Extra, she placed an ad in the classified section of one of the afternoon papers. It asked for a

WOMAN to care for 2 children (ages 6, 3) of working mother. Also light housekeeping. Hours 8–6. Wages by arrangement. CEdar 0983.

June Weed was the only person who answered the ad. Morris Bird III's mother hired her without asking too many questions. There just isn't anyone anymore to do that sort of work, she told her husband. Any port in a storm.

Then she tried to smile. It didn't amount to an awful lot.

Even though he'd not seen June Weed in almost a year, Morris Bird III remembered her very well. He remembered the odor of her hair. He also remembered the fragrance of her Juicyfruit. She never would give him any of her Juicyfruit. I'm not *made* out of Juicyfruit, she liked to say.

When June Weed came to the house on Edmunds Avenue, she said she was twentytwo years of age, but Morris Bird III's mother wasn't about to believe *that*. If she's twentytwo years of age, said Morris Bird III's mother, then I'm Dorothy Lamour.

This made everyone laugh. Morris Bird III's father laughed the loudest.

June Weed was fond of holding long telephone conversations with people she said were her girlfriends. Sometimes Morris Bird III listened in. He heard June Weed argue about the lyrics to songs. He heard her talk, giggling from time to time, about that absolute *rascal* of an Errol Flynn. But mostly June Weed and her girlfriends discussed Sailors. Morris Bird III and his little sister Sandra eventually got to know a lot about Sailors. This was because, starting in the summer of 1943, once June Weed had become really settled into her routine, a Sailor came to the house just about every other day or so. Always, however, a different Sailor. They all wore funny floppy trousers, and sometimes they gave candy or gum to Morris Bird III and Sandra. Once one of them gave Morris Bird III a quarter and then laughed aloud. He laughed so loudly that June Weed also had to laugh. After a time, so did Morris Bird III, although he didn't have the slightest idea what he was supposed to be laughing *about*. They all laughed so loudly that they awakened Sandra from her nap upstairs. Blinking, rubbing her eyes, she came downstairs. After she saw what they all were doing, she joined in. It was a nice loud time.

Morris Bird III's parents never were home when the Sailors came calling on June Weed. Go upstairs, you two, she would say to the children, and play with your Erector Sets or something. Then June Weed and that particular Sailor would bray and whoop, and Morris Bird III supposed this was because he had no Erector Set.

Sometimes, when he and Sandra went upstairs, he told her stories. But he didn't know too many stories. So mostly they just sat. One time he went to the front upstairs window and told Sandra: You got Plymouths. I'll take Fords. First to get twentyone wins.

He sat at the window and counted Plymouths and Fords. The final score was Ford 21, Plymouth 3. Sandra cried a little, and so he supposed she hadn't particularly liked the game. Oh well. Some people were like that. Couldn't take it.

Then, one Saturday in the autumn of 1943, Morris Bird III's mother became ill at work and was sent home. (It was a time and a half day too.) Morris Bird III's father was not home. One of the younger announcers at WCCC had been drafted, and everyone was working overtime until a replacement could be found.

Only Morris Bird III and Sandra and June Weed were at home.

And one of June Weed's Sailors. Naturally, June Weed hadn't expected Morris Bird III's mother home so early. The children were upstairs. The first they knew their mother was home was when they heard her start to holler. Her voice came from downstairs, and she was hollering at June Weed. "You filthy oar!" she hollered. "You filthy filthy *oar!*"

A loud hollow sound from June Weed.

"Out!" hollered Morris Bird III's mother. "Out! Out! And I mean right now!"

Morris Bird III and Sandra ran to the head of the stairs.

"On the sofa!" hollered Morris Bird III's mother. "The sofa! How dare you! Out! Out!"

"Aw, shut up!" hollered June Weed. "We're going!"

Morris Bird III and Sandra stared at each other. For some reason, he looked around. There was a bookcase up there at the head of the stairs. Three of his mother's china owls were on top of it. One of them was purple. It frowned at him. He wished he had the nerve to go break it.

Then they heard the front door slam.

Morris Bird III and Sandra ran to the upstairs front window. June Weed and the Sailor were walking fast. June Weed's hair was going all this way and that, and never mind her Permanent. She was buttoning her coat, and the Sailor was doing something with the front of his funny floppy trousers. Their faces didn't appear to have an awful lot of color.

Then Morris Bird III's mother came upstairs. She was weeping. Morris Bird III didn't like the sound of it. She hugged Morris Bird III and Sandra. "Oh my babies . . . my poor darling babies . . . your mother has been a bad mother . . . now, now, there, there . . ."

Morris Bird had no idea what his mother was talking about. He and Sandra blinked at each other, peeking around their mother's bosom.

That night he asked his mother what an oar was. She shook her head and said something that meant Never You Mind Dear.

MORRIS BIRD III'S MOTHER stayed home for a few weeks and took care of the children. Then she telephoned Grandma, and Grandma agreed to move from Paradise Falls to Edmunds Avenue. Morris Bird III and Sandra were delighted.

A night or so later, Morris Bird III's mother and father had an argument. It came late at night, and Morris Bird III was upstairs in bed, but the sound of it awakened him. He heard the words very clearly.

"Oh *drop* it!" shouted his mother.

"Every time I talk about you and your great love of money, you tell me to drop it!" hollered his father. "What's the matter? You got a guilty conscience?"

"Sh! They'll hear you!"

"*Me?* What about *you?* You think you're *whispering?*"

"Sh!"

Morris Bird III's father lowered his voice, but it still was audible. After all, he *was* the Voice of Cleveland & Northeastern Ohio, and the sound of him just naturally carried well. Nothing much he could do about it. "Well," he said, "I just can't understand it. We're not on relief."

"Nobody's asking you to understand it. Some day you'll be glad I earned the Extra."

"Sure."

"Ah. Hey. A real answer. The man says Sure. What a rejoinder. What a vocabulary."

"Ho ho ho. You slay me."

"Really?" said Morris Bird III's mother. "How nice."

MORRIS BIRD III'S MOTHER returned to work the day after Grandma came to live with them. Her disposition improved immediately. There were no more arguments, or at least none that Morris Bird III heard.

But the important thing was that Grandma was living with them. Morris Bird III and Sandra both loved Grandma. When she spoke to them, most of the things she said made sense. This certainly was an improvement over June Weed, who had seldom made sense. Maybe this had had something to do with June Weed having been an oar, but now there was no way of knowing for sure.

Morris Bird III understood very little about age, but he supposed Grandma was quite young for a grandma. Nancy Reese, who lived across the street, had a grandma staying with *her* too, but this appeared to be a very old grandma. This grandma had a crinkly face and brown spots on her hands. Her gums were orange, and she had declared war on cats. She was forever chasing them off the Reeses' front lawn. You're not going to leave any mess on *this* lawn! she hollered. Ugh! Filthy beasts! And then invariably she pursued them with a broom. Vile! she shouted. Dirty! Ugh! And invariably the cats ran.

In the autumn of 1943, when Grandma came to live in Edmunds Avenue, she said she was fiftyone years old. She liked to tell people she thought she had lived a good life. She was slender, and her hair wasn't hardly white at all. She had had seven children, and she didn't mind laughing now and again. Her gums were pink, and her hands had no brown spots, and she could take cats or leave them alone. She seldom said Never You Mind Dear. If she was asked a question, most of the time she tried to answer it. She had a soft voice (she had been born in Virginia), and it had sort of a grin in it, something like the voice of Smiling Jack Smith, the radio singer. Naturally, from time to time she couldn't answer questions. After all, she was only human, and she didn't know everything. An example of this was the day Morris Bird III walked into the kitchen and asked her what an oar was.

"A what?" said Grandma.

"An oar," said Morris Bird III. "When June Weed went away, Mamma called her a filthy oar."

"Oar! Oh. *Oar.* Well now."

"You know what it is?"

Something was pulling and grabbing at the corners of Grandma's mouth. She turned away from Morris Bird III and began fussing with a pot. "Uh, *well*," she said. She cleared her throat. "Uh. A oar. Yes indeed." Then she shook her head from side to side. Her voice was pinched. "No. No. Can't say as I do."

"Maybe it's like something you row a boat with?"

"Maybe," said Grandma, fussing with the pot.

"Or maybe it's like what they dig in Wisconsin."

"You mean iron ore? Uh, it's dug in Minnesota."

"Mrs. Dallas says it's very important to the war effort."

"Yes," said Grandma. "Oh yes." She took a handkerchief from a pocket of her apron. She wiped her eyes. Then she again cleared her throat.

"I looked it up in the dictionary," said Morris Bird III. "All I could find was oar like in boats and ore like what they dig."

"Um," said Grandma. "Very peculiar." She sniffled, blew her nose.

"You got a cold?"

"Yes," said Grandma. "A little cold."

"Aw," said Morris Bird III.

Grandma turned and faced him. She went to him and hugged him. She was laughing. "Thank you," she said. "Thank you. Thank you."

Morris Bird III hugged Grandma back. He hugged her and hugged her. She smelled good. The tighter he hugged her, the more she laughed. "How come you're laughing?" he asked her.

"Tickles," said Grandma, laughing.

"Oh," said Morris Bird III.

Grandma was fond of food, *Time* Magazine and radio daytime serials. Even with the rationing, she prepared meals the likes of which Morris Bird III had never experienced. Casseroles, stews, meatloaves . . . she stretched the ration points with great skill, and everyone in the house got to smiling more often, even Morris Bird III's father. The stews were Morris Bird III's favorites. All that juice, and the round little bloobers of fat. *Bloobers* was one of his madeup words. He enjoyed making up words that described better than real words did. After more than a year of June Weed's reluctant little lunches of hotdogs and peanutbutter sandwiches, he fell to Grandma's bloobery casseroles and stews and meatloaves with immense vigor. He'd never had such an appetite. He spent more and more of his time in the kitchen. As for Grandma, well, *she* spent almost all *her* time in the kitchen. She liked the kitchen because it was the sunniest room in the house. She'd always been very fond of sun, she told Morris Bird III. It's something that's larger than the earth, she said, and you can feel it, and that's good. She had brought a little radio with her from Paradise Falls, and she kept it in the kitchen. There, Monday through Friday, she listened to all her daytime serials. Her favorite was *The Guiding Light*. She loved dear Pappa Bauer. One day she wrote a threepage letter to the producers of *The Guiding Light*, telling them how much she admired dear Pappa Bauer. The letter never was answered, but this did not lessen Grandma's love for the program and Pappa Bauer. Nothing could have. If you love a thing or a person, she told Morris Bird III you shouldn't hold back. Who cares that they never answered my letter? They're very busy. They get a lot of letters.

ABOUT HIS NAME:

He realized that Morris Bird III was a dumb name, but he managed to live with it. There were worse things than dumb names. Speedometers in the belly for instance. Or salami sandwich incidents. And anyway, there was no one around he could blame. The fault lay with his father's father, but the original Morris Bird had been dead for some time, and there wasn't much sense wasting time being mad at a dead man. The damage had been done. You went on from there.

The original Morris Bird had been a newspaper editor in Paradise Falls. His mother's maiden name had been Morris, but she'd been the last of her line. This was why she named her son Morris. In a way, she was perpetuating her family. So, inexorably, Morris Bird was followed by Morris Bird II, and now Morris Bird III. There was only one catch. Morris Bird III had more trouble with his name than either his father or grandfather had had. This was because people, especially small boys, got a big charge out of calling him Morris Bird The Turd, or sometimes simply Bird Turd.

But he didn't particularly care. It wasn't everyone who had a Roman Numeral after his name. He thought of himself as Morris Bird The Three. Occasionally he thought of himself as Morris Bird The Eye Eye Eye, but mostly Morris Bird The Three. It wasn't right to think of himself as Morris Bird The Eye Eye Eye. That made him sound too much like a King, and this was a democracy. He didn't want people to think of him as a King. In the books he'd read, most Kings hadn't been worth much. Like that man with the big appetite. The one who had chopped off the heads of so many of his wives. That fat King whose name had been Henry The Vee Eye Eye Eye.

HE HAD A LARGE field of knowledge. People had told him he had A Good Mind, and maybe there was something to what they said. Certainly he knew a lot of facts. In his mind, he called them Items. There was a real mess of them—

ITEM: Mr. Wysocki, the C sticker man, owned the only Packard on Edmunds Avenue. It was a '36, but Mr. Wysocki had taken good care of it.

ITEM: George Case, an outfielder for the Cleveland Indians, was the fastest man in the American League.

ITEM: Veronica Lake and Alan Ladd were not married to each other.

ITEM: The Knickerbocker Theater, on Euclid Avenue near East 81st Street, was sometimes called the Niggerbocker because of the large numbers of colored people who went there.

ITEM: Arlene Kovacs, who lived three doors away and was sixteen, stuffed funny things down the front of her dress. One day in the summer of 1944 she dropped her purse on the sidewalk in front of Morris Bird III's home. She was wearing a lowcut dress. When she stooped to pick up the purse, one of the funny things fell out. She gave a little shriek, quickly stuffed the funny thing back down the front of her dress. Then, after she had straightened up, she saw Morris Bird III standing on his front porch. She glared at him, called him a NASTY LITTLE SNOT! She'd not spoken to him since that day. Whenever he saw her, he backed away and hid.

ITEM: Stapleton was the murderer in *The Hound of the Baskervilles*.

ITEM: When you pitched baseball gum cards against a wall, you got two for leaners.

ITEM: There were no such people as Charlie McCarthy and Mortimer Snerd.

ITEM: There lived on the next street a crazy man who caught leaves as they fell from the trees in his front yard.

ITEM: Mr. Pisani, the man who was dying of cancer, shrieked a lot. Everyone said he would be better off dead.

ITEM: Spring smelled best.

ITEM: Army had the best football team in the country.

ITEM: It was very humorous when people asked each other why Errol Flynn didn't hurry up and win the war.

ITEM: A 6B boy named Hank Moore was the best athlete at the Hough Elementary School.

ITEM: Next to baseball, the best game in the world was Guns. Morris Bird III had an automatic and two revolvers, plus a set of holsters for the revolvers. His father had a *real* automatic. Naturally, Morris Bird III wasn't permitted to touch it. (It was kept in a bureau drawer in his parents' bedroom, and sometimes he sneaked in there to take a look at it. It was very shiny, and it always smelled of oil. His father cleaned it at least once a week, sometimes oftener. We need protection, his father said. This neighborhood has seen better days.)

ITEM: Republicans were terrible people. Everyone said so. Or anyway, almost everyone.

ITEM: Errol Flynn's indictment for statutory rape did not mean he had raped statues.

ITEM: ABCDEF meant American Boys Club to Defend Errol Flynn.

ITEM: People who had double boxes of Crayola crayons put on the dog.

ITEM: At the Astor Theater, they gave you a candybar on Saturday afternoons if you left after one show.

ITEM: The Astor Theater was where Morris Bird III had fallen in love with Veronica Lake. It had happened one Saturday afternoon in 1942. She had stood up so bravely to that big fat awful Laird Cregar in *This Gun for Hire.* It had been a great movie. Alan Ladd's death at the end had been especially gratifying.

ITEM: A boy named Stanley Chaloupka had been the goofiest person at the Hough Elementary School. Also the smartest.

ITEM: The worst thing you could meet up with was guilt.

Physically, Morris Bird III was dark, small for his age. He was, however, probably the thirdbest baseball player in the 4A at the Hough

Elementary School. There were two 4A rooms (Miss Lundberg's and Mrs. Dallas'), and so to be the thirdbest baseball player was not exactly a thing to be sneezed at. His favorite position was shortstop. There always was a lot happening at shortstop. A person was kept on his toes.

Actually, although they called it baseball, the game they played was handsoccer. Morris Bird III had no idea where the name came from, but it was a good one. What you did was: you socked the ball with a hand. There was no bat, nor was there a pitcher. The "batter" hit a rubber ball by throwing it up with one hand and socking it with the other. He was out if a) he missed the ball altogether, or b) the ball was caught on either the fly or the first bounce, or c) he was thrown out at first base, or d) he was hit (or "pegged out," as it was called) by a thrown ball, or e) he hit to right field (anything over the first baseman's head was an automatic out, which meant that lefthanded handsoccer hitters didn't really have an awful lot of value). This being the case, the most important positions in handsoccer were third base, shortstop and left field. And Morris Bird III was as good a shortstop as there was. He was especially skillful at pegging out runners between bases. He usually got them in the belly. Sometimes the head, but mostly the belly.

He had one other significant athletic accomplishment. He could dropkick a football farther and with more accuracy than any other boy at the school, and never mind just the 4A. He didn't know how he did it, but he did it. It probably was a matter of rhythm and timing, but, *whump*, however he did it, three times out of four he was able to dropkick the ball a good twenty yards, and on a straight line most of the time. Sometimes he and dumb old Alex Coffee, The Human Garbage Can, would borrow Alex's brother's football and walk over to Rockefeller Park, where Morris Bird III would dropkick the ball for hours and hours. Alex didn't seem to mind chasing it and tossing it back. Sometimes he even caught it on the fly, but those times weren't frequent. Besides being The Human Garbage Can, he was clumsy. Not to mention dumb.

OF ALL THE PEOPLE at the Hough Elementary School, the one Morris Bird III admired the most was Hank Moore, the 6B boy who was such a tremendous athlete.

Hank Moore was thick and husky. His hair was so blond as to be almost white, and some of the 6B and 6A girls had been heard to remark that he was Cute. He had played second base for the Gordon Park Keltners in the sandlot Class F division in the summer of 1944. His team had won eight games and had lost only four; he had hit six home runs, and his batting average had been .778 (28 hits for 36 times at bat). The reason Morris Bird III knew all these statistics was that Hank Moore hadn't let him forget them.

One Saturday afternoon late in September of that year, Morris Bird III and Hank Moore walked over to the schoolyard and played catch for several hours. They played until Morris Bird III's arm began to hurt. Then he begged off. Grinning, Hank Moore told him: "Okay, kid. You did good. Real good."

Hank Moore called everyone Kid. At twelve, his voice was just beginning to change. It had a hoarse and splintered quality that made everything he said sound tremendously authoritative. He lurched rather than walked. His legs were bowed, and he rested his weight on the outside part of his feet. The way he walked made it appear that he had piles, but no one ever had pointed this out to him. No one was that stupid.

Hank Moore lived over on Crawford Road, a couple of blocks from Morris Bird III's home. They walked together north along East 90th Street. Morris Bird III had to sort of run to keep up.

Hank Moore pounded the baseball in his glove. He spat into the glove, rubbed the spit into the leather. "Yessir," he said. "You do real good for a little kid."

Morris Bird III didn't know whether to say thank you or what, so he said nothing.

"You ought to keep yourself in shape," said Hank Moore, croaking.

"Um," said Morris Bird III.

"You're what now? 5B?"

"4A."

"Okay. So in a couple years you'll be ready for Class F."

"Um," said Morris Bird III, thrusting a hand in a pocket and scratching a leg.

"I'm going to be in the major leagues by the time I'm fifteen."

"Huh?"

"You hear me. I'm going to be in the major leagues by the time I'm fifteen. Just like Joe Nuxhall."

"Who?"

"Joe *Nux*hall. He's a lefthanded pitcher, and this summer he started a game for the Cincinnati Reds, and he was only fifteen."

"That so?"

"You don't believe me?"

"I believe you."

"He started a game, and his name was in the box score, and that's something nobody can take away from him."

"Um," said Morris Bird III, nodding.

"Maybe it don't mean nothing to *you*, but it's a real big—"

"No. No. It means a lot to me."

"I'm going to do it too."

"Do what?"

"Pitch in the major leagues when I'm fifteen."

Morris Bird III didn't say anything. He looked off toward some-body or other's house.

"You don't believe me?" said Hank Moore.

"Sure I do," said Morris Bird III.

"I'm twelve. I got three years. Every night I work out. And I mean *work out*. I run around the block ten times. Up Crawford to Rosalind, down Rosalind to Holyrood, back on Holyrood to 90th, then up 90th to Crawford. Ten times, and it's a long block, and then I do pushups. Running for the legs. Pushups for the arms. And the old wind. You got to remember the old wind."

Morris Bird III nodded.

Hank Moore's splintered voice became louder. He glared at Mor-ris Bird III. "And don't think I'm kidding. And I'll do better than Joe Nuxhall. He got knocked out of the box, and they sent him down to Lima of the Ohio State League. Nobody's going to send *me* down. I got three years. I'll make it. Some scout'll see me, and that'll be that. You just wait and see. That'll be 1947. You'll open your paper and you'll read a box score, and there it'll be—Henry Larkin Moore, *ma-jor leaguer*. You better believe it."

"I believe it," said Morris Bird III.

"A guy goes 28 for 36, he's got a future."

"Yes," said Morris Bird III.

"Everybody said I was too good for Class F."

"Yes."

"I never told nobody about this before."

"Oh."

"Sometimes at night I can't sleep."

"Um."

"Henry Larkin Moore, *major leaguer.*"

Morris Bird III nodded.

"People'll say: Hank Moore, he's that kid who's only fifteen but hits all the home runs. He sure must be some kid."

"Yes," said Morris Bird III.

Now they were at the corner of East 90th and Edmunds. Thumping his glove, Hank Moore stared at Morris Bird III. "Thanks, kid," he said.

"For what?"

"You know what."

"Um," said Morris Bird III.

Hank Moore lurched away, on down East 90th. He kept thumping his glove. Morris Bird III watched him and thought of loneliness and heroism. He thought of people who ran around the block ten times every night because of their dreams. He rubbed an elbow and went on home.

LOVE AND BRAVERY: MORRIS BIRD III understood neither. *Really* understood, that is. He figured he had an *idea* of what they meant, but it was only an idea, not real knowledge. He loved Veronica Lake. He loved Suzanne Wysocki. He loved his family—and this even included, reluctantly, his little sister Sandra. At one time, he'd probably loved a boy named Stanley Chaloupka. And maybe, although he resisted it, he loved the lonely Hank Moore. And then of course there was Mrs. Dallas. He certainly didn't *want* to love *her* (who in his right mind loved a *teacher?*), but how could she be resisted? So what if teachers *were* The

Enemy? Maybe somehow, if you tried hard enough, you could manage to ignore that awful fact.

There was one thing, though, for sure—Mrs. Dallas was the best teacher he'd ever had. She was the prettiest, and she was the nicest, and she had more to say. Sometimes he wished she didn't have quite so *much* to say, but then you had to make allowances.

Her full name was Helene K. Dallas, and she'd told the children she was of Greek ancestry. Sometimes, when she was upset, she would speak to them in Greek, and this always made them giggle. The words made her sound as though she had a cold in her head.

But don't get the wrong idea—Mrs. Dallas was by no means a nasty teacher. (Morris Bird III considered himself something of an expert on nasty teachers. For instance, back in the 1A his teacher had been a nasty old biddy named Miss Outhwaite. She was about three hundred and fifty years old, and she was so skinny that when she turned sideways she just about vanished from view. Every hour on the hour she'd made the children take what she called Deep Indian Breaths. You bent forward until your head was practically between your knees. Then you sighed and panted and wheezed as though maybe you were about to die. Some fun. Her name was Gertrude C. Outhwaite, and whenever you were Bad she made you come to the front of the class while she took your paper, or your drawing, or your valentine, or whatever it was you'd made a botch of, waved it in front of the class and then, frowning and tight of lip, tore it up, saying: *This is what we do with lazy work in *this* room! And *this!* And *this* and *this* and *this!* And then she dropped the shredded pieces on the floor and made you pick them up and put them in the wastebasket. She died one April morning in 1943. She was doing Deep Indian Breaths with her class. She gave a little shriek and fell from her chair. The children all ran whooping from the room. Only one child, a boy, stopped where Miss Outhwaite lay, and he only stopped long enough to kick her. Later the word got out that Miss Outhwaite had died from a burst bloodvessel in her head. She was forgotten within a week.)

Mrs. Dallas was almost pretty. She had quite a large mouth, and her lips were thick and most of the time moist. Her eyes were brown, moist too. Her hair was dark, done in a long pageboy. If you didn't count Veronica Lake's hair and Suzanne Wysocki's hair, Mrs. Dallas' hair was the prettiest in the world.

As for the rest of Mrs. Dallas, well, just say she wasn't hard to notice. Sometimes she wore dresses that didn't seem to give her much room to breathe in, and Morris Bird III had heard some of the 6B and 6A boys make liquid sounds when discussing her. He wasn't so dumb that he didn't have kind of a good idea why.

Mrs. Dallas' desk had an open place where her legs went. Sometimes she didn't sit quite the way she should have. This brought dimples to her knees. They put Morris Bird III in mind of human faces. He remembered seeing photographs in *Life* Magazine of knees that looked like faces, but none of those faces had been as sharp and clear as the faces on Mrs. Dallas' knees.

There was only one thing that made Mrs. Dallas almost pretty instead of all the way pretty. That was her mustache. Not that it was much of a mustache, but it was there, and there was no sense saying it didn't exist. You saw it when you stood close to her. Ah, but then there was no law that said you had to look. When Morris Bird III stood close to Mrs. Dallas, he did not look at her mustache. Instead he smelled her perfume. It was always the same perfume, and it put him in mind of grass on a warm day after the rain. It was a very green smell, but in no way did it knock you down. Instead, it made your breath feel good, and Morris Bird III for one was never happier than when his breath felt good.

Mrs. Dallas' husband was with the merchant marines, and from time to time she brought the children postcards her husband had sent from strange places called Murmansk, Naples, Liverpool. Except for the ones from Murmansk, most of the postcards had pictures of great big old churches. She usually tacked the postcards on the bulletinboard, but she never let the children see what was written on the back. Morris Bird III supposed this was because sometimes husbands told their wives things they didn't want anyone else to know.

THE WAY SHE TALKED made you know Mrs. Dallas was fully as brave as Hank Moore.

There's nothing at all the matter, she liked to say, with doing something you think is right even though nobody wants to help you, even though people actually try to stop you. As long as you don't hurt anybody, and as long as you honestly *know* what you're doing is *right* and *moral* and *just*, then go ahead and do it. We know about George Washington and the other men who founded this nation. They could have sat back and done nothing. Most of them were rich men. Why was liberty so important that they were willing to risk their lives and their fortunes and their sacred honor so they could have it? It was important for only one reason—its *rightness*. If a principle is right, if it is a thing of faith and honor, then it is worth the taking of risks. Why do you think we're at war with the Germans and the Japanese? For *that* reason, and *that* reason *only*. It has nothing to do with our size or our strength. We're not trying to prove anything. We're not trying to show off, to make the world afraid of us. No, we're fighting for a principle, a thing of *rightness*. Do you know what the word Virtue means? The word Virtue means being good. Well, in this war we are the ones with Virtue—and Virtue is a thing of rightness. We—and the British and the Russians and the Chinese, all of us—are the ones who are dying because we have committed ourselves to Virtue, to being the good guys. This is very brave and fine. We aren't fighting for the sake of fighting; we are fighting for the sake of *rightness*. We have had to stand up and be counted. But don't for a minute think this is only a thing of nations, of armies and wars and all that. Standing up and being counted is a thing that can happen anywhere—in this room, in the schoolyard, on the street, anywhere at all. If you're right, and you *know* you're right, then in order to be a good human being you *have* to stand up and be counted. When you see a big boy beating up a little boy, what should you do? Should you stand there and say Oh *my*, what a *shame*, and not lift a hand? Or should you go help the little fellow, even if people laugh at you and criticize you for not minding your own business? And they *will* laugh. And they *will* criticize. You can bet on *that*. But you shouldn't let them bother you. Bravery is the best thing there is—and the smartest. It makes you able to live with yourself. It's smart to be able to live with yourself. Helps you sleep nights. Helps you—ah, oh *my*, I *have* gone on. Pardon *me*. This isn't telling us much about James A. Garfield is it?

• • •

OF ALL THE PEOPLE Morris Bird III knew, only Mrs. Dallas and Grandma had ever spoken about bravery. Because of the salami sandwich betrayal of Logan MacMurray, he tried to pay attention to their words. He knew that some day he would have to do something about the salami sandwich betrayal. A thing can eat at you and eat at you only so long.

IN THAT OCTOBER OF 1944, Mrs. Dallas had all the children engaged in a Special Project. It was entitled *Ohio's Contribution to the Civil War.* Each of them had been given a topic and was expected to deliver a fiveminute talk. Morris Bird III's topic was Ulysses S. Grant.

Since his last name began with a B, he had to give one of the first talks. He did the research at the Hough-Crawford library. He read up a great deal on old Ulysses S. Grant. When the time came for his talk, he spoke at great length on Grant's days at West Point, his business and farming failures, the battles of Fort Henry and Donelson and Shiloh and Vicksburg and The Wilderness and the siege of Petersburg, his election to the Presidency, his failure there, and finally the writing of the *Memoirs*, and the talk consumed a good fifteen minutes, and at recess a few of the boys accused him of having A Big Fat Long Brown Nose, and their words didn't bother him a speck. At the conclusion of his talk, Mrs. Dallas had said Very Good Morris, and the sound of the words had been like the green smell of her perfume—they had made his breath feel good. (She had a wonderful voice, this Mrs. Dallas. It was soft, slow, quite distinct, with clean clipped sibilants. She never hollered at children who were slow. She often used her hands when she spoke. They described gentle parabolas. They were pink, not bony, and the eyes of Morris Bird III never tired of following the parabolas.)

The life of Ulysses S. Grant had been very interesting to him. He'd not anticipated this. Why should he have cared about some old Civil War general? But, sitting there in the vague and not unpleasant yellowgray light of the Children's Reading Room of the Hough-Crawford library, looking up from time to time and sniffing the fine thick odor of a generation of caps and coats and mittens and boots (a good damp comfortable fragrance), Morris Bird III felt himself being pulled toward the crusty and funnylooking old general. Poor old sloppy Grant (the children's librarian, a Miss Silberman, fetched him every book the place had on the subject, and even a few of the Adult books), old bearded Grant and his cigars, his way of saying precisely what he meant, his insistence on doing a thing even if it took all summer, his refusal to die until the *Memoirs* were finished and his debts paid . . . yes sir, you read about this man, and this was a man the way people *thought* of men, and Morris Bird III took to staring with great intensity at pictures of the old rip. Such a homely face, and it was a face of bravery. You closed your eyes, and the face followed you. It said: Look. Study me. I did not betray. I would have gone to Mrs. Ochs. I would not have let the terrible thing happen to Logan MacMurray. I would have looked her straight in her mean old eye and I would have said: I did it. I, Ulysses S. Grant, threw the salami sandwich.

Which maybe was the reason Morris Bird III gave such a good talk. He'd not once lost his place in his notes. And he'd not felt selfconscious. This was the first time he'd not felt selfconscious when standing in front of the class and giving a talk. The first time *ever.* Usually he hated giving talks. He'd always thought that one of the curses of his existence was that his last name began with a B. This time, though, he wouldn't have cared if it had begun with an A.

HIS GRANDMOTHER'S BELIEF IN bravery did not lend itself so much to speeches, but it was just as intense. His mother and father had never taken Morris Bird III to church, but Grandma did. She took little Sandra too. The first time Sandra went, she became so nervous she wet herself. But after that she was all right. It was an Episcopal church. The minister's name was Gar P. Pallister, and he looked like a benign Boris Karloff. He was quite tall, and he kept his hair cut short, and his voice had the sound of boulders rolling in a cave. Morris Bird III liked to listen to the Rev. Mr. Pallister talk. He also liked the music. The Rev. Mr. Pallister never made God seem scary. Grandma often talked about the Rev. Mr. Pallister. More ministers should be like him, she

said. After all, God is Love. There is no need to make Him out to be
Something that frightens people half to death. Then, staring at Morris
Bird III: You listen to him when he talks. He knows what he's talking
about. And never mind the fact that his first name is the name of a fish.
That's not *his* fault, poor man. He understands goodness. And he be-
lieves in it. Don't ask me how I know. I just *know*, that's all. I've lived
long enough so that I can trust my instincts. They've been pretty accurate over the years. They made it so I married your grandfather, and
that was the best thing I ever did. He was a fine brave man. Always
said his piece. In '28, when everyone was making so much money, he
warned people it wouldn't last. He told them too many of them were
doing too much borrowing. He told them it would all catch up with
them. They didn't like to hear it, and they made fun, and they insulted
him, but you want to know something? Not for a minute did he shut
up—and not for a minute did he get mad. That's bravery. That's the
sign of a man of worth. Your grandfather was a man of worth. He had
no bank balance, but he was a man of worth, and you'd just better
believe me. I know. I bore his children. There were no secrets. Brave
people don't believe in them. So you take my word about Mr. Pallister.
He is a brave man too. His sermons are the best I've ever heard. Last
Sunday, when he talked about what he called The Sin of Withdrawal
from Commitment, you know what he meant? He meant: Do what
has to be done. Don't hold back. Forget what the people down the
street will say. If a thing is right, it is right. Don't turn your back on it.
Don't put comfort ahead of duty.

Come to think of it, maybe Grandma's belief in bravery did *too*
lend itself to speeches.

Oh well, she was the best of her kind a person could hope for. And
Morris Bird III didn't mind the church and the Rev. Mr. Pallister the
slightest bit. He especially liked the part they called Versicles. It put
him in mind of something wet and delicious at the end of a stick.

AND THEN OF COURSE there was President Roosevelt, who knew something about courage too.

This was because of a man named Thomas E. Dewey. Morris Bird

III didn't understand Thomas E. Dewey. It seemed Thomas E. Dewey hated President Roosevelt. In this fall of 1944 Thomas E. Dewey was running against President Roosevelt, trying to throw President Roosevelt out of office, and he was calling President Roosevelt old, tired and defeated. And, every time you turned on the radio, you heard somebody say CLEAR IT WITH SIDNEY, whatever that meant.

Clearly, this Thomas E. Dewey—and a man named John W. Bricker, who was governor of the state of *Ohio* for crying out loud— really couldn't stand President Roosevelt. But only Nazis and the dirty little Japs were supposed to hate President Roosevelt. If you were an *American* and hated President Roosevelt, what did that make you?

(Old? Tired? Defeated? How come, if President Roosevelt was all those things, our side was winning the war? Well, you had to make allowances. After all, the people who said such things were Republicans, and everyone knew Republicans were sort of thick in the head. They're aginners, his grandmother told him, and aginners never make much sense.)

Huh. Thomas E. Dewey and John W. Bricker and the rest of those Republicans made no sense at all. Who could possibly have wanted that Dewey instead of President Roosevelt? That mustache and all. Fooey.

Not that President Roosevelt minded, though. Morris Bird III read the papers, and President Roosevelt was concentrating on winning the war, paying no mind to the silly Republicans with their thick heads, and this meant that he was a brave man. They were calling him old and tired and defeated, but he was above them. He was so brave that he could afford to ignore them. That was some brave, and Morris Bird III was very proud of him. (And so was just about everyone else in the neighborhood. President Roosevelt was a Democrat, and the neighborhood was full of Democrats, and this was nice to know. As long as there were so many Democrats around, there was some hope for the world.) So, in order that everyone knew where Morris Bird III stood in the political arena, he wore a button that said

ROOSEVELT

on his jacket, and another button that said

ROOSEVELT-TRUMAN

next to the watchpocket of his trousers, and a little plastic donkey-shaped pin that said

FDR

on the front of his shirt, and sometimes he caught Mrs. Dallas looking at him and grinning. Well, let her. He enjoyed rooting for things and people—baseball teams and the President and whatever. It was good to be interested. It made it so you didn't suffer from The Sin of Withdrawal from Commitment. As his grandmother said: Get involved in things. Don't let the world pass you by. Don't be ashamed to get up on your hind legs and whoop and holler. This *Time* Magazine that I read every week, it's full of bushwah up to its eyeballs, but you want to know something? I don't care. The important thing is that it takes stands. It gives me the news, which means that I can Keep Up (provided I take what it says about the President with a grain or two of salt), and if the man who owns it—his name is Luce, and his wife used to be some sort of writer or actress or something—if the man who owns it wants to give me some halfbaked Republican propaganda, let him. It's his right. It's his magazine. And anyway, I like the movie reviews.

One day Morris Bird III asked his grandmother what CLEAR IT WITH SIDNEY meant.

She was peeling potatoes. She smiled at him, but her smile was not warm. It was simply a lot of teeth, nothing more. "It's just the Republicans being nasty," she said.

"Huh?"

Grandma laid aside her knife and her potatoes. "Sidney is a Jewish name," she said. "The President has a friend named Sidney. The Republicans are trying to get the votes of people who don't like Jews."

"Jews? Like Mr. Rubinstein who runs the used funnybook store?"

"Yes."

"Mr. Rubinstein shrugs his shoulders a lot. Is that why people don't like Jews?"

"It's as good a reason as any," said Grandma.

"He's different."

"Yes," said Grandma, "and people are afraid of people who are different."

"I'm not afraid of Mr. Rubinstein."

"Well, that's because you're *you*—you're not just *people*."

Morris Bird III went to Grandma and hugged her. "Thank you," he said. "Thank you."

"My pleasure," said Grandma.

STANLEY CHALOUPKA HAD BEEN different too. As a matter of fact, Stanley Chaloupka was the most different person Morris Bird III had ever known. He was also his closest friend. This is not to say that Morris Bird III had no other friends. He had plenty. Despite the Ulysses S. Grant incident when some of the boys had accused him of having A Big Fat Long Brown Nose (and despite a few others, such as the time he dropkicked Johnny Sellers' football through an open window of an apartment building next to the schoolyard), Morris Bird III got along very well with his classmates, even though none of them was a Stanley Chaloupka. (The football never was recovered. Someone in that apartment building made off with it.) But the previous summer Stanley Chaloupka had moved away. Stanley's father had been drafted, and Stanley and his mother had gone to live with her parents, who had a home on East 63rd Street, away over by St. Clair Avenue, which was farther away than the end of the world. (Several of the boys went into the apartment building and made inquiries, but none of the people who lived there owned up to finding the football. Johnny Sellers wept, calling Morris Bird III a dumb showoff.) Stanley Chaloupka was attending another school, and Morris Bird III didn't suppose he'd ever see old Stanley again. (Johnny Sellers' big brother, who was in the eighth grade at Addison Junior High, encountered Morris Bird III on the sidewalk the next day and kind of talked him into forking over a dollar for a new football. Morris Bird III had anticipated the encounter. He had the dollar with him, all ready to be forked over. He'd fished the money that morning from his Porky Pig bank. He'd not minded doing this. The previous night, he'd not slept a bit well. He'd thrashed. Grandma had heard him thrash. She came into his bedroom and asked him what the trouble was. Heartburn, he told her. Well, we'll just take care of *that*, said Grandma, and she fetched him a tablespoonful of Phillips' Milk of Magnesia. He made a face, choked it down, bawled himself out for telling such a stupid lie. Next time he would *think* before he lied. He got up early in the morning, and half an hour later he had coaxed the money from the Porky Pig bank with his penknife. The penknife had been a Christmas present from his Uncle Alan, but he wasn't allowed to carry it with him. It makes my flesh run cold, said Grandma. He didn't argue with her about it. The truth was—it kind of made *his* flesh run cold too. When he encountered Johnny Sellers' big brother that day, he handed over the money before the fellow had hardly said ten words. Two quarters, three dimes, a nickel and fifteen pennies. Here, said Morris Bird III, thrusting the coins toward Johnny Sellers' big brother. The boy blinked several times before taking the money. Ah, he said. Yes. Well. All *right*. And, smiling, Morris Bird III proceeded unmolested. Footballs just like Johnny Sellers' were selling for 58 cents at Woolworth's, but this was all right. That night Morris Bird III slept well, and that was what was important.) As for Stanley Chaloupka, Morris Bird III missed him more than he liked to admit. (For several months after the thing with the football, Johnny Sellers referred to Morris Bird III as Old Bird Turd the Showoff.) Stanley Chaloupka had owned the most elaborate layout of Lionel O Gauge trains it had ever been Morris Bird III's pleasure to see. Next to sports and Guns, his favorite activity was electric trains, and Stanley Chaloupka's magnificent layout had been enough to suck away the breath. Now the layout was in a house somewhere over by East 63rd Street or wherever. (He always glared when he passed the apartment building where the football had disappeared. A couple of times he went into the vestibule and examined the names on the little plates where the doorbell buttons were. The football had gone into a secondfloor hallway, and so it stood to reason someone who lived on that floor had made off with it. There were four suites on the second floor. They were occupied by people named Israel, Roberts, Cox and Marshall. He kind of suspected Israel, probably because he'd never heard of such a peculiar name.) Stanley Chaloupka's father had set up the layout in the basement of their old home, which had been on Rosalind Avenue, a narrow little street a shade more than a block from Edmunds Avenue. The main track ran in an enormous L, with loops at either end for turning the trains around. There were numerous passing tracks, sidings, stations, crossinggates, little lead cows and horses and automobiles and trucks, and even a roundhouse with a real operating turntable. (One day Morris Bird III got up his nerve and rang the Israel doorbell, but no one answered.) In his days at the Hough Elementary School, Stanley Chaloupka was undoubtedly the worst handsoccer player in the history of the world. He was even worse than clumsy old Alex Coffee, The Human Garbage Can. He was what the other boys called A Slop. There was no worse name to be called than A Slop. In choosing up sides, it was traditional to pick Stanley Chaloupka last. And, when the number of available players was uneven, Stanley didn't get to play. Not that he minded. If the others wanted him to play, fine—he played. But, if they didn't, that was all right too—he enjoyed sitting on a swing and thinking. Not that he swung. He didn't. All he did was think. Sometimes he grinned, but no one except Morris Bird III ever found out what he was grinning *about.* It took Morris Bird III a long time to find out, and when he finally did, he wasn't really very comfortable with the information. At any rate, Stanley Chaloupka didn't Fit In very well. Sometimes the other boys called him Goofy instead of A Slop, but mostly they ignored him. If he wanted to sit on a swing and think and grin, let him. They were too busy to care. (Morris Bird III never did get around to ringing the Roberts, Cox and Marshall doorbells. He'd had only so much nerve, and it all had been used up in the ringing of the Israel doorbell.)

THE FRIENDSHIP OF MORRIS BIRD III and Stanley Chaloupka had more going for it than simply Stanley's superb O Gauge layout. A great deal more. For one thing, it enabled them to sort of protect themselves against most of the other kids. This was because they both were known as Brains. No one in his right mind—except maybe a *girl*—wanted to be thought of as A Brain. Better to be thought of as A Slop than A Brain. After all, if you were A Slop, you probably couldn't help it. But if you were A Brain, obviously you *could* help it. You could hide it. Which was what Morris Bird III most of the time tried to do. Occasionally, such as the time he gave the lengthy speech on old Ulysses S. Grant, he forgot himself, but that sort of lapse didn't happen very often. Most of the time, he was quite skillful at losing himself in the crowd. Stanley Chaloupka, on the other hand, was not good at all in being inconspicuous. He was A Slop *and* A Brain, which made him probably the Number One Goof in the whole school. And it certainly didn't help matters that he *looked* like a Goof. He was overweight, and he wore glasses (they had no rims, and he could barely see without them), and they looked like the bottoms of pop bottles. He had red hair, and it always curled around his ears like a girl's. His pants always hung below his belly, and he carried breadcrusts in his pockets. Sometimes he fed the breadcrusts to sparrows, but most of the time he ate the breadcrusts himself. One day when Morris Bird III asked him what was so great about breadcrusts Stanley said: I like them.

"CHALOUPKA?"

"Yes?"

"Kids laugh at you."

"I know that."

"So why don't you do something about it?"

"I can't."

"Why?"

"I'm me."

The above conversation took place one day in February of 1944. Morris Bird III and Stanley Chaloupka were walking to school together. It was the only time Morris Bird III ever tried to talk his friend into getting lost in the crowd. He was never again that rude.

ALMOST EVERY MORNING STANLEY CHALOUPKA had yellow boogers in his eyes when he came to school. They were not small either. They couldn't have been. If they had been, you wouldn't have been able to see them through his glasses. And then there was his hat. Not a cap. A *hat*. It was a regular wide-brimmed *felt hat*, like the kind grown men wore. He was the only pupil at the Hough Elementary School who wore a hat. And, for that matter, he was the only pupil at the Hough Elementary School who wore a vest. A blue vest, with large buttons, and sometimes people asked him what office he was running for. He always smiled at the question, never answered it. You got the feeling he was in on some great big secret. Like maybe how to blow up the world. He was bigger than most of the others, but his bigness was gelatinous. It wouldn't have scared a rabbit. When he did the exercises in gym class, all the parts of him went in every which direction, and the older boys laughed at what they called his boobies. Sometimes they called him Jane Russell. He never seemed to mind. At least no one had ever seen him cry.

"CHALOUPKA?"

"Yes?"

"How come you think so much?"

"I like it."

"That why you grin?"

"Yes."

The above conversation took place one day in June of 1944, shortly before Stanley Chaloupka and his mother moved out of the neighborhood. Stanley had been sitting on the porch steps of his home. His glasses were off, and he was cleaning them with a gray handkerchief, and he was grinning. Morris Bird III sat down beside him and asked him the questions. The answers made Morris Bird III nod. They didn't reveal much to him, but they did make him nod.

THERE WAS SOMETHING PECULIAR about the friendship. After all, Morris Bird III *was* a good handsoccer player and far and away the best dropkicker in the entire school (which meant he was in no way A Slop), and yet there he was—stuck with his fondness for old Stanley Chaloupka. One day, because of the fondness, he almost did a very

peculiar thing: he almost chose Stanley Chaloupka *first* for a handsoccer game. Stanley Chaloupka's name was right there, waiting to pop
from his mouth, but then at the last possible second he chose Kenny
Haas. There was an uneven number of players that day, and of course
Stanley Chaloupka didn't get to play. He went to a swing and sat there
and grinned. Morris Bird III played very badly, and that night it took
him a long time to get to sleep. Two words kept going through his
mind: YOU STINK. Over and over again: YOU STINK. YOU STINK. YOU
STINK. Not that Stanley Chaloupka minded. Or, if he did, he never said
a word. Whenever the subject came up, all he said was this: I know I'm
no good, so don't let it get you. I don't think it's my fault I'm no good,
but it's not *your* fault either, so you listen to me. Don't let it get you.
I'd just as soon sit on the swing. No kidding. I like to think. It's mostly
about my trains. I close my eyes, and there they are, and it's almost
as good as being home with them. I make up trains in my head. I ask
myself What kind of a train is it going to be tonight, freight or passenger or what? I've got it down real good. I make up the whole train.
A boxcar maybe, and a gondola, and two tankcars, and a cattlecar,
with the caboose at the end, with the whole thing pulled by maybe the
little 0–4–0 switcher, the one that says PENNSYLVANIA on its tender.
The tender is the coalcar, the car right behind the engine. It's really
part of the engine. Not everybody knows that. So, anyhow, that's what
I do most of the time when you see me sitting on the swing. I love
my trains. They make me feel big. When I grow up, you know what
I want? I want to be rich. You know why I want to be rich? Because
then I can have my own private railroad car. I can lie in bed and get
pulled around the country. You ever lie in bed in a train? Makes you
feel like King of the World. You're warm, and nobody wants anything
from you, and outside your window the whole world goes by. Like in a
movie. The telegraphpoles are nice. *Whisk whisk whisk*, a nice sound.
And the sound of the tracks. And all the houses and streets so tiny and
quiet. It's all there in front of you, and no one wants to hurt you. It's
your own little world, and nobody wants to get mean to you. I mean,
nobody cares how smart you are, I mean, it's so good sometimes I
want to cry.

● ● ●

"CHALOUPKA?"

"Yes?"

"You're my pal."

"Thank you."

"You'll always be my pal."

"You too."

"What?"

"*You'll* always be *my* pal too."

The above conversation took place the day in July of 1944 when Stanley Chaloupka and his mother moved out of the neighborhood. He and Morris Bird III were standing in the empty basement of the Chaloupka place on Rosalind Avenue. The layout had been disassembled and carried out in boxes. The basement seemed so much bigger now. Morris Bird III felt small and almost frightened. He knew he was being a dummy. A lot of good it did. He sort of punched Stanley Chaloupka in the belly, and Stanley Chaloupka grinned at him, and then they went upstairs.

STANLEY CHALOUPKA'S GRIN HAD been almost too much of a grin. It had been almost scary. Morris Bird III knew he was being a ninny when he remembered his friend's grin as being almost scary. After all, Stanley Chaloupka wasn't Bela Lugosi. He just grinned funny. He grinned like Stanley Chaloupka. Nothing more, nothing less. Still, when he thought back on the friendship, Morris Bird III did shiver—sort of— when he remembered Stanley Chaloupka's grin. He knew he wasn't being fair, but since when did a shiver understand fairness? Ah, it surely was a peculiar friendship, and Morris Bird III hadn't ever really got it all straight in his mind. There were so many *parts* to it, so many different *things* he felt (friendliness, then mystification, then fear, then sympathy, and so forth and so on and so forth), and all these things jostled each other in his mind, and sometimes they were just about enough to give him a headache. But about Stanley Chaloupka's grin: Morris Bird III wasn't the only one who was frightened by it. The other children almost always brought it up when they discussed Stanley Chaloupka. *He looks like he's waiting for the man in the white* coat, they said. Or maybe like he's just swallowed a fly. Huh, how'd you like to meet *that* in a dark alley? Well, Morris Bird III didn't particularly want to agree with the other children, but he did. Stanley Chaloupka had been his best friend and all that, but . . . ah fooey, what good did it do to try to figure him out? If Stanley Chaloupka knew the secret of blowing up the world, let him know it. Life was too short. The best thing to do was take things as they came and not try to figure out so many Whys. It was enough that Morris Bird III liked Stanley Chaloupka. It was enough that Stanley Chaloupka had that great layout of O Gauge trains. Three or four times a week Morris Bird III went to Stanley Chaloupka's home to play with the trains. (Before that day in July of 1944, that is. Since the day Stanley Chaloupka and his mother moved away, Morris Bird III hadn't heard a word from him.) But it surely had been fun playing with those trains, and Stanley Chaloupka's parents had been just as pleasant as anything. Morris Bird III and Stanley Chaloupka spent most of their time in the basement. They played quietly, and Stanley Chaloupka always let Morris Bird III be the engineer. He stood and watched Morris Bird III work the transformer, and from time to time the grin appeared, and it was as though he were maybe off on the moon. Morris Bird III tried to pay no attention. Instead he sat behind the little control box and concentrated on all the levers and switches and all. He learned a lot. Before getting to know Stanley Chaloupka, he'd understood very little about trains and railroads—the difference, for example, between a little 0-4-0 switcher and a great big 4-6-4 freight engine. But Stanley Chaloupka understood that kind of stuff, and he explained it so that Morris Bird III understood it. The first number represented the number of little wheels that were in front of the drivewheels (the drivewheels were the big wheels that made the locomotive go). The second number represented the number of drivewheels. The third number represented the number of little wheels that trailed behind the drivewheels. Thus, it stood to reason that a 4-6-4 was a whole lot bigger than an 0-4-0, and Morris Bird III knew something he'd not known before. Not that he'd particularly minded not knowing what the 0 and the 4 and the 0 of an 0-4-0 meant, but oh well, he supposed his Horizons had been expanded a little. (Teachers liked to talk about Expanding Your Horizons, whatever *that* meant, and maybe they were important.) The name of Stanley Chaloupka's railroad was the Atlantic & Pacific. There were stations at each end of the L—one for the town of Atlantic, one for the town of Pacific. Ten times the distance between the loops at the ends of the L represented the distance between the two towns. Stanley Chaloupka ran his railroad on a rigid schedule. At 6:45 each morning (except Sundays; the Chaloupkas were Catholics and attended early Mass), a freight train ran from Atlantic to Pacific. At 7 o'clock, a passenger train ran from Pacific to Atlantic. At 6:45 and 7 in the evening, the schedule was reversed. Stanley Chaloupka never deviated from it. He owned an extremely accurate Mickey Mouse pocket watch with a leather fob, and he checked it every morning by telephoning GReenwich 1212 and listening to a lady talk about the tone and the time. He saw nothing strange in the precision with which he ran his railroad. If you're going to run a railroad, he told Morris Bird III, you should do it right. Otherwise you shouldn't bother. Of course there were other trains that ran on the Atlantic and Pacific, but Stanley Chaloupka designated them as Extras. He kept a record of all trains—regulars and Extras—in an old Spiral stenographer notebook. All the trains Morris Bird III operated were, naturally, Extras. At first he was a little scared to sit at the controls, and sometimes, when the train moved too slowly, Stanley Chaloupka would frown at him. Open it up, he would say. Open it *up.* You're running behind schedule. So, obediently, Morris Bird III would open it up. The first few times he was engineer, he took the curves too fast, which meant that some of the cars tipped over. Stanley Chaloupka would then have to assemble a work train, complete with wreck crane, and come clear the debris and restore mainline traffic. After the first three or four wrecks, Stanley Chaloupka taught Morris Bird III a little trick. He taught Morris Bird III to make up a train so that the heavier cars were immediately behind the locomotive. Always put flatcars at the end of the train just in front of the caboose, he said. That way, there won't be so much tipping. And, sure enough, this was true. After learning the little trick, *and* after learning to slow down the train on the curves, Morris Bird III had no further trouble with wrecks. Sometimes Stanley Chaloupka helped the trains make their sounds. *Ch ch ch ch ch,* he

said under his breath, *ch ch ch ch, woo woo, ch ch ch ch ch.* Morris
Bird III never said a word about these sounds. As a matter of fact, they
were sort of fun, and sometimes he made them himself. *Ch ch ch ch
ch.* You could time them to the rhythm of the drivewheels, and the
whole operation made you feel better than anything. The truth was:
Morris Bird III really enjoyed himself when he visited the Chaloupka
home—and not just because of the trains either. He liked Stanley
Chaloupka's father and mother a whole lot. Before going into the
Army, Edward H. Chaloupka had been a display advertising salesman
for the morning paper. He was large, wore glasses that were just as
thick as his son's, but there was nothing a bit shy about *him.* Back in
the late 1920's he'd played professional football for a team called the
Akron Terriers. A picture of the 1928 team hung in a frame over the
mantel. A young Edward H. Chaloupka stood in the second row,
fourth from the left. I was only a kid that year, he told Morris Bird III,
but I hung in there. I was a first team man, started every game. Twenty
dollars a game we got, if we was lucky. Sometimes it was ten, and
sometimes it was nothing at all, but listen, I'll tell you something: we
had fun. Heh. First team man. Heh. Count the players in the picture.
It comes to nineteen. I couldn't of been much else *but* a first team
man, could I of? But I will say this: I played every minute of every
game. I was the center, and we played about twentyfive games, so I
guess playing every minute of every game wasn't such a small thing at
that. And you know something? I'm proud of that. Maybe I shouldn't
be, but I am. Can't help it. Yessir, every minute of every game, and I'll
tell you something else: I'm still in shape. Maybe I can't move around
as fast as I could when I was a kid, but that don't mean I don't take
care of myself. I got this friend, and we belong to the Y, and twice a
week him and I go there and work out. And I mean *work out.* Mostly
the old handball. Best exercise in the world. Good for the old muscle
tone. And it keeps your brain alert too. Makes it so you don't get old
so fast. In this life, the worst thing in the world is getting old, and
don't you forget it. So keep in shape. Exercise. The old muscle tone.
And, uh, your wife appreciates it too. A man who's in good shape is a
man who can make his wife happy. With these words, Edward H.
Chaloupka looked at his wife and gave her a broad grin. Mrs. Cha-

loupka, a pretty woman with red hair, turned her face away and said: Oh *you*. Morris Bird III liked her very much too. She was tiny, but she was very very pretty, and she had a fluted birdlike way of talking. She often brought milk and Hostess chocolate cream cupcakes down to the railroad magnates in the basement. She couldn't say six words without smiling, and she behaved in no way like any mother Morris Bird III ever had known, but you didn't hear him complain. Once, when he went upstairs to go to the bathroom, she took him aside and said: You're a good boy, young Mr. Bird. Stanley really likes you. I hope you really like him. No, I take that back. It's an insult. I *know* you like him. You're an honest boy. You wouldn't come here if you didn't like him. His father and—he's nothing at all like us, and . . . well, *you* know . . . I mean, sometimes we think maybe it's our fault he doesn't make so many friends. So *many?* Huh! Until you came along, he hadn't ever made a one. Not a one. He's eight years old, and eight years is a long time when you're a kid, and in all those eight years not a one. My husband built that layout in the basement. Ever since Stanley's been able to put words together, it's been trains trains trains. Trains and all the books he reads. And Eddie slaved like a dog on that layout. Every night after work. You should have seen him. He loves his son. I mean, you don't have to understand someone to love him. Stanley's not mean anyway; he's just different, so *smart* and all. When he's not down there with his trains, he's reading some book. Oh. Oh I'm sorry. I'm not saying what I want to say. Can you . . . uh, oh I'm *so* sorry. Mrs. Chaloupka bent down and quickly kissed Morris Bird III on a cheek. You're a love, she said, and then she went away. He frowned, rubbed the cheek. He decided it wasn't easy for people whose only kid was a Stanley Chaloupka. Too complicated. He was undoubtedly the best friend Stanley Chaloupka had ever known, but old Stanley threw him for a loss too. He did the most peculiar things. The spelling bee, for instance, back in the spring of 1943 when they'd both been in the 3B. The spelling bee and the arithmetic contest. There were to be these two competitions, and the winners were to get Easter baskets full of eggs and candy and all that. Not that Morris Bird III had much of a chance. Even though he probably *was* A Brain, he wasn't much of a speller, and he didn't think he had the concentration for the arithmetic contest. In arithmetic, it was all concentration, and in the springtime he had a hard time concentrating on much of anything besides baseball. Their teacher that semester was a Miss Steingass, who was sort of fat and giggly. The idea of the Easter baskets was hers. She bought them with her own money, and she did not let the children forget her generosity. Still, for all that, she wasn't a bad person for a teacher. So what if she did make a lot of noise? At least she didn't hit people, and she didn't bother with Deep Indian Breaths. Well, at any rate, there was a lot of fuss connected with the spelling bee and the arithmetic competition. You'd have thought the winners were going to receive special berths Up There Where God Was. The arithmetic competition came first. Morris Bird III didn't disappoint himself. He was eliminated on the eleventh problem. At the end of the twentieth problem, only two children—Stanley Chaloupka and a girl named Dolores Bovasso—were still in the running. This Dolores Bovasso was thin and prim, the sort of girl who forever sucked in her breath whenever someone did something she thought was bad. This was a fretful and aggravating sound, prissy and oldmaidish, and Morris Bird III despised the sort of people who made it. These people were Goody-goods, and Dolores Bovasso was the prize Goodygood of the world. She even had a double box of Crayola crayons. On the twentyfirst problem, Dolores Bovasso had to multiply 9 by 12. She got 98. Stanley Chaloupka got 108. Which meant that was that. Giggling and chattering, Miss Steingass gave him an Easter basket. Dolores Bovasso made a thin sound that came from her nose. (Most of the children had been pulling for old Goofy. They'd had enough of Dolores Bovasso. That afternoon, a number of them congratulated Stanley Chaloupka as he walked home with his Easter basket. By the time he arrived home, he had given away every piece of the candy and all but two of the eggs.) Next day the spelling bee began, and it turned out to be what everyone called a lulu. Morris Bird III survived the first ten words, and he survived the second ten words, but on his twentyfirst turn he spelled Soap *Sope*, which of course did him in. At the end of the fifth set of ten words, only Stanley Chaloupka and that hissing little priss of a Dolores Bovasso were still in the running. Miss Steingass was by this time giving them words hardly anyone had *heard* of, let alone knew how to *spell*. Words such as *Nonetheless* and *Niggardly* and *Flaccid* and *Antidote*, all sorts of exotic polysyllabic words that made the children gasp and cluck. On her twelfth word, Dolores Bovasso spelled *Thankful* Thankfull, but Stanley Chaloupka also missed, coming up with Paralell for *Parallel*. Dolores Bovasso had begun to sniffle after missing her word, but then when—miracle of miracles—Stanley Chaloupka missed *his*, she forgot her sniffles. She looked at him and then she actually grinned. Everyone saw it. She didn't try to hide it at all. In the back of the room, someone said: Boo. Stanley Chaloupka blinked at her, and the corners of his mouth were moist. He rocked back and forth on the balls of his feet, and his hands were thrust deep in his pockets. Morris Bird III supposed the poor goof maybe was playing with his breadcrusts. Dolores Bovasso and Stanley Chaloupka stood flanking Miss Steingass' desk. Dolores stood rigidly, and her face had no color. All Stanley Chaloupka did was blink and rock. The sniffles had made Dolores' eyes a little pink. After her grin went away, she began sneaking timid little glances at Stanley Chaloupka. Her eyes became small, and Morris Bird III saw that the glances were hateful more than timid. He wanted to rush to the front of the room and clap Stanley Chaloupka on the back, but of course Miss Steingass would have had a heart attack, and so he stayed in his seat. Dolores did *Thoughtful* correctly, and Stanley Chaloupka got past *Jasmine*. Miss Steingass told the class that goodness, she was now giving Dolores and Stanley *junior high* words. She hoped they all understood what remarkable pupils Dolores and Stanley were—being only 3Bs and all that. Ah, that Miss Steingass certainly did like to talk. Did she really think she was telling them something they didn't already know? Dolores Bovasso was the biggest studier and memorizer and Pill in the school, so what did Miss Steingass expect? Naturally Dolores knew how to spell all those big words. She certainly studied enough. As for Stanley Chaloupka . . . well, Stanley Chaloupka was just plain *smart*. So it stood to reason that the two of them would do well. Morris Bird III and the others would have fallen over if Dolores and Stanley *hadn't* done well. Miss Steingass flipped the pages of the book, gave Dolores *Youthful*. Dolores didn't hesitate. Out it came, and it was correct. Stanley Chaloupka got *Wily*. He didn't hesitate either. Out it came, and it was correct. Everyone was leaning forward, and Morris Bird III's breath hurt. He was rooting for old Stanley Chaloupka as hard, if not maybe harder, than he'd ever rooted for anything or anyone in his whole life. He glared at prissy Dolores Bovasso and wished she would fall over dead. He looked around, and he could see that everyone else was rooting just as hard for Stanley Chaloupka. Maybe old Goofy didn't know it, but right at that moment he had a lot of friends. Morris Bird III couldn't see Stanley Chaloupka's eyes (the glasses were too thick), so he didn't know whether Stanley Chaloupka understood what was happening. Ah, but Stanley was A Brain. Surely he understood what was happening. Great would be the delight when he won the second Easter basket. Sooner or later, Dolores would make a mistake. She was no real match for Stanley Chaloupka. No one was—not at this sort of thing. Now Dolores' hands were shaking a little, and she kept opening and closing her fingers. They put Morris Bird III in mind of little worms. Her next word was *Withhold*. She spoke up quickly, her voice squeaking. It came out Withold. No Dolores, said Miss Steingass. I'm sorry. Dolores blinked at Miss Steingass for a moment. Then there came from Dolores a sequence of shudders, then a snort, then a sort of whine. Her nose began to run. She took a handkerchief from a sleeve, turned her back on the class, blew her nose. She walked to the blackboard, rested her forehead against it. Now *Dolores*, said Miss Steingass. Dolores paid Miss Steingass no mind. Miss Steingass started to stand up, then thought better of it. She gave a shrug, smiled at Stanley Chaloupka and asked him to spell *Gingerbread*. He rubbed his tongue over the wet corners of his mouth, glanced at Dolores. He opened his mouth but nothing came out. He swallowed, smiled at Miss Steingass. *Gingerbread*, said Miss Steingass, frowning. Dolores turned from the blackboard. That's an *easy* one! she hollered. She folded her arms over her chest. She was trembling. Miss Steingass glared at Dolores. You be a Good Sport, she said. Dolores swallowed, nodded. Yes Miss Steingass, she said. Again the handkerchief came from her sleeve. This time she wiped at her eyes. Morris Bird III and the others looked at Stanley Chaloupka. The dampness had gone out of the corners of Stanley Chaloupka's mouth, and now he was showing Miss Steingass his teeth. Uh oh, something peculiar was about to happen. Morris Bird III wasn't fooled by the grin. He knew Stanley Chaloupka too well. Stanley Chaloupka glanced briefly at his hands (they had just come from his pockets), rubbed them together, then, very slowly and distinctly, spelled *Gingerbread* Gingerbred. His grin had become wider than the sky. All of a sudden Morris Bird III understood what was happening. Again he wanted to run to the front of the room, only this time he wanted maybe to hit Stanley Chaloupka in the belly and call him a dumbhead. Miss Steingass was frowning at Stanley Chaloupka, and Morris Bird III supposed *she* understood too. She shook her head from side to side and told Stanley Chaloupka no, that's incorrect. Dolores Bovasso promptly began to cough. She coughed so vigorously she had to bend forward. Finally Miss Steingass excused her from the room. She staggered out to the Girls' Toilet for a drink of water or something. When she returned, she was smiling, and she had combed her hair. She knew what Morris Bird III knew, what Miss Steingass probably knew, what anyone in the room with any brains also probably knew. Her eyes were as dry as anything, and her face had all sorts of color. Her next word was *Alfalfa*, and she had no trouble spelling it. Stanley Chaloupka's word was *February*, and speaking very carefully, enunciating clearly, he spelled it Febuary. Dolores Bovasso giggled and did a happy little dance when Miss Steingass gave her the Easter basket. Stanley Chaloupka stood grinning at Dolores, and of course she paid no attention to him. No one asked her for any of her eggs or candy. For several months thereafter, almost everyone referred to her as That Pill. Then, what with memories fading, everything went back to being what it had been before. Morris Bird III didn't quite know what to think. He knew the word Love, and he knew the word Pity, but what did they have to do with Dolores Bovasso? What had she ever done to deserve them? Ah, that Stanley Chaloupka . . . how come he knew so much? Maybe he was a midget. Maybe he was really about fifty years old. Goofy Chaloupka: what was the secret? Which meant that, no matter how nice Stanley Chaloupka's parents were, no matter how much fun it was being engineer for the Extra runs of the Atlantic & Pacific Railroad, no matter how interesting Mr. Chaloupka's hearty football talk was, no matter how many hurried little kisses Mrs. Chaloupka gave him on the cheek, Morris Bird III never really relaxed when he visited the Chaloupka place. He liked being there, and he didn't like being there, and he was being a ninny, and he knew he was being a ninny, but the thing was—sometimes he wished he'd never met goofy old Stanley Chaloupka and the Love or Pity or whatever . . . goofy old Stanley Chaloupka with his dumb vests, his breadcrusts, his Spiral notebook . . . goofy old Stanley Chaloupka with the boogers in his eyes and his grin that was all teeth . . . goofy old Stanley Chaloupka with his big flopping boobies . . . what could you do about goofy old Stanley Chaloupka if, when all was said and done, you loved him? Aw, fooey. Morris Bird III tried not to spend too much time considering this problem. He couldn't afford to. He owed Stanley Chaloupka too much—and forget the trains. It was Stanley Chaloupka who got Morris Bird III to read *The Hound of the Baskervilles*. It was Stanley Chaloupka who introduced Morris Bird III to the works of Rudyard Kipling. It was Stanley Chaloupka who loaned Morris Bird III his vast collection of the adventures of Lamont Cranston, known more familiarly as The Shadow. It was Stanley Chaloupka who showed Morris Bird III how to read a compass. It was Stanley Chaloupka who explained to Morris Bird III how a pump worked. It was Stanley Chaloupka who made Morris Bird III understand the beauty of *knowing* things. Not because you *had* to. Just because they were interesting. But then Stanley Chaloupka went away. In January of 1944 Stanley Chaloupka's father was called up for his third physical (he'd flunked the first two because of bad eyesight). This time he was classified 1-A, and the following month he was inducted into the Army. He was sent to a camp in Georgia. After his basic training, he was assigned to the post cadre as a calisthenics instructor. By the time Stanley Chaloupka moved away in July, Edward H. Chaloupka had attained the grade of Technician Fourth Grade and had been named coach of the camp football team. Stanley Chaloupka was very proud of all this, and his grin just about split his face whenever he spoke of it. The day Stanley Chaloupka and his mother moved to East 63rd Street, Morris Bird III helped Stanley pack several boxes with all the track, rolling stock, outbuildings and equipment of the Atlantic & Pacific Railroad. He didn't say much, and neither did Stanley. They told each other they always would be pals, and Stanley said something about East 63rd Street not being the end of the world, and that was about the extent of the conversation. Morris Bird III still didn't understand why Stanley and his mother had to move. Mrs. Chaloupka had tried to explain, but Morris Bird III hadn't paid much attention. The thing was—he hadn't *wanted* to pay attention. With my husband in the army, Mrs. Chaloupka had said, there just isn't enough money coming in. My mother has offered to take us in, and . . . well, I can't afford to turn her down. We're going to miss you, young Mr. Bird. You'll have to come visit us. East 63rd isn't so far away. And who knows? Maybe when the war's over we'll come back here to live. I like it here. I always have. I like the neighborhood. And so does Stanley. Maybe *you* don't know that, but he's told me. Just the other day he came to me and he said: Mother, I know we have to go, but I don't *want* to go. And then he had to take off his glasses and wipe his eyes. And he's not a bawler. Not by any manner or means. How about that, huh? But don't you say anything to him. He wouldn't like knowing I'd told on him. Nodding, Morris Bird III promised Stanley Chaloupka's mother he would keep the secret. Not that there was so much to tell. So Stanley Chaloupka had almost cried. So big deal. So Stanley Chaloupka was a member of the human race. When you moved away from a place where you'd lived for a long time, there was something wrong with you if you didn't at least *almost* cry. Lord knows, on the day Stanley Chaloupka moved away Morris Bird III wasn't above a little sneaky sniffling. Especially at that moment when the movingvan pulled away. His chest hurt, and so did the back of his neck, and so did his eyes. He wasn't proud of himself, but he wasn't ashamed either. He didn't believe people should go around bawling and puling like his little sister Sandra over the slightest thing, but now and then where was the harm in warm eyes and maybe a sniffle or two? He stood on the sidewalk with his hands on his hips, looked at the house, watched Stanley and his mother emerge. Mrs. Chaloupka was carrying a suitcase. Well, she said, coming toward Morris Bird III, this is it. He looked away from her. He looked down the street. The movingvan turned onto Crawford Road and then disappeared. Mrs. Chaloupka carried the suitcase to her car. It had an A sticker, and it was a '38 Chevrolet. She put the suitcase in the trunk,

then smiled and said: I hope we don't have an accident. I'm a real
Nervous Nellie of a driver. Stanley Chaloupka got into the car without
saying anything. Morris Bird III walked to the car and placed a foot
on the runningboard. Mrs. Chaloupka got in the car, started the engine. Uh, said Morris Bird III, I got a foot on the runningboard. Mrs.
Chaloupka looked at him. Yes, I know, she said. Goodbye, said Morris
Bird III. Goodbye, said Mrs. Chaloupka. Goodbye, said Stanley Chaloupka. He examined the dials on the dashboard. Yes, said Morris
Bird III, and his foot came off the runningboard. The car moved away.
Stanley Chaloupka's right arm came out of his side window in a sort
of waving gesture. Then the car turned onto Crawford Road and disappeared in the direction the truck had disappeared. Walking home,
Morris Bird III had all sorts of peculiar thoughts. He began to count
the seconds. When he got to one hundred, he said to himself: One
hundred seconds ago everything was all right. Then he got to thinking
about the movers. They had had no trouble at all carrying out the
boxes containing all the track, rolling stock, outbuildings and equipment of the Atlantic & Pacific Railroad. Morris Bird III supposed it
was all in a day's work for them, but he'd wanted them to make some
sort of acknowledgment. They'd made no acknowledgment. They'd
been bored. They'd just wanted to get it over with. If only one of them
had yelled: Hey, this is some railroad, some *heavy* railroad! If this had
happened, then . . . aw beeswax, Morris Bird III was thinking beyond
himself, and he knew it. He grinned. He was a ninny. He thought
about Stanley Chaloupka's vest and his felt hat. This helped nothing.
That night he didn't eat well, and naturally his grandmother asked
him was he off his feed. He assured her he was all right. He went to bed
early and surprised himself by sleeping well. He had dreams, though.
They were full of trains, and all the trains went *Ch ch ch ch ch*.

BUT DON'T GET THE wrong idea.

The departure of Stanley Chaloupka in no way dropped the bottom out of Morris Bird III's life. He still had all the friends anyone
would have wanted. The only thing was—he had no real buddy. The
distance between a friend and a real buddy was large. With a friend,

you had to watch yourself. With a real buddy, you didn't. It was that simple, and the distance was that large.

But please don't get the wrong idea.

For friends Morris Bird III had Kenny Haas. And Ted Karam. And clumsy Alex Coffee who ate so much and whose breath was so bad. And Tom Pisani, youngest son of poor Mr. Pisani who was dying. And Freddy Carlson. And even a colored boy named Hoover Sissle. So none of them was a Stanley Chaloupka. So who said life had to be perfect all the time?

And anyway, there was always so much to *do*.

Besides school, there was handsoccer, and the joy you felt when you let go a good throw and pegged out a runner, the cries of
HERE
Throw it HERE!
Come ON!
Get him!
You're OUT!
It hit you BEFORE you got to the base, you Slop!

And there were the times you crooked chalk and wrote

FOOEY ON DEWEY

on sidewalks and walls, the letters skinny and tottering.

And there were the Crooking Expeditions, the times when you walked into Woolworth's with your arms full of schoolbooks, wandered oh ever so casually, maybe even whistling through the openings between your teeth, to the section where the *Big Little Books* were sold (Dick Tracy was your favorite), looked around, nonchalantly set your schoolbooks on top of the *Big Little Book* of your choice, then picked up the schoolbooks *and* the *Big Little Book* and meandered out the door and ran snickering down Hough Avenue toward home and an excellent literary feast.

And there were the Saturday matinees at the Astor Theater, and there in the serial you again encountered Dick Tracy, and the actor who played Dick Tracy was named Ralph Byrd, and you couldn't see

Ralph Byrd in any other sort of movie without thinking of him as Dick Tracy (and of course you wished your name were Morris Byrd III), and business was so good at the Astor Theater, what with the war and all, that the management gave you, free for nothing, a candy bar—if you left after seeing only one complete show.

And there were the times in winter in Rockefeller Park when the police closed off the upper part of East Boulevard, and you could hug your sled to your belly, then slam it down in the snow (after running with all your might to get up good momentum) and coast maybe a hundred yards, with your breath tasting like pins and the wind making your face red and your eyes wet.

And there were the times when you and maybe halfadozen of your friends went exploring in the old abandoned brewery at Hough Avenue and Ansel Road, and this was a very very old brewery, and it had been closed ever since the beginning of something people called Prohibition, and everything inside it was all dusty and collapsed and splendid, and you and your friends strapped on your holsters and played Guns inside that old brewery, and terror clung sweetly to the roof of your mouth, and

BAM!

you shouted, and

BLAM! BOOM! YOU'RE DEAD!

your friends shouted, and sometimes you were cut by broken glass, and sometimes you scraped your hands on old bricks, but who in his right mind would have cared?

And there were the hilarious radio times, of Red Skelton (you and your friends all called him Red Skeleton, and the horrid crimson image of such a thing as a Red Skeleton made you all whoop and shriek), good old Red Skelton and his Mean Widdle Kid, not to mention Clem Kadiddlehopper, of Fred Allen and Titus Moody (howdy bub, *ah*), of Jack Benny and Rochester and the poor doomed Gas Man down there in the cellar where The Vault was, of George Burns and Gracie Allen and how could one woman be so dumb?, of Baby Snooks, of Charlie McCarthy and Mortimer Snerd and that ridiculous tightwad of an Edgar Bergen. (And there was this one program, called *Easy Aces*, that you didn't understand but was loved by Grandma. It was about a man with an adenoidal voice who kept saying *Naow Jane* to a woman who had a screechy voice and all the time said dumb things. Oh well, if it made Grandma laugh . . .)

And of course there was love. So please don't get the wrong idea.

He supposed maybe his love was larger than most people's. It even, reluctantly, included his little sister Sandra. He wasn't so stupid that he admitted this to anyone, but he did admit it to himself, which was all that mattered.

But oh boy, in that fall of 1944 she surely was a trial.

Such a puler and whiner the world had never seen. You looked funny at her and she burst into tears. She was about 43 percent as brave as a baby mouse, and this was giving her the benefit of the doubt. She was small for six, and she had dark hair, and people said she was pretty, but how in the world did they know? Her face was always all screwed up, because of tears or fear or both, and no one was pretty whose face was always screwed up. Poor Sandra. He supposed life eventually would get the best of her.

But was this his worry?

He didn't see why it should have been, but it was. His parents and his grandmother had taken care of *that*. They had made him *responsible* for her.

Responsible—

If there was one word Morris Bird III had no use for, that was it.

Huh, he told himself. Huh. *Responsible*, my clavicle.

THIS THING—THIS *RESPONSIBLE* business—was inflicted on him every school day. On weekends, Sandra more or less had to fend for herself, but five days a week Morris Bird III was charged with looking after her.

His daily routine didn't vary an awful lot. It began with what Grandma called his Ablutions. Such as they were. The only thing he really liked about his Ablutions was brushing his teeth. The family used Pebeco toothpaste, and it had a fine clean astringent taste. He brushed his teeth with such vigor that almost every morning he splattered the bathroom mirror. Now and then his mother yelled at him for this, but most mornings she didn't get up that early. She was fond of what she called Sleeping In (she didn't have to be at work at the Cleveland Bolt & Screw Co. until 9:30, and she didn't have to leave the house until 9:15, when a man named Watzman, her driver in a car pool, picked her up), which meant that Morris Bird III usually was out of the house before she went into the bathroom. As long as he got out of the house in time, he was in no trouble. He wouldn't be seeing his mother until evening, and by that time she'd usually forgotten about it.

Morris Bird III didn't believe in wasting much time with Ablutions. He usually was downstairs no more than ten minutes after getting out of bed. He ate breakfast in the kitchen with Grandma and Sandra. These breakfasts did not vary. First orange juice, then a bowl of hot Fit-for-a-King oatmeal, then a glass of milk. Morris Bird III detested Fit-for-a-King oatmeal, but he was always hungry, so he ate it despite himself. Fit-for-a-King oatmeal, ugh! If he ever became President, his first official act would be the issuance of an order to round up all the people responsible for Fit-for-a-King oatmeal. When this was done, he would have them taken to the nearest stone wall and shot down like the dogs they were.

Show no mercy, men!

Ready!

Aim!

Fire!

BLAM!

Make sure they're all dead, Lieutenant.

Anyone who twitches, give him a bullet in the head.

Still, he did manage to force it down. Hunger is hunger. Sometimes he had been accused of being too shy, but he'd never been shy about eating. You, his grandmother told him one day, have the appetite of a sackful of gorillas. Ah, a pretty good figure of speech if I do say so myself.

Morris Bird III looked at her, grinned, helped himself to more

French fries.

Yes indeed, said his grandmother, it'll be a cold day in a certain warm place when you don't clean your plate.

Morris Bird III kept grinning and eating.

His grandmother came around the table and hugged him.

Thank you, said Morris Bird III, chewing.

His grandmother shook her head, and her smile reached to the next block.

At any rate, he had what you'd have to call a good appetite. Even for Fit-for-a-King oatmeal. His daily routine was never without it, so he had to make his peace with it. He had his choice of either Fit-for-a-King oatmeal or nothing at all, and anything was better than nothing at all. He was always starved in the morning. Old inner soles would have been better than nothing at all.

After breakfast, the next phase of his daily routine was the ritual known as Bundling Up. The extent of the Bundling Up naturally depended on the weather. In this month of October, it usually consisted of cap and jacket. If the day were cold and/or rainy, scarf, mittens and galoshes were added. Everything had to be attended to; everything had to pass Grandma's inspection. He wore a black leather aviator's cap with goggles, a bright green and orange jacket, a clean white shirt and corduroy knickerbockers. (His grandmother called them "knickies." Morris Bird III wouldn't have called them "knickies" for anything, but Grandma was Grandma, and she didn't mean any harm. He'd never once known her to mean any harm. Wasn't in her. There were people like that.)

Once his own Bundling Up was attended to, Morris Bird III had to help Grandma get rotten little Sandra ready. This meant helping Sandra into her coat, checking her mittens to make sure they were attached to their strings, making sure she had a fresh handkerchief (not that she'd ever been known to *use* one), inspecting her galoshes when the weather was bad, determining whether the right galosh was on the right foot, the left galosh on the left foot, and so on and so forth and so on, praise the Lord and give us all strength.

And, wouldn't you know it, Grandma always made him take Sandra *by the hand* when they went off to school. *By the hand!* A person would have thought Sandra was maybe not right in the head. There they went every morning, and oh my wasn't it ever *sweet*, dear little Morris Bird III leading his dear little snot of a sister by her dear little hand as they went, tra la la, hippity hop, off to school.

Oh what a picture. Ugh.

Hand in hand.

Ah, the world was gray and bleak, and no one suffered the way Morris Bird III suffered.

Tra la la, hippity hop.

And he couldn't even complain to Sandra about it. All he had to do was look at her sideways and it was boo hoo, sniffle sniffle. *When in doubt, bawl*: this was old Sandra's motto. She bawled as often as other people wiped their noses, oftener maybe, and that was a fact. Tiny and whimpering, she hung onto him as though he were some sort of great prize, and he wanted to fall through a crack in the sidewalk.

She had some favorite remarks. Such as:

You hate me.

I'm going to tell Grandma.

If you do that, you're going to *get* it.

Come *on*, we have to get to school.

Come *on*, we have to get home.

You're supposed to share your gum with me. Grandma said so.

You said a bad word. I'm going to *tell*.

I *seen* you picking that booger.

And naturally he heard about it from his socalled *friends*. They hollered and brayed at him, and of course they had all sorts of real bright comments. Such as:

Hey, Bird Turd, who's your girlfriend?

Boy, I wish *I* was so popular with the girls!

How come you're holding her hand? You two going steady?

Haw! Haw! Haw! Can you ever *pick* them!

It was some fun. Sure it was. There were burdens and there were burdens, and he supposed maybe the salami sandwich incident and the speedometer in his stomach and all the rest of his stupidities and cowardices were catching up with him.

He thought about these things a lot.

He knew he was being a dumbhead, but he couldn't help it.

Sometimes he kicked at leaves. He looked at everyone else, and everyone else was normal, and so the leaves went spinning.

THEN ONE DAY HE got an idea. It came from Mrs. Dallas. She was talking about President James A. Garfield, who had been born near the village of Orange, which now was a Cleveland suburb. "None of you," she said, "can imagine what life must have been like in those days. It was the Nineteenth Century, and—ah, before I get started, do all of you know what the Nineteenth Century is?"

Just about everyone looked blank.

Not Dolores Bovasso, though. She raised her hand.

"Yes, Dolores?" said Mrs. Dallas.

"The Nineteenth Century is all the years that begin with Eighteen," said Dolores.

Mrs. Dallas smiled. "Not quite."

Everyone grinned at Dolores Bovasso, who was blinking at Mrs. Dallas.

"The Nineteenth Century," said Mrs. Dallas, "was the hundred years that began in 1801 and ended in 1900." She looked at Dolores. "Ninetynine of those years began with Eighteen, but the hundredth began with Nineteen."

Dolores Bovasso looked at her hands.

Morris Bird III wanted to leap up and put his fingers in his mouth and whistle through his teeth the way people in the movies did when they called a taxicab. But he didn't know how to whistle that way. And besides, he didn't have the nerve.

Mrs. Dallas was standing at the blackboard, and the sunlight caught at her hair. He was almost ready to believe he could smell her perfume. She wore a plain black dress, and her arms were folded across her bosom. "Well," she said, *"anyway*, back in the Nineteenth Century, when James A. Garfield was a boy and grew to manhood, life was a great deal different. A great deal harder. There were no roads the way *we* think of roads, no telephones, no radios, no streetcars, no buses or cars. Out here in Ohio there was only a deep woods, the deepest woods you can imagine. The forest primeval. Here and there were little settlements and farms, but they were about it. Transportation was so inadequate that a person could live an entire lifetime and never venture more than twenty miles from his home. So . . ."

Dolores Bovasso's hand was up.

Mrs. Dallas sighed. "Yes?"

"Didn't they have trains in at least half of the Nineteenth Century? And wasn't the telegraph invented?"

Another sigh from Mrs. Dallas. "Yes. But it wasn't until the very last years of the century that those things came into general use."

Dolores Bovasso nodded, "Yes, Mrs. Dallas. I just wanted to make sure. That's all."

Morris Bird III snickered.

Mrs. Dallas continued. "So, as I was saying, there weren't many of the conveniences we know today. A *few*, as Dolores has pointed out, but not *many*. Which meant what? Which meant that if a person wanted to do a thing, he had to do it through his own hard labor. He had precious few mechanical conveniences to help him. Now then, I don't want you to get the wrong idea. I certainly *like* our conveniences, but sometimes I think people had more . . . well, sometimes I think people had more *courage* in those days."

Uh oh, said Morris Bird III to himself, here we go again. He was thinking of Mrs. Dallas' weakness for speeches.

Mrs. Dallas' face had no expression. "You just think about that for a moment," she said. "For instance, in those days the children sometimes had to walk miles to school. And I mean *miles*. Have any of you walked even so much as *one* mile? I doubt it. Not that I blame you. Why walk when you can go wherever you want in a streetcar or a bus? Only stupid people walk when they can ride. Isn't that right? Isn't that what people are always telling you? Feet were invented before wheels, but so what? Getting somewhere on wheels is more comfortable, and that's what progress is all about, isn't that so? But is comfort all that good? Doesn't comfort maybe make us lazy? That's something to think about, isn't it? What I mean is—we all want to accomplish something. That's the secret of what everything's all about—this business of wanting to accomplish something. But if everything is made too easy for us, how can we accomplish? I mean *really* accomplish. The more things we have helping us, the harder the accomplishing. We get too spoiled. We give up too easily. We . . ."

A girl named Julie Sutton raised her hand.

"Yes?" said Mrs. Dallas.

Everyone frowned at Julie Sutton. She was small and dark, and she took piano at the Institute of Music, and music was all she cared about, and in an ordinary week you couldn't get ten words out of her. "You mean like Beethoven?" she said.

"I beg your pardon?" said Mrs. Dallas.

Julie Sutton's voice was tiny. "At the Institute, my piano teacher Miss Diehl says Beethoven was a great composer because it was hard work, because it didn't come easy."

"Yes," Mrs. Dallas said, "that's exactly what I mean. Exactly. A fine example. Thank you for bringing it to our attention." Then Mrs. Dallas looked toward Dolores Bovasso.

Everyone else looked toward Dolores Bovasso.

"A really intelligent contribution to the discussion," said Mrs. Dallas.

Dolores Bovasso studied her inkwell.

"We need more such intelligent contributions," said Mrs. Dallas. "Some people raise their hands just for the sake of showing off. Other people have something to *say.* I hope we all understand the difference."

Dolores Bovasso made fists.

Mrs. Dallas' eyes turned to Julie Sutton. "Julie, are your piano lessons easy for you?"

Julie Sutton was blushing. She shook her head no.

"But you like them?"

Julie Sutton shook her head yes.

"Why do you like them?"

A blank look from Julie Sutton. She scratched the back of her neck.

"Could it be because they *are* hard?"

Julie Sutton's eyes took on a sort of glint. Her brows went up.

"Julie, isn't it possible that when you learn to play a piece, and the learning is hard, isn't it possible that the learning is worth more because it *is* hard?"

"Oh," said Julie Sutton, and for the first time in about sixty years she smiled. She shook her head yes.

Mrs. Dallas looked at the others. "Julie knows what I mean."

Julie Sutton beamed.

Mrs. Dallas unfolded her arms and made a series of gentle swooping gestures. "Yes," she said, "one of the best feelings there is is the accomplishing of something that's difficult. It's something that's *yours*. It's something no one can take away from you. And it's brave too, very brave. Determination means courage, and courage means you're a real person. And it doesn't have to be the most earthshattering act either. It could be telling yourself you're going to walk a mile and then going out and *walking* it. Or two miles. Or telling yourself I'm not going to chew gum for a week and then keeping your word to yourself. This is called dignity. It helps your selfrespect. It . . ."

Mrs. Dallas continued speaking for some time, but Morris Bird III had stopped listening. He'd heard all he'd needed to hear. She had provided him with the idea. The word that kept nibbling at him was SELFRESPECT. He glanced at Julie Sutton, and Julie Sutton was leaning forward on her elbows with her hands clasped tightly together. She looked as though she had seen an Angel of God. He forced his eyes away from Julie Sutton. He glanced out a window and watched a Hough Avenue trackless trolley go past. He counted a dozen cars, and five of them were Chevrolets. Then he looked toward the front of the room. He read the words

BUY U.S. WAR STAMPS

that Colleen Cleveland, a colored girl who had the best penmanship record in the room, had fastidiously printed with red, white and blue chalk. Then he glanced at the huge rollup map that hung over the blackboard, repeating to himself the lovely and musical words

MERCATOR PROJECTION

with silent salivary delight. He thrust his hands in his pants pockets and scratched the backs of his legs. There wasn't any doubt now of his love for Mrs. Dallas (not that there'd ever been *much* doubt), and high in his chest was a warmth that just about made him burst.

The idea was just as clear as clear could be.

He would visit his friend Stanley Chaloupka.

East 63rd Street wasn't the end of the world, and he would walk there.

Walk there.

Never mind the number of miles.

The more miles, the larger the accomplishment.

He would plan very carefully, and nothing would get in the way. He couldn't wait to get started.

He set his mind to work on the planning. He scratched his legs, paid no attention to Mrs. Dallas, spent the rest of the day frowning and figuring. Gradually the plan came. It was a good one.

DATE OF THE IDEA: Friday, October 13, 1944.

So what if it *was* Friday the thirteenth. So big deal. Superstition was for dumbheads. And anyway, Morris Bird III had too many things on his mind to waste his time with *that* sort of fear. There were more than enough other sorts.

As, for example: what would happen to him if he really went through with it?

Ah, but that was no way to be thinking. He had set himself a thing to do, and he would do it. Nothing would get in the way. He would be brave. And with no help. He would be like old Ulysses S. Grant. He would do a thing no matter what.

Maybe then somehow he would be able to make it up to Logan MacMurray. And for upchucking in the Loew's Stillman. And for believing in the stomach speedometer.

It came out SELFRESPECT.

FIRST HE HAD TO learn what Stanley Chaloupka's address was. The exact address.

Mrs. Chaloupka had written the address for Morris Bird III on a slip of paper. A telephone number too. But he'd lost the slip of paper. His grandmother had put his pants in the wash the next day, and that had been that. For a number of weeks he'd waited for Stanley Chaloupka to telephone *him*, but there had been no call.

And of course looking in the telephone book did no good. Only the old Chaloupka listing, the one on Rosalind Avenue, was there. And anyway, they'd moved in with Stanley's *mother's* people, which meant their name wasn't Chaloupka. Stanley had mentioned it once—Szuk or Szek or something like that.

On Saturday, October 14, 1944, Morris Bird III examined the telephone book. He found no Szuk. He found no Szek.

On Sunday, October 15, 1944, Morris Bird III telephoned the residence of a Paul Szulc, who lived on East 41st Street. A woman answered the phone. No, she'd never heard of anyone named Stanley Chaloupka. Furthermore, she told Morris Bird III, she was perfectly content to go to her grave without hearing of anyone named Stanley Chaloupka. So sonny, she said, go play your practical jokes on someone else.

The answer to the problem of Stanley Chaloupka's address and telephone number didn't come to him until the afternoon of Monday, October 16, 1944. He was walking home from school. He had his little sister by the hand. "Hey!" he shouted, and he began running.

"Stop that!" hollered Sandra, stumbling behind him.

"Come on!" hollered Morris Bird III, pulling.

Sandra began to weep.

He slowed down. "Cut that out," he said.

Sandra wept more loudly.

"Shut up," he told her.

She began to scream.

Morris Bird III looked up toward God or Whoever. He stopped, looked down at Sandra and said: "Okay. Okay. Okay. I'm sorry."

She grinned up at him through her tears. "All *right*," she said. "All *right*." She wiped her nose with her sleeve, and you wouldn't have known anything had happened.

They went home. Morris Bird III ran into the diningroom where the telephone was. He didn't even bother to take off his coat. He heard his grandmother in the kitchen. He had to hope she wouldn't come in. There was no other place to make the call. He grabbed the phone book and looked up the Chaloupkas' old Rosalind Avenue number. The listing:

Chaloupka Edw H   *9211 Rosalind . . . RA 5721*

Morris Bird III grinned. He took off his cap, lifted the receiver and dialed the number. There was a buzz, another buzz. Then clicking sounds.

"What number were you calling please?" It was a woman's voice, and it was like a day with no sun.

Morris Bird III cleared his throat. "Uh. Yes. Well. Uh, R-A—five-seven-two-one."

"Randolph five-seven-two-one?"

"Yes."

"Thank you. One moment please."

Morris Bird III waited.

"Sir?"

"Yes?"

"That number has been changed to Henderson four-four-one-eight."

"Henderson! That H-E?"

"Yes."

"Four-four-one-eight?"

"Yes."

"Thank you."

"You're welcome, I'm sure," said the woman. She broke the connection.

Morris Bird III hung up. He dug a pencil and a slip of paper from a pocket and wrote down the number. Then he dialed it.

"Allo?" Another woman's voice. This one older and very Foreign.

"Uh . . ." said Morris Bird III, again clearing his throat.

"Allo?"

"Is this H-E—four-four-one-eight?"

"How?"

"Is this H-E—four-four-one-eight?"

"Yes. You dial good. You win the grand prize."

"Is . . . uh, is Stanley Chaloupka there?"

"Yes. Who this? You speaking to Eva Szucs. Who I speaking to?"

"Morris Bird III," said Morris Bird III. His face was warm. He supposed this was because of the compliment on his dialing. And maybe it had something to do with the fact that this woman was crazy.

"What you say your name is?"

"Bird."

"Bird?"

"Yes."

"Bird. Ho. Ho. Ho. Such a name. Bird."

He wanted to tell this crazy woman he didn't think anyone with a name like Szucs had a right criticizing anyone else's name, but he decided maybe it was better if he let the subject drop. It was impossible to win arguments with crazy people. Finally he said: "Can I just speak to Stanley?"

"Stanley in the basement."

"Uh, could you . . ."

"He know you?"

"Yes."

"He know someone name of *Bird?*"

"*Yes.*"

"My."

Morris Bird III was about to say something, but there was a thumping sound. The woman had dropped the receiver. Probably against a bass drum, judging from the way Morris Bird III's ear felt. He rubbed the ear, listened to find out what would happen next.

She came on the line. "He be right up."

"Thank you."

"He in basement playing with trains."

"Thank you."

The crazy woman's breathing was loud. "Bird," she said. "My. Bird. Some name."

"Mm," said Morris Bird III.

The woman sniggered.

Morris Bird III glared at his knees.

There was a rustling sound, and then Stanley Chaloupka came on the line. "Hello?"

"Chaloupka? Stanley Chaloupka?"

"Yes."

"This is Bird. Morris Bird."

"Oh."

"Uh, how are you?"

"Fine."

"Good," said Morris Bird III. "I . . . uh . . ."

Silence from Stanley Chaloupka's end of the line.

"Well," said Morris Bird III, "uh, how you been?"

"Fine."

"Uh. Well. That's good. Yes."

Silence from Stanley Chaloupka's end of the line.

"Chaloupka?"

"Yes?"

"You're still there?"

"Yes."

"Good," said Morris Bird III. His skin felt damp.

Silence from Stanley Chaloupka's end of the line.

"Uh," said Morris Bird III, squirming, "the reason I called . . ." He hesitated.

"Yes?"

"I'm getting to it. It's about your address."

"My address?"

"Yes. I know it's East Sixtythird, but I don't know the number."

"It's six-seven-oh."

"Six-seven-oh?" said Morris Bird III. "Just a second. I want to write that down."

He wrote it on the slip of paper that had the Chaloupka telephone number.

"It's near the lake," said Stanley Chaloupka.

Hey, Morris Bird III said to himself, old Stanley *volunteered* something. Aloud he said: "Near the lake?"

"Yes. North of St. Clair Avenue. You know where St. Clair Avenue is?"

"Yes. I mean, I could find it on a map."

"I can see the lake from my window," said Stanley Chaloupka.

Morris Bird III spoke quickly. "I, uh, I thought I'd come see you."

"Come see *me?*"

"Yes."

"All right," said Stanley Chaloupka.

"Friday maybe? Friday be all right?"

"This coming Friday?"

"Yes."

"Sure. Friday's fine."

"Friday after school?"

"Sure."

"The trains okay?"

"They're fine."

"Chaloupka?"

"Yes?"

"How come you got nothing to say? I ask you questions and all you say is yes and sure and fine."

"This hasn't ever happened to me before," said Stanley Chaloupka.

"What?"

"It's the first time anyone's ever called me on the telephone."

"The first time *ever?*"

"Ever," said Stanley Chaloupka. "And it sounds funny. A person's voice sounds funny on the telephone. Someone I know, I mean."

"Uh," said Morris Bird III, "well, yes, I guess that's so." He hesitated, then: "Friday then? Friday afternoon? Maybe three o'clock or so?"

"All right."

"See you."

"Yes," said Stanley Chaloupka.

Morris Bird III hung up.

● ● ●

HE CHOSE FRIDAY BECAUSE it was the day Mrs. Dallas' room was supposed to visit the Cleveland Museum of Art. He figured there was a chance he might not be missed. Not that he particularly cared. In order to be brave, you have to be brave all the way. You have to understand that you must take the consequences for an Unexcused Absence.

As for the Cleveland Museum of Art, Morris Bird III could take the place or leave it alone. He and his classmates already had visited the Cleveland Museum of Art several times over the past few years. The visits were called Field Trips, and big deal.

Oh well. They beat sitting in school.

The only thing was—you almost had to feel sorry for the teacher. For a teacher, a Field Trip was about as much fun as pulling out fingernails. Whenever a Field Trip was made, it was the teacher's responsibility to

LOAD all the children aboard a Hough Avenue trackless trolley;

SEE TO IT that they all paid their fares and bought penny transfers;

KEEP the children in reasonable order and thus protect the property of the Cleveland Transit System;

UNLOAD all the children at East 105th Street;

MARCH them down the brick steps that led from the Hough Avenue bus barns to the East 105th Street streetcar stop, past the place where a fat blind man stood playing an accordion;

LOAD them aboard an East 105th Street streetcar;

SEE TO IT that they all surrendered their penny transfers and obtained free transfers;

UNLOAD them at Euclid Avenue;

LOAD them aboard a Euclid Avenue streetcar;

SEE TO IT that they all surrendered their free transfers;

UNLOAD them at the Adelbert Road stop;

COUNT NOSES to make sure no one was lost strayed stolen dead wounded or otherwise harmed or made off with;

PAIR them off, two by two;

MARCH them along East Boulevard north from Euclid Avenue to the Cleveland Museum of Art, which sat behind a big pond where swans swam in the summer;

SHUSH them when they entered the museum;

KEEP them from climbing on or into the suits of armor;

KEEP them from touching the mummy case;

KEEP them from whooping (the echo in those large highceilinged rooms was an awful temptation);

KEEP them all together;

MAKE SURE those who had to Go to the Toilet were given the opportunity;

COUNT NOSES again, and then, finally face grim and eyes narrow.

DO IT all over again, only this time in reverse.

MORRIS BIRD III COULD understand why teachers looked tired after an afternoon of this sort of thing. Conducting a Field Trip was probably as enjoyable for a teacher as carrying an armful of warm snakes, and Morris Bird III didn't think it did too much harm to pity the poor teacher. At least a little. And, in the case of Mrs. Dallas, more than a little. Especially now that he was pretty sure he loved her. So, in that sense, maybe in not going on the Field Trip he was doing her a favor, which meant he was showing her his love. And anyway, how many times did a person have to *go* to the Cleveland Museum of Art? As far as Morris Bird III was concerned, he'd already seen everything that was to be seen there. The exhibits and such were quite clear in his mind, and he had no need to see them again. Suits of armor were suits of armor, and mummy cases were mummy cases. When you saw one suit of armor, you saw them all. Same with mummy cases. And besides, there was this idea of doing Mrs. Dallas a favor. His absence would mean one less nose for her to count, one less straw on the camel's back. It was a nice thought.

THE AFTERNOON OF TUESDAY, October 17, 1944, Morris Bird III nonchalantly wandered into Albrecht's Drug Store at the corner of Hough Avenue and Crawford Road. He waited until no one was looking, then crooked a city map off a rack next to where the postcards were. That night, alone in his bedroom, he unfolded the map and traced out a route from his house to 670 East 63rd Street. As close as he could figure it, the distance was about four miles. He used a black crayon to draw a faint line along the streets he wanted to follow. Most of them were back streets. He had no desire to run into the police or people like that. He would take as few chances as possible.

THE MORNING OF WEDNESDAY, October 18, 1944, he was up early. He went to work on his Porky Pig bank with the evil penknife that had been given to him by his Uncle Alan. He extracted 94 cents. That afternoon, after bringing puling little Sandra home from school, he walked to the candy-store at Hough Avenue and East 93rd Street. There he bought a jar of Peter Pan Peanut Butter and a toy compass.

THE AFTERNOON OF THURSDAY, October 19, 1944, he rooted around in his closet and came up with about three dozen funnybooks and twenty or so *Big Little Books*. He took them to Mr. Rubinstein, the Jewish man who operated the used funnybook store at Hough and East 89th. Mr. Rubinstein gave him a penny apiece for the lot. Walking home, Morris Bird III counted his money, and it came to $1.07. He figured this was enough to cover any kind of emergency.

THAT NIGHT HE TOOK inventory. He would take along with him:

ONE jar of Peter Pan Peanut Butter (in case he needed to replenish his energy);

ONE toy compass (in case he lost his way);

ONE evil penknife (for protection and emergency use);

ONE map of the city (to augment the compass);

THE SUM of $1.07 (you never could tell when money would come in handy).

In addition, he would take along:

THE PICTURE of Veronica Lake (for morale purposes);

THE ALARMCLOCK from his bedroom (he owned no watch, and he figured it would be important that from time to time he *know* the time).

NATURALLY, HE COULDN'T SLEEP. He called himself all sorts of names, including SCAREDYCAT and COWARD and YELLOWBELLY and FRAIDYPANTS, and a lot of good they did. Then he got to thinking that maybe he would need even more protection than the evil penknife. He sat up in bed and listened for voices. He heard his parents' and his grandmother's. They came from downstairs. He slid out from under the covers and tiptoed across the hall to his parents' bedroom. He went to the dresser and opened the drawer where his father's automatic was. He lifted the automatic. It was very heavy. He pressed it to his face. He winced from the cold feel of the metal. He ran his fingers over the gun's oily surface. Some of the oil got on his fingers. Holding his breath, he pressed the muzzle of the gun to his right temple. "Boom," he said. "Farewell, cruel world." Then, shuddering and trembling, he put the gun back in the drawer, closed the drawer and left the room. He went into the bathroom and washed the oil from his hands. Then he cleaned out the sink. He didn't want to leave any traces of oil for his parents or his grandmother to discover. Then he returned to his room and slid back under the covers. He closed his eyes, and the first thing he saw was the word SCAREDYCAT. He squeezed it out, making a face. The next word he saw was HERO. Its letters were red and they were white and they were blue and they glowed in the dark. He smiled, hugged his belly. He reviewed the reasons for the thing that would happen tomorrow. He thought of people and their talk of courage. His grandmother and Mrs. Dallas especially. He thought of love. He thought of old Ulysses S. Grant. He thought of Stanley Chaloupka. He thought of Logan MacMurray. Do this thing, they said. Start it and finish it. Know honor. And Morris Bird III said: Yes. I will. I am no SCAREDYCAT. I am no YELLOWBELLY. *You'll* see. He pulled the covers up over his ears. It was a gray day, and there were cold winds. Suzanne Wysocki was with him, and they were eating their supper in the diningcar of the Atlantic & Pacific Railroad's most crack passenger train, the Twentieth Chaloupka Limited. Outside, the air was full of frost, but Morris Bird III was perfectly comfortable, and so was Suzanne Wysocki. *Ch ch ch ch ch* went the train, and Morris Bird III couldn't have been happier if he'd been King of the World. He grinned at Suzanne Wysocki. I love you, he said. She was eating a bowl of Fit-for-a-King oatmeal. Even though it was suppertime, she had insisted on ordering a bowl of Fit-for-a-King oatmeal. She looked up from the bowl and she was frowning. Never mind *that*, she said. What I want to know is—are you serious? Morris Bird III sighed. Always with Suzanne Wysocki the big word was *serious*. It wasn't enough for her just to enjoy the comforts of the Twentieth Chaloupka Limited. She had to bring in outside things. He sighed again. Serious? I think so, he said. How do you *know*? she asked him. I don't, he said. Don't you think maybe you ought to find *out*? she wanted to know. It's *that* important, I mean *really*? he asked her. Yes, said Suzanne Wysocki. Oh, he said. Don't just say Oh. *Do* something about it. Here, help me with this, said Suzanne Wysocki. Whereupon she plopped some of her Fit-for-a-King oatmeal, all lumpy and hideous, on Morris Bird III's plate, right splat on top of his porterhouse steak, and then she smiled at him, and his stomach churned, and of course that was when it came to him that he was having a nightmare. He woke up all hot and dopey. And scared.

FRIDAY, OCTOBER 20, 1944, was, as dates go, rather an important one. The war news, for instance, was excellent. On this date American troops, commanded by General Douglas A. MacArthur, landed on the island of Leyte in the Philippines. On the other side of the world, U. S. Army units entered the German town of Aachen. The Axis was getting a good flogging, and naturally everyone in Cleveland and the rest of the nation was delighted. Maybe the war would be over by Christmas. Or at least the war in Europe. And who knew? Maybe the Pacific war too. The headline in the morning paper—MACARTHUR LANDS IN PHILIPPINES—certainly wasn't *pessimistic*, now was it? Good old Dugout Doug back in the Philippines—hot *dog!* Yes indeed, it was an encouraging day. In Cleveland, the weather was fine. The day began with clouds, but the Weather Bureau promised a sunny afternoon, with temperatures in the middle forties and a gentle wind from the southwest. Morris Bird III was up at 6 o'clock, and so was a retired furrier named Leo Bernstein who lived on Massie Avenue, a couple of miles northeast of Morris Bird III's home on Edmunds Avenue. It looks like maybe it'll be a good day, Bernstein told his skinny little wife. Think maybe I'll rake the leaves. Bernstein's wife, Naomi Segal Bernstein, shrugged. All right, she said, so have a heart attack already. A grin from Leo Bernstein. He patted his wife on her fanny, went into the bathroom to wash and shave and brush his teeth. He was just turning on the HOT spigot when, a good four miles to the south, in an upstairs bedroom in a fine house in the fine green suburb of Shaker Heights, a woman whose name was Mrs. Josephine Brookes groaned in her sleep. She flung out an arm, slapped her husband Tom on his belly. He snorted, rolled free of the arm. Mrs. Brookes was dreaming about an optician named G. Henderson LeFevre. It was rather a romantic dream. Ah, but then Mrs. Imogene Brookes, the former Imogene Pinkerton of the Adrian Michigan Pinkertons, was rather a romantic *person*. She always had been. This probably had something to do with her good looks. Goodlooking women had a weakness for romance—and, if she was nothing else, Imogene Brookes was a beauty. People were forever telling her how strongly she resembled Loretta Young . . . *the* Loretta Young, the movie actress. This was true. Mrs. Imogene Brookes was tall, slender, dark, fragrant, graceful. At thirty, she had never looked better. A great beauty, people said, and they were right. Her eyes were brown, and they were set widely apart. They were very large eyes. Her cheekbones were high and strong, but they were not so high and strong that they made her appear hatchet-faced. Her skin was pale, and she was unable to take too much sun, but she loved her skin. Its texture was so terribly smooth, and the paleness made her feel so very much a great lady. Ah yes, a great beauty and a great lady: people stared at her. But don't for a minute think she didn't understand how fortunate she was. She did understand, and for that reason she wasn't as vain as she could have been. Oh she was vain *enough*, but most people could get along with her. She felt this was not an insignificant accomplishment. All in all, she should have been a happy young woman. Tom was a trust officer for the National City Bank, and they both had inherited money, which meant they had no trouble meeting the financial obligations of their life here in this fine house in the fine green suburb of Shaker Heights. Together with their two children (Karen, four; Mark, two), they moved in an atmosphere of comfort and ease and unending warmth. She was an excellent dancer and bridgeplayer, did volunteer work for the Red Cross, and since September of 1943 she had been having an affair with the optician, this fellow whose name was G. Henderson LeFevre and who just happened to live next door. G. Henderson Le-Fevre! Now *there* was a name to go echoing down the corridors of recorded time! And yes, he *looked* like a G. Henderson LeFevre. He was bald and skinny, and the very idea of having an affair with *him* was pre*pos*terous. The only thing was—when she was with him, he made her feel like the Wife of Bath. She should have laughed, but she couldn't. No man had ever made her feel like the Wife of Bath. Now, as she lay groaning, she began grinding her teeth. She had been grinding her teeth in her sleep for some months. Sometimes she ground them with such force that she woke up with aching jaws. What was it? Was it because Tom and the children (Karen, four; Mark, two) weren't enough to occupy all her time? She had given this a great deal of thought, and she supposed the absolute flat truth of the matter was that she was dying of boredom. Which was why she was planning to run off with her passionate optician. The way she saw it, it was something to do. She and her passionate G. Henderson LeFevre met often. Seeing as how they lived next door to each other on Southington Road in Shaker Heights, it wasn't difficult for them to arrange the meetings. Still, it was unfortunate that G. Henderson LeFevre's wife was so fond of Imogene Brookes. Not that Imogene Brookes had encouraged the woman. But, want it or not, Imogene Brookes had a fervent admirer in G. Henderson LeFevre's wife, whose name was Marva and who was from the Souf—Alabama to be exact. Oh that Marva. She talked a great deal, and she didn't know which end was up, and sometimes Imogene Brookes and her passionate optician just had to laugh and laugh. Imogene was quite good at imitating Marva's Alabama accent. Ah, she and G. Henderson LeFevre laughed very loudly. But there was something the matter with their laughter, and you didn't have to be much of a genius to know what it was. Groaning again, Imogene Brookes rolled over, punched her pillow and kept grinding her teeth. Next to her, Tom breathed easily, serenely. In a house over on East 63rd Street, Stanley Chaloupka was in the basement. He sat at the control box and guided his regular morning passenger train around the layout. He was grinning, and the corners of his eyes were thick with boogers. Washed and shaved, Leo Bernstein sat in his kitchen and read the morning paper. His wife asked him when he was going to get to work on those leaves. He grinned at her, told her the whole world hated a nag. Out in Shaker Heights, Imogene Brookes came awake at seven. Considering the unsatisfactory sleep she'd had, she felt rather good. She slid out of bed without awakening her dear stupid husband. Her two children (Karen, four; Mark, two) already were stirring. She put on her robe and slippers and went downstairs to fix them some breakfast. She hummed, and her mind was full of visions of her passionate optician. She felt quite strong and alert. She didn't know why, but she had a hunch today would be interesting. Maybe she would even get up the nerve to tell her husband she was leaving him. Once she did this, then her optician would have to tell his wife. The thing would be settled, and hooray. Arrangements would be made, and then all concerned would be able to go on from there. Next door, the passionate optician, G. Henderson LeFevre, sat in the breakfast nook with his wife Marva and listened to her talk about the good war news. Oh those boys, said Marva. I hope and pray they'll be coming home soon. Won't that be a blessin though? I mean, since when has war proved anythin? G. Henderson LeFevre listened to his wife's foolish creamy voice and he didn't listen to it. He glanced out the window and saw Imogene Brookes moving about in the kitchen next door. He cleared his throat, asked his wife for the sports section. In a house on East 63rd Street, not far from the house in which Stanley Chaloupka lived, a legless man named Casimir Redlich decided he would practice today on his trumpet. He was working on the lovely solo in Auber's *Fra Diavolo* Overture. He wheeled himself to a closet and got the trumpet and the sheet music. Grinning, he settled back, wet his lips, lifted the trumpet. In the kitchen, his wife groaned. At the Palace

Theater, Charlie Spivak's orchestra was opening a week's engagement. Charlie Spivak had never heard of Casimir Redlich. And vice versa. In a house on East 66th Street, ten blocks or so south of the place where Casimir Redlich lived, two little twin girls named Vicki and Viola Oravec argued over a coloring book. They were five. They loved arguing. Their mother ran to them, made an exasperated clucking sound, shooed them both outside. They went to the door with their arms around each other. They wore coats and mufflers and stockingcaps, and when they got out to the sidewalk they made sure not to step on any cracks. To the north, in a house on Norwood Road, a retired schoolteacher whose name was Miss Edna Daphne Frost fed her goldfish. Farther to the north, on East 62nd Street, Mrs. Barbara Sternad decided to clean house. She fixed breakfast for her nephew, Harry Wrobleski (they lived alone together; Mrs. Sternad's husband was in the Army, and poor Harry's parents had died last year in an automobile accident; his mother had been Mrs. Sternad's sister). Then she kissed Harry goodbye, sent him off to his classes at East High School. He told her he would be home late this afternoon. East High was playing Central High in football. Back down on Norwood Road, two nasty boys named Dickie Fristoe and Allie Sandwick talked of cutting school. When they walked past Miss Frost's home, they saw her electric automobile parked in the driveway. They laughed. They hated Miss Frost. She had been their teacher in the fourth grade, and she had let them get away with nothing. They were in the eighth grade now, but they had not forgotten. Dickie Fristoe stuck out his tongue and made a wet rude sound. Allie Sandwick laughed. Over in the house on Edmunds Avenue, Morris Bird III went over everything for about the millionth time. He wouldn't begin his walk to Stanley Chaloupka's place until after lunch. This morning he would go to school as usual. The Field Trip to the Cleveland Museum of Art wasn't scheduled until the afternoon. He would come home for lunch, then start back in the direction of school. But somewhere between his home and the school he would change his direction and set off. As for Sandra, there would be no problem. He'd deliver her into the custodianship of one of his friends. She probably wouldn't like it, but that was her tough luck. As soon as he got rid of her, he would set off. He would pay attention to his map, and he would do this thing he had set out to do. Equipped with map, compass, alarmclock, the evil penknife, his best Gun (an afterthought, and a good one), the jar of Peter Pan Peanut Butter, the picture of Veronica Lake and his ready capital of $1.07, he would walk every inch of the distance that lay between his home and 670 East 63rd Street. *Walk* it. Just like James A. Garfield and all the rest of those people. No mountain would be too high. He was no YELLOW-BELLY. No sir. Gas tanks or no gas tanks. Explosion or no explosion.

THE FIRST THING HE did that morning was make a last-minute check. All the stuff was in the closet. Or almost all of it. The alarmclock he would leave right where it was. He didn't want his grandmother making his bed and asking him at noon why the alarmclock had disappeared from the table by his bed. So he left the alarmclock on the table. He went to his small bookcase by the door and removed his copy of *The Kid from Tompkinsville*. He took the picture of Veronica Lake from between the pages. He held the picture by the edges, so as not to smudge it. He went to the closet. All his gear was hidden at the bottom of the box that held his rubbers and galoshes. It was far back in the darkest corner of the closet. He dropped to his hands and knees, crawled inside the closet, fumbled for the box. He reached under the rubbers and galoshes for the map. He unfolded the map, carefully placed the picture inside the map, then refolded the map, taking care not to bend or otherwise damage the picture. He replaced the galoshes and rubbers, emerged from the closet. He stood up, walked to where the alarmclock was, stared at it. It was ticking slowly, running down, about to stop. Good. That was the way he had planned it. When he left this afternoon with the alarmclock under his jacket, he didn't want his grandmother to hear him tick.

He went into the bathroom and took care of his Ablutions. The Pebeco tasted especially good this morning. It tasted so good he brushed his teeth twice. He did not particularly splatter the mirror. Particularly.

Ten minutes later he was dressed and in the kitchen.

He drank his orange juice, then began his daily battle with Fit-for-a-King oatmeal. Grandma was fussing at the stove, and Sandra had a white mustache from the milk she'd been drinking. She'd never learned how to drink milk without making a white mustache. But then she was only six, and a person had to make allowances. Sure. Allowances. You-bet.

Grandma glanced out the window. "Might rain," she said, yawning. She put a hand over her mouth. She always yawned in the morning. She called herself a slow getterupper.

"Might," said Morris Bird III, slopping his Fit-for-a-King oatmeal with his spoon.

"Don't play with your food," said Grandma.

"Sure," said Morris Bird III, and he forced down a mouthful. Part of it stuck to the roof of his mouth. He washed it down with some milk.

"I like rain," said Sandra.

Morris Bird III took another mouthful. This time he swallowed it without letting too much come into contact with his palate. He'd practiced this maneuver for a number of years. He'd mastered it pretty well. What you tried to do was—you tried to swallow it all in one lump. That way, you didn't have to taste much of it. (The aftertaste of the Pebeco helped too.)

"I like rain when I'm going to sleep," said Sandra.

"Big deal," said Morris Bird III, gulping. The lumps of oatmeal felt like golf balls. He put a hand over his mouth, just in case he made a funny sound.

"All pingy and all," said Sandra.

"Great," said Morris Bird III from behind the hand.

"*Now,*" said Grandma.

"He picks on me all the time," said Sandra to Grandma.

"You hush too," said Grandma, yawning.

Sandra frowned. She blew into her milk. Blub.

The golf balls slid from Morris Bird III's gullet into his stomach. He was almost ready to believe he could hear them splash. He took the hand away from his mouth, again slopped the oatmeal with his spoon.

Grandma shook her head at him. "Eat your oats," she said.

"Neigh," said Morris Bird III.

"I know you're not a horse, but eat your oats anyway," said Grandma.

(This happened every morning. First Grandma said Eat your oats. Then Morris Bird III said Neigh. Then Grandma said I know you're not a horse, but eat your oats anyway. The words came out like a set of prayers. Like the Versicles at the Rev. Mr. Pallister's church. Morris Bird III and Grandma said them without hardly knowing they were saying them. Which was right and proper. At that hour of the morning, who was original? Who had that much of the old pep?)

Morris Bird III forced down the rest of his Fit-for-a-King oatmeal. He cleaned out his mouth with two glasses of milk. He decided he felt pretty good, even though maybe there *was* too much thickness and warmth in his neck and chest. But this was to be expected. It wasn't every day a person set out to do the sort of thing he was setting out to do.

He stood up. "Come on," he said to Sandra.

He led her into the front hall, where he began helping her into her various wraps and accouterments. When it came to Bundling Up, no one in the world was more of a draggy slowpoke than Sandra. And no one was more careless. He didn't have to be told any more to give her a hand. Helping her into her wraps and accouterments was as inflexible a part of his daily routine as the battle with Fit-for-a-King oatmeal. (One morning a couple of weeks ago Grandma had complimented him on it, calling him a Good Little Soldier. Ahhhhh, big deal. All it was was a lot of buttering him up.)

He inspected Sandra's buttons, made sure her mittens were on the proper hands. Then he put on his jacket and cap. He looked down, and the button that said

ROOSEVELT

was firmly attached to the front of his jacket. He'd already made sure that the button that said

ROOSEVELT TRUMAN

was decorating his pants, and that the little donkeyshaped pin that said

FDR

was in its usual prominent place on his shirt. In no way did he want this day to be unusual. Not that he wouldn't have worn the buttons and the pin anyway, but this day it was especially important that he do nothing unusual. If he'd forgotten the buttons and the pin, his grandmother might have suspected something. That wouldn't have done. His plan was delicate, and the slightest slip could send it down the drain.

Grandma came to the front door just as Morris Bird III and Sandra were leaving. "Be good, you two," she said. "Watch the streets."

"Uh huh," said Morris Bird III. He took dear little Sandra by the hand, dragged her out the door. Grandma closed it behind them.

They were going down the front steps when the door opened again.

"Morris?" said Grandma.

"Huh?" he said, looking back.

"It might rain," said Grandma. She was holding Sandra's boots. "Here. Help your sister put them on."

Morris Bird III sighed. He went back up the steps and took the boots from Grandma.

"You're welcome," said Grandma.

"Oh," said Morris Bird III. "Uh, thank you."

Grandma smiled. She started to close the door, but then she frowned. "You know," she said, "I think you'd better wear your rubbers. I'm going upstairs. I'll get them from your closet. I'll toss them down the stairs to you. We'll see how good a catcher you are."

Another sigh from Morris Bird III. He handed the boots to Sandra, went inside.

Grandma walked across the vestibule and started up the stairs. She was at the top of the stairs when Morris Bird III just about had a heart attack.

His stuff in the closet!

He went up the stairs two at a time. "I'll get them!" he hollered. "I'll get my rubbers!" He caught up to Grandma in the hall just outside his room. He pushed past her before she could say ah, yes or no.

He fell to his hands and knees and rooted in the closet for his rubbers. He glanced back over a shoulder.

Grandma stood at the bedroom door. Her hands were on her hips.

He scrabbled for the rubbers, finally came up with them. He backed out of the closet, stood up and slammed shut the door. His head hurt. He opened his mouth to say something, then thought better of it.

"You gone out of your mind?" said Grandma.

Quickly he shook his head no.

"You've got something hidden in there, haven't you? Something you don't want me to see."

"No."

"Don't fib. The world hates a fibber."

"I . . . don't . . . I don't have anything in there."

"Do you mind if I take a look?"

"Yes!"

"Oh? And why?"

He said nothing.

"Well?" said Grandma. "Speak up. Be a man. Tell me."

Morris Bird III looked at his hands, and the hand that was holding the rubbers was damp. He opened his mouth. "Uh," he said, "well . . ."

"Yes?"

"I . . . I can't . . ."

"Now, Morris. I love you. Whatever it is, it can't be that bad."

Morris Bird III blinked. He didn't want to be a baby and bawl, but—and then came . . . pure and golden and beautiful . . . the greatest brainstorm he'd ever had! It was the brainstorm of all brainstorms, and it was guaranteed to bail him out! Next Thursday was his grandmother's birthday! Oh hot dog! Oh joy! Oh rapture supreme! Slowly a grin came. It was the biggest, warmest, truest, most virtuous, most generous, kindest, bravest, most loyal grin the world had ever seen. It was a grin of all grins, guaranteed to turn all in its path to butter. "Uh, well, you see," he finally said, "it's a . . ." Here he allowed himself a shy pause. "It's . . . well, I sort of want it to be a surprise."

"Are you talking about my birthday?"

"Yes . . ."

"Really?"

"Yes."

Grandma unfolded her arms. Her eyes had been quite small, but now they weren't. "And this surprise is in the box with the rubbers and galoshes?"

Morris Bird III nodded.

"That's the truth?"

Another nod. His mouth felt like a sackful of chalk.

"Well," said Grandma, and she smiled, "what do you know about that?"

Morris Bird III sat on the edge of the bed and put on his rubbers. He wiped the sweaty hand on his pants. He stood up, stamped down the loose places where the rubbers and his shoes weren't in proper alignment. "You won't look?" he asked her. He didn't know how he'd gotten up the nerve to say the words, but there they were. Out.

"No," said Grandma, "I won't look."

"I want it to be a surprise."

"I won't look. I give you my word."

Naturally, by this time Morris Bird III was unable to look into his grandmother's eyes.

Still smiling, Grandma backed out of the doorway and went down the hall to the bathroom. A few seconds later he went out into the hall. He was about four inches tall.

"WHAT'S GOING ON OUT THERE?"

Morris Bird III gave a little shriek, jumped back.

The voice had come through the closed door of his parents' bedroom. It was The Voice of Cleveland & Northeastern Ohio. It was irritable and thick and full of sleep and very loud, and never mind the closed door.

"Nothing," said Morris Bird III under his breath.

"WHAT?"

"Nothing."

"SO THEN KEEP IT DOWN TO A LOW ROAR ALL RIGHT?"

"Yes," said Morris Bird III, and he scurried down the stairs.

But not before he heard Grandma's voice from the bathroom. "I'm sorry!" she shouted. "It was my fault! Don't blame the boy!"

Morris Bird III's height shrank to two inches.

Outside on the porch, Sandra was sitting on the steps. She had very skillfully managed to put her left boot on her right foot, her right boot on her left foot.

"Oh *great*," said Morris Bird III. It took him almost five minutes to struggle with her and get, lo and behold and gloryosky, the left boot on the left foot and the right one on the right. He trotted her off to school, and she whimpered all the way, and they just made the third bell. (If you weren't in your classroom by the time the third bell rang, you were charged with a Time Tardy, and the next day you had to bring a note from your parents. Morris Bird III had never been charged with a Time Tardy in his whole entire life, and oh boy, that Sandra. A Time Tardy would have been all he'd needed—especially on *this* day. It was bad enough that he would be socked with an Unexcused Absence this afternoon; he certainly didn't need a dumb old Time Tardy as well.)

He was breathing hard when he came into Mrs. Dallas' room, and the third bell was clonging away like maybe there was an air raid.

He ducked into the cloakroom, hung up his cap, shucked himself out of his jacket, ran out to his desk. All the other children stared at him. Even Mrs. Dallas stared at him. He slid into his seat just as the last terrible clonging echo of the third bell faded away.

"*Well*," said Mrs. Dallas.

Morris Bird III looked at nothing in particular.

"It's a good thing no one was in your way, Morris," said Mrs. Dallas. "Would have meant certain death. Talk about your steamrollers."

The other children whickered.

Mrs. Dallas smiled. "Perhaps we should give you a nickname. How does Flying Flash sound?"

More sniggers.

Morris Bird III looked at her, and then he decided he might as well snigger too.

Still smiling, Mrs. Dallas opened her copy of the spelling book, and they started in on Drills. Morris Bird III let his mind wander. He looked down at his feet. He had forgotten to take off his rubbers. He thought of his grandmother's trust. She wouldn't inspect the closet. He knew she wouldn't. He knew this as surely as he knew his own name. He wished he could run home and kiss his grandmother and tell her the truth. He hadn't wanted to lie to her—but what else could he have done? This afternoon he *would* go on that walk. Nothing could be allowed to get in the way. Even if he had to reduce his height to two inches, he still would go on that walk. He closed his eyes for a second or two, and the word he saw was LIAR. Quickly he opened his eyes. He looked around. Mrs. Dallas was conducting the Drill in the usual way. Starting with the first child at the first desk in the first row, each child had to spell the word read by Mrs. Dallas. The first row had done its reciting. So had the first four children in the second row. Just ahead of him, his friend Teddy Karam was spelling something. Then it was Morris Bird III's turn. Mrs. Dallas asked him to spell *Fried*. "F-r-i-e-d," he said. Mrs. Dallas nodded, went on to the next child. Morris Bird III relaxed, again let his mind wander. Again he saw the word LIAR. He pushed it away. He replaced it with FLYING FLASH. Now *there* wasn't a bad name at all. It certainly beat Old Bird Turd. Huh, and it certainly did go to show you something. This was the latest to school he'd ever been in his whole entire life, and all of a sudden he was someone special. Well, he supposed this was something he needed. Took his mind off his lying. Huh. It surely did beat anything he'd ever heard of. Ordinarily he was so punctual that sometimes the other children called him Old Early Bird. What are you looking for? they asked him. To catch the worm? But this morning Old Early Bird had changed his spots, or something. He'd almost been late, and so now he was someone special—Morris Bird III, the FLYING FLASH. Sure was funny. Peculiar and ha ha both, he supposed.

THE REST OF THE morning, though, was nothing special. Mrs. Dallas handed back the arithmetic test papers from Wednesday. Morris Bird III's grade was 88, which he didn't think was bad at all, considering all the pondering and planning that had been distracting him. At about 10 o'clock, Mrs. Dallas set aside fifteen minutes for the cleaning out of desks. For Morris Bird III, this was about as much fun as eating worms. Half the time he couldn't even get his desk *open*, let alone clean it out. There was always too much stuff jammed inside. It interfered with the hinges, which meant that he had to grunt and strain to force the desk open. Which was what happened now. He had to strain every muscle to get the stupid thing open. Ever since the beginning of the semester, he'd been stuffing things inside. For the past week or so, he'd been able to open the desk only an inch, maybe two. Well, now was the time of reckoning. He examined the desk's contents. Two boys with wastebaskets circulated up and down the aisles. Morris Bird III disposed of several anonymous paper wads, four broken pencils (it was one of these broken pencils that had jammed one of the hinges; the other had been jammed by a crayon), half of an old apple that smelled like Dog Mess and made several children at neighboring desks glare at him, two old spelling tests, an outofdate current events outline, the wornout and bent metal strip from the edge of a ruler, a globby piece of old gum that he'd hastily hidden a couple of weeks ago when he'd caught Mrs. Dallas glaring at him, several pieces of string, two broken rubberbands and a paper clip. It all went into one of the wastebaskets. Then he arranged his tablets, notebooks, pencils and crayons in neat little rows. He blew out some dust, sneezed, asked himself: What would she say if she knew? He was looking at Mrs. Dallas as he asked himself the question. He was thinking of his walk. He decided she would have approved. She almost had to. Otherwise, she would have had to go back on the things she was forever saying about courage. Then, at 10:15, it was time for recess. Everyone ran outside. The girls gathered to compare grades in the arithmetic test. He overheard Dolores Bovasso tell someone she'd received a 96. Good old Dolores Bovasso. You could always count on her. He glared at Dolores Bovasso for a moment, remembering Stanley Chaloupka and all the stupid love Stanley Chaloupka had shown. Then he sighed, ran to join the other boys for a little football. Boys from all the grades were playing football all over the yard. Everyone whooped and hollered. Little rubber balls were used as footballs. Morris Bird III was picked on a team captained by Hoover Sissle, the colored boy. It won, 12-0, and both touchdowns came on passes from Quarterback Bird to Right End Sissle. All around them, children ran and yelled just for

the sake of running and yelling. On the last play of the game, just before the bell rang to signal the end of recess, Morris Bird III fell and
scraped his left knee. But so what? He got up without even wincing.
A person who proposed to walk all the way to 670 East 63rd Street
didn't let such a small thing as a scraped knee bother him. Wouldn't
have been consistent. He ran to Hoover Sissle, clapped him on the
back, told him Nice Game. Hoover Sissle grinned, and they went back
inside the school. From 10:45 to 11:15, Mrs. Dallas spoke to them
about I before E except after C, and for crying out loud Morris Bird
III had learned that *last* year. But apparently, from the way some of
the others frowned, the lesson hadn't taken with everyone. So for half
an hour he sat there and listened (or at least tried to *show* that he was
listening) to a lot of silly—ah, now, now, there was no sense getting
worked up. Morris Bird III glanced out the window, concentrated on
the Hough Avenue traffic. He saw a Packard. Then, at 11:15, it was
time for gym class and volleyball. As sports went, volleyball was at the
bottom of Morris Bird III's list. Somehow it seemed witless, a game
that only girls should play. You hit a ball up in the air, and then somebody else hit the ball up in the air, and who cared? Oh well, it was
better than listening to a lot of talk about I before E except after C.
And anyway, he was just in a grumpy mood. He wanted to get on with
the walk. As soon as he did, the grumpiness would go away. He told
himself to be patient, concentrated on the volleyball game. The gym
smelled like varnish. There was another smell, a high and thin smell,
and he decided it had something to do with children and exercise
and sweat. He didn't much like either of the smells. Ah, but there he
went—being grumpy again. He took a deep breath, found himself a
place near the net. His team won the first game, 21–8. He didn't touch
the ball. He ran back and forth and jumped a few times, but he never
once touched the ball. His team lost the second game, 4–21, and this
time he touched the ball at least a dozen times. He didn't once knock
it over the net. His team won the third game, 21–17, and everyone
said it was very exciting. Huh. Exciting. Sure. Very exciting. He hit the
ball three times, and once he even hit it over the net. Sure. Exciting.
You bet. Then it was 12:15 and time for lunch. Mrs. Dallas gathered
them all together, reminded them to bring carfare that afternoon for

the Field Trip to the Cleveland Museum of Art. Everyone nodded. Even Morris Bird III nodded. Then they ran to their room, got their wraps and went home for lunch. Morris Bird III rounded up Sandra and dragged her on home. His throat was all tingly, and every time he opened his mouth his voice sounded funny. He didn't have to bother wondering why.

LUNCH WAS NOTHING SPECIAL either.

It consisted of wieners and beans, which didn't exactly represent Grandma at the top of her form. But you had to remember the war, and Morris Bird III knew it wasn't right to complain.

And anyway, he couldn't be bothered with complaining. Too many other things were on his mind. It was getting along about That Time, and—

"Have a nice time at school this morning?" Grandma wanted to know.

"It was all right," said Morris Bird III, stabbing at a wiener.

"You weren't late?"

"No."

"He *dragged* me," said Sandra.

"Learn how to put your boots on and I won't have to drag you."

Sandra began to sniffle.

"Stop that," Grandma told Sandra.

Sandra stopped sniffling.

"I certainly am curious," said Grandma.

"Huh?" said Morris Bird III. "You talking to me?"

"Yes. I'm talking about that birthday present you have for me."

He looked at her.

"No," she said, "I stayed out of the closet."

He smiled. He didn't know how good a smile it was. All he could do was hope for the best.

"A handkerchief?" said Grandma.

"Uh . . . well . . . *maybe* . . ."

"No. It's not a handkerchief. You're just trying to throw me off the track."

"Okay."

"If it *was* a handkerchief, you wouldn't say maybe."

Morris Bird III sighed, shoveled in some beans. "Okay," he said. "Okay. Okay."

"Don't be so crosspatch."

"Okay."

"I mean that, young man. I've had enough of crosspatches this morning. Your father and mother were a couple of bears. I mean that—a couple of honest dyedinthewool *bears.* Not enough butter on his toast, your father says, and the coffee isn't strong enough. A lot he cares about the war. And your mother complaining because the electric bill is maybe a dollar more than it was last month, accusing me of using . . ." A hesitation. Grandma got up and went to her little radio and turned it on. "My," she said, "I almost forgot." Presently the radio was filling the kitchen with the troubles of Our Gal Sunday, the girl from the little mining town who was seeking happiness as the wife of Lord Henry Brinthrop.

Morris Bird III ate his wieners and beans.

"More," said Sandra, holding her plate in Grandma's general direction.

"Eat all your beans," said Grandma. "You can't have another wiener until you've eaten all your beans."

"I don't *like* beans."

"Eat. Your. Beans."

Sandra scraped at her beans.

Morris Bird III looked at Grandma, and his face was hotter than anything.

Her head was inclined toward the radio.

First he'd lied to her, and now he was being a crosspatch.

Sandra fiddled with her beans.

Grandma was smiling at the radio.

"Grandma?" said Morris Bird III.

"Yes?" Absently.

"I love you."

● ● ●

HE SNEAKED UPSTAIRS JUST before he was due to return to school with Sandra. He crawled into the closet and dragged out all the gear he would take with him. He slipped the map and the enclosed picture of Veronica Lake inside his shirt. His best Gun, a .38 automatic that could fire a string of six caps, was stuffed under his belt. The compass and the $1.07 went into a pants pocket. The evil penknife went into the other pants pocket. He shoved the jar of Peter Pan Peanut Butter into a side pocket of his jacket. The pocket was just deep enough to accommodate the jar. He went to the bedside table and got the alarmclock. It had run down. Good. Grandma would not hear him tick. He placed the alarmclock inside his jacket, then buttoned up the jacket. He shoved a hand inside the pocket where the jar of Peter Pan Peanut Butter was. By pressing the jar against the alarmclock, he kept the alarmclock from falling out the bottom of his jacket. He went into the bathroom and examined himself in the mirror. He didn't think he looked particularly fat. Maybe this was wishful thinking, but it couldn't be helped. He went downstairs. Keeping the one hand in the pocket, he helped Sandra Bundle Up. Grandma came out from the kitchen just as he was opening the front door.

"Wait," said Grandma.

MISS EDNA DAPHNE FROST opened her telephone book and looked up the number of Mount Sinai Hospital. She dialed the number, asked the girl who answered for the condition of Miss Katharine Arthur. Miss Frost had known Miss Arthur for more than thirty years. They'd taught in the same school. Earlier this week, Miss Arthur's left breast had been removed. The girl told Miss Frost to hang on for a moment, then came back on the line to report that Miss Arthur's condition was Satisfactory. Does that mean she can have visitors? Miss Frost wanted to know. Yes, said the girl. Visiting hours are from 1 to 2. Thank you very much, said Miss Frost. She hung up, washed her hands and face, put on her hat and coat, checked all the doors to make sure they were locked, glanced outside, decided to take along her umbrella, fetched the umbrella, then went out to her electric automobile. There was a florist over on Superior Avenue. She would stop there and buy some flowers for her friend. On Massie Avenue, Leo Bernstein had a fried egg and a cup of tea. Outside, about half his leaves had been raked. He lit a Between the Acts cigar, told his wife he was feeling pretty good these days for an old gink. Sure, said his wife, so when are you going to finish with the raking? Leo Bernstein grinned. In a *min*ute, he said. Maybe two minutes. But first I got to enjoy my cigar. His wife made a face. Some cigar, she said. Uck. I could throw up already.

MORRIS BIRD III HESITATED. Then, slowly, he turned around—keeping Sandra between him and his grandmother. His stomach felt funny.

Grandma was smiling. "Give us a hug," she said, holding wide her arms.

"Kachoo!" said Morris Bird III, and he forced his nose to run.

"My goodness," said Grandma. She let her arms drop. "You have your handkerchief?"

He nodded. He managed to pull his handkerchief from the pocket where the money and the compass were. His other hand was tight on the jar of Peter Pan Peanut Butter. The alarmclock was heavy against his stomach. He blew his nose, making a great fuss of it.

Grandma was standing practically on top of him. "You feel all right?"

"I feel fine," he said. Actually, he felt as though any second he would throw up.

"I didn't know you had the sniffles."

"They just came on," he said. Which was just as true as true could be.

"Well, you take care this afternoon."

"All right."

"And thank you for saying what you said—about loving me."

He nodded. He was looking down. He didn't dare look up. If he did, he certainly would see the underbelly of a snake.

Grandma bent over him and kissed him on a cheek. Then she kissed Sandra on a cheek. "Watch the streets," she said.

Morris Bird III nodded. He dragged Sandra out the door.

"What's going on?" said Sandra.

"Never mind," said Morris Bird III.

"Huh?"

"Never *mind.*"

Grandma closed the door behind him. He dragged Sandra down the front steps. Now he was one inch tall. He sighed, letting his breath whistle through the openings between his teeth. The way he saw it, he had only one thing going for him. He *had* told Grandma the truth once today. He *did* love her. Which was the reason for all the lying. In doing this thing, in taking this walk, in going *through* with it, he would make everything all right again. He would learn SELFRESPECT. He would show the love.

"You got something wrong with you?" said Sandra.

A growling sound came from deep in his throat.

She looked at him, and whatever it was she saw made her silent.

NOW ALL MORRIS BIRD III had to do was find someone to escort Sandra back to school. He dragged her along Edmunds toward East 90th Street and looked around for a likely victim. He wanted someone who wouldn't laugh too much. If there was one thing he wouldn't be able to take right now, it was someone who laughed too much.

Children walked in little groups. Most of them chattered and shrieked. Girls especially. Girls were such goodygoods in the classroom, but once they were outdoors, oh *boy.* They skipped, and they waved their arms, and their voices were like police whistles. Morris Bird III ignored the girls, looked for a boy to take Sandra back to school. The boys were just as loud, he supposed, but their loudness was different—to him anyway. It meant more. It was more important. It had nothing to do with dolls or arithmetic test grades. Eyes narrow, he inspected the boys. He saw no one he was willing to trust. He saw no one he even knew very well. Back down the street was Hoover Sissle, walking by himself, but Hoover Sissle was colored, and Morris Bird III figured Sandra would bawl if she were given to Hoover Sissle.

Blinking, Morris Bird III looked ahead, toward the corner of Edmunds and East 90th. And there he saw Teddy Karam, and he knew Teddy Karam would do just fine.

He grinned, dragged Sandra forward at a trot. "Marak!" He yelled. "Wait up!"

"Not so *fast*," said Sandra.

He paid no attention to her.

Teddy Karam was standing on the opposite side of East 90th— just in front of his house, which was right at the corner. "Drib!" he hollered.

Morris Bird III dragged Sandra across East 90th.

"Olleh," said Teddy Karam.

"Olleh yourself," said Morris Bird III.

Teddy Karam was chunky and dark. He had very white teeth. He was a Lenabese. Or Lebanese. Morris Bird III hadn't ever been able to get the pronunciation straight. Not that it mattered. With Teddy Karam, nothing was straight. His favorite pastime was saying things backwards. He said just about everything backwards. Which could be sort of aggravating. And a strain. Sure, it was *interesting* and all that, but sometimes . . . well, sometimes it just about wore a person out to hold a conversation with him. So much heavy frowning and all. (Teddy Karam had a favorite saying. It was: Able Was I Ere I Saw Elba. Which meant nothing at all, except that it came out the same way backwards as forwards. Big deal.)

"Woh si Ardnas?" said Teddy Karam.

"Nettor, ekil syawla," said Morris Bird III, thinking as quickly as he could.

Teddy Karam grinned. "Oot dab," he said.

"What?" said Sandra.

"Shut up," said Morris Bird III.

"Emoc no," said Teddy Karam, starting off in the direction of school.

Morris Bird III didn't move. "Uh, just a second."

"Huh?" said Teddy Karam. He looked back. Huh was one of his favorite words, along with Otto and Bob and deed and pip and poop.

"Talk frontwards for a minute, okay?"

Teddy Karam shrugged. You didn't need a lantern to see his disappointment. "Okay," he said.

Morris Bird III pulled Sandra forward. "You take her to school for me?"

"What?"

"You take her to school for me?"

"No."

"I'll give you a dime."

"A dime?"

"Uh huh. All you got to do is take her to school."

"Why don't *you* take her to school?"

"I'm not going."

"What?"

"Sssss," said Sandra drawing in a prissy mouthful of wet breath and sounding for all the world like Dolores Bovasso.

"Be quiet," Morris Bird III told her.

"A dime?" said Teddy Karam.

Morris Bird III reached in his change pocket, came up with a dime. He held it out. "Here."

"Where you going?" said Teddy Karam, not reaching for the dime.

"That's got nothing to do with you."

"You're not going on the Field Trip?"

"No."

"You look fat. You got something under your jacket?"

"Never mind."

"You crazy?"

"No."

"A dime huh?"

"A dime. Just for walking her to school."

"So what about *after* school? You going to take her home from school?"

Morris Bird III's mouth dropped open. He'd never thought of *that*. "You can take her home. I'll give you another dime." His hand returned to the change pocket. He found a second dime, held both dimes out to Teddy Karam.

"Just a minute," said Teddy Karam. "It'll cost you a quarter."

"A quarter?"

"You heard me."

"Robber."

"That's me," said Teddy Karam, grinning.

"You're holding me up."

"How'd you guess?"

Sandra spoke up. "No," she said.

They looked at her.

"I'll *tell*," she said.

"Be quiet," Morris Bird III told her.

Sandra's eyes were moist. She inclined her head toward Teddy Karam. "You're not going to leave me with *him*."

"I'll leave you with whoever I *want* to leave you with."

"I'll *tell*. I'll run and holler and tell everybody all about it."

"Tell what? You don't know where I'm going."

"I'll scream."

"You'll what?"

"I'll scream. I'll run home, and I'll scream all the way, and Grandma'll catch you, and it'll be the worst thing ever happened to you."

"You won't do—"

"If you take me with you, I won't tell. I won't scream either."

"What?"

"I'm going to scream," said Sandra. "One. Two. Three. AHH-HHH!"

"CUT THAT OUT!"

"AHHHHH!" screamed Sandra.

"BE QUIET!"

"AHHHHH!" screamed Sandra.

Across the street, three little girls were staring at them. "What's the matter?" one of them hollered.

"NONE OF YOUR BEESWAX!" hollered Morris Bird III.

Sandra's eyes were shut, and her face was all knotted and wrinkly. "AHHHHH! AHHHHH! WAAAAAH! WOOOOO! I WANT MY MOMMY! EEEEEK! AHHHHH!"

Teddy Karam was sniggering to beat the band.

Morris Bird III glared at the three little girls across the street. "Go away!" he hollered.

"WAAAAAH!" screamed Sandra. "WOOOOO! EEEEEK!"

Morris Bird III sighed. "All right," he said. "All *right*." Sandra stopped screaming. She smiled. "Thank you," she said quietly.

"You won't make it."

"Huh?"

"You'll poop out. It's going to be a long walk."

"Then you can carry me."

"Carry you?"

"Uh huh. You want me to scream again?"

"You don't even know where we're going."

"I don't *care* where we're going. I just want to *go*."

Teddy Karam spoke. "Can I say something?"

"Why not?" said Morris Bird III, grunting.

"She's not going to school with me, right?"

"Right."

"And that means you aren't going to pay me anything, right?"

"Right."

"I got an idea."

"Big deal."

"It's a good idea."

"Great," said Morris Bird III.

Several children walked past them. Teddy Karam said nothing until they were out of earshot. "Now, this has got to be quick. I got to get to school, so make up your mind in a hurry." He nodded toward Sandra. "You don't want to carry her if she poops out. So, for half a dollar, I'll rent you my wagon."

"Half a dollar?"

"Take it or leave it."

"Crook!"

"Right," said Teddy Karam, grinning.

Sandra giggled.

Morris Bird III glared at her. "I haven't got half a dollar," he said to Teddy Karam.

"Okay," said Teddy Karam. He turned and started walking away. "See you."

"Wait a second!"

Teddy Karam hesitated, looked back over a shoulder. "Something on your mind?"

"Okay."

"Okay what?"

"Okay I'll give you half a dollar."

"Now that's using the old bean," said Teddy Karam.

"Crook. Lousy dirty crook."

"Ah. Ah. Ah. Sticks and stones," said Teddy Karam, sniggering.

Sandra clapped her hands together and began a little singsong. "Sticks and stones may break my bones," she sing-songed, "but names will never hurt me."

The words

CRIMSON STREAK

were printed in bright white letters on the side of Teddy Karam's little red wagon. The left rear wheel had a flat place. It went tiddlelump. Teddy Karam had a name for his wagon. He called it.

NOSMIRC KAERTS

Morris Bird III and Teddy Karam *carried* the wagon from the Karam garage. They could not risk pulling it. Teddy's mother might have heard the tiddlelump.

Sandra smiled when she saw it.

They set it down on the sidewalk a couple of doors from the Karam place.

"Half a dollar," said Teddy Karam, holding out a hand.

Morris Bird III nodded. He fished for the money in his pocket, gave Teddy Karam four dimes, a nickel and five pennies. "Crook," he said.

Happily Teddy Karam nodded. "Ain't it the truth?" he said. He pocketed the money. "Well, os gnol." He walked off toward school.

He was whistling. He did not look back.

Morris Bird III glared at his sister.

Doog dlo Ardnas. Hah! Gubmuh!

HE PLACED THE ALARMCLOCK and the jar of Peter Pan Peanut Butter in the wagon. Sandra asked him if she was going to get to ride. He told her to shut up. He pulled the wagon with one hand, held onto Sandra's hand with the other. Tiddlelump went the wagon. He was stuck with her, and that was all there was to it. And he was out half a dollar. This reduced his ready capital to just 57 cents. Oh boy, some luck. Well, why complain about it? Didn't do a bit of good. The thing to do was make the best of the situation. If he'd not agreed to take Sandra along, she'd have run home to Grandma, and Grandma would have called the police, and the name of Morris Bird III, Master Criminal & Dangerous Fugitive, would have been broadcast to every police car in the city. Which meant he *had* to have this wagon, this dumb old flatwheeled thing Teddy Karam called NOSMIRC KAERTS. Sandra would sooner or later poop out. Probably sooner. He didn't want to have to carry her on his *back* for crying out loud. He would let her ride in the wagon. He would make the best of the situation. He would carry on. He would do this thing no matter what.

THE ROUTE MORRIS BIRD III had chosen for his walk did *not* represent the shortest distance between Edmunds Avenue and 670 East 63rd Street. It was crooked and oblique, and it kept him away from most main streets. He didn't want to have much to do with main streets. Schools were located on main streets. Policemen could be found on main streets. And there were more just plain *people* on main streets. The fewer people he encountered, the safer he would be. People sometimes asked nosy questions. He had no answers for such questions.

According to the map he'd crooked from Albrecht's Drug Store, the logical route from Edmunds Avenue to 670 East 63rd Street involved walking west on Hough Avenue to East 79th Street, north on East 79th to St. Clair Avenue, west on St. Clair to East 63rd, then north to

Number 670. But he wasn't about to follow this route. It passed at least two schools that he knew of—Hough Elementary School, at Hough and East 90th, and Addison Junior High School, at Hough and East 79th. North of Addison, the lay of the land was unfamiliar to him, but he figured it was a pretty good bet that several more schools were up there somewhere.

So, a side street route was called for.

It began right there at the corner of Edmunds and East 90th. Instead of turning south toward Hough Avenue, Morris Bird III turned north. Pulling his sister and NOSMIRC KAERTS, he walked one short block to Crawford Road, crossed Crawford Road, continued northwest on a street called Harkness Road for one long block to East 86th Street, turned south on East 86th for one short block to a street called Linwood Avenue, then turned west on Linwood. They were moving parallel with Hough Avenue a block north of it. It was a residential street, and it had no policemen. The first large thing that happened was the riot.

SANDRA DIDN'T DISAPPOINT HIM. She pooped out in the fourth block. They had just turned off East 86th. They were walking west on Linwood. The trees smelled dry and clean.

"I want to ride in the wagon," she said.

"Okay. Get in."

Sandra sat down in the wagon. She grinned.

He tugged on the handle. Now the wagon was harder to pull. The tiddlelump was louder. At Linwood and East 84th Street, they passed the house where Dolores Bovasso lived. Morris Bird III had attended a Halloween party there a couple of years ago. They had all bobbed for apples, and a boy named Roy Mollenkopf had pushed Dolores in the tub. Dolores' mother had been furious and had ordered everyone out. Old Roy Mollenkopf had been quite a hero. But old Roy Mollenkopf wasn't around anymore. He was blind now, attending some sort of school for blind children.

Now that Morris Bird III didn't have to hold his sister's hand, he kept a hand in the pocket where the evil penknife was. His fingers were curled around it. For some reason he was afraid it would pop open. He supposed this was a dumb way to feel, but he couldn't help it.

As he walked and pulled, he thought of the route. So far, so good. This early part of the route he had committed to memory. But, when he came to the corner of Linwood and East 82nd Street, he stopped.

"We . . . something wrong?" said Sandra.

He paid her no mind. He dropped the wagon handle, unbuttoned his jacket and shirt and removed the map. Then he took the compass from his pocket. He checked the map against the compass. Yes, everything was all right. They would continue west on Linwood, all the way to East 66th Street. There, at East 66th, they would turn north.

He held the compass steady. North was where it was supposed to be. He smiled. Then he took the picture of Veronica Lake from inside the folds of the map. "It's going to be all right," he said.

"What?" said Sandra.

"Nobody was talking to you."

"Then who you talking to?"

"Never mind," said Morris Bird III. He refolded the map around the picture, slid both back inside his shirt. He put away the compass, buttoned his shirt and jacket, picked up the wagon handle. Tiddle-lump, they crossed East 82nd, made a short dogleg north, then continued west on Linwood.

"Where we going?" Sandra wanted to know.

"I was wondering when you'd ask."

"So where we *going*?"

"None of your beeswax."

"I'll scream."

"Go ahead."

"Huh?"

Morris Bird III halted. Again he dropped the wagon handle. He turned around. "If you don't like it, go home."

"I don't know the *way!*"

"I know you don't."

"You'd *leave* me here?"

"Uh huh."

Sandra dug at a nostril with a mittened thumb. She was crying. "You're *mean* . . ."

"Uh huh."

Sandra opened her mouth to scream.

He broke in. "I wouldn't do that. If you do, I'll run. I'll leave you sitting in the wagon and I'll run away. So somebody hears you and comes. So still it'll take whoever it is a long time to get you home. And then what are you going to tell Grandma? That I'm gone? So big deal. So you'll tell her I'm gone. But you won't know where I've gone *to*, will you? So yell. Do me a favor. One yell is all I need. One yell and I run away."

Sandra closed her mouth.

Morris Bird III squatted next to the wagon. He looked his sister squarely in her damp little eyes. His breath tasted sweet. "Now you listen to me real close," he said. "We got a long way to go today, and I been planning this a real long time. *Before*, when we were back there with Teddy Karam, okay, so if you'd of kept screaming or run off and told Grandma, then *sure*, I wouldn't of been able to go. But now I don't care *what* you do. We're far enough away so it doesn't matter. You got that?"

She nodded.

He rocked on the balls of his feet. "If you keep quiet, you can come along. Otherwise, goodbye, it's been good to know you."

"I'll be quiet."

"Promise?"

Sandra nodded.

He straightened up. "And no questions."

"But where we *going*?"

"I said no questions."

Nodding, Sandra rubbed her eyes with her mittens. "Morris?"

"Yeah?"

"Be . . . be nice to me. I'm . . . scared."

The sweetness went out of his breath. He wet his lips. He coughed, then: "Yeah. Sure. Okay."

"Thank . . . you."

"Ahhhhh," said Morris Bird III. He picked up the wagon handle. Tiddlelump. He looked at trees, and he looked at houses, and he looked at the sidewalk, and as he did these things he asked himself a question. He asked himself: Hey friend, aren't you something? It takes a lot of the real stuff to pick on your sister who's just six. Who you going to bully next? Somebody's baby in a crib?

He looked up at the sky, exhaled in such a way that his lips flapped loosely. Like a horse.

Well, at least the sky was clear. Grandma's threat of rain had gone away. But something of a wind had come up, and it was making the day colder. The hand that was curled around the evil penknife in his pocket was warm. The hand that pulled the wagon was not warm. He wondered when he'd begin getting tired. He'd not counted on pulling this stupid old wagon, this NOSMIRC KAERTS. All right, so maybe Sandra was small; this didn't mean that she was particularly *light*. And half an hour from now he would be feeling it. In his shoulders, his back. (There was only one consolation that he could see. In talking about that fellow Beethoven, Mrs. Dallas had said something to the effect that difficult achievements were the best. Well, now that Morris Bird III had to haul Sandra along, the doing of this thing would be a lot harder. It had been difficult enough to begin with, but now . . . well, *now* it would be like getting water to run uphill.)

He snorted, told himself to stop feeling sorry for himself.

Sandra sat with the alarmclock and the jar of Peter Pan Peanut Butter in her lap. "Morris?"

Still pulling, he glanced back at her.

She nodded toward the stuff in her lap. "How come we got this?"

"None of your beeswax."

"Every time I ask you something, you say none of my beeswax."

"Be quiet," he said. He looked forward again.

Sandra sniffled.

Sighing, Morris Bird III shook his head.

A fat woman came toward them. "Hello, little girl," she said to Sandra as she walked past. She was smiling, and several of her upper teeth were missing.

"Morris?"

"Yeah?"

"That lady, she smelled like lavender."

"Great."

"Can I have some peanut butter?"

"After."

"When after?"

"When I say so."

"Oh," said Sandra, and then she was silent. Not even a sniffle.

The sidewalk dipped. Morris Bird III rested the wagon handle against the back of a leg and let the wagon coast to the bottom of the dip. Then he shifted hands, transferring the penknife too—from one pocket to the other. Now his cold hand was wrapped around the penknife and his warm hand was pulling the wagon. Tiddlelump, and somewhere someone was burning leaves.

They were coming to the intersection of Linwood and East 79th Street. There was a little candystore at this corner. It had COCA-COLA and LUCKY STRIKE and BABY RUTH signs in its window. Morris Bird III had heard it said that one of the most inspiring events of the war had been the sending of Lucky Strike Green off to serve its country. He didn't quite know whether to believe this. *Lucky Strike Green has Gone to War*—big deal. Hot spit.

They were about fifty feet from the little candystore when the riot began.

MRS. BARBARA STERNAD'S HUSBAND, Ralph, was stationed in England. Before the war he had been a motion picture projectionist, and so naturally the Army had put him in charge of the laundry facilities in a hospital just outside London. He had the grade of T/4, and he was complaining about not a thing. A V-Mail letter had come from him this afternoon: *I dont guess after the war Ill do much bragging about what I done here, but it beats getting shot. In this hospital we got plenty of guys who was shot. I havnt heard a one of them say it was fun. I love you Barb. All I care about is getting Home.* Mrs. Sternad read the letter five times, then carefully folded it and put it in a shoebox with all the rest of his letters. Then she sat down in the livingroom. It was past noon, and she still hadn't started her housecleaning. Lazy, she said to herself. Go on. Get up off your fanny. Smiling, she stood up. She patted her tummy, decided maybe a Bromo would get her going. She went into the kitchen and fixed it. Downtown, in the Rose Building, G. Henderson LeFevre stared out his window and tried to guess when he would get up the nerve to tell Marva he wanted to divorce her. He closed his eyes, and there was Imogene Brookes. He gasped. Then his secretary rang and told him a Mrs. Garling had arrived for her fitting. Over on Massie Avenue, Leo Bernstein had gone back to his raking. The brisk air felt good to him. He grinned at the sky, counted himself lucky to be enjoying such a fine day, then toppled over dead.

A man came running across East 79th Street and disappeared inside the little candystore.

Another man came running across East 79th. He was almost hit by a bus.

A skinny and coatless old woman emerged from the front door of a house on the other side of Linwood. Her skirt flapped. She beat her arms across her bosom, hobbled across Linwood and into the little candystore.

A boy of about sixteen came around the corner from East 79th.

A police car careened up. It squealed to a stop, just like in the Boston Blackie movies. Two policemen leaped out, ran inside the little candystore.

Now shouts were coming from the little candystore.

Seven men ran out of an apartment building next to the little candystore. Two of them had thrown overcoats over pajamas. One was actually barefoot. They arrived all at once at the door to the little candystore. They jostled each other, and someone stepped on one of the barefoot man's bare feet. He shrieked and did a little dance. Elbows and arms went in every which direction.

Wiping his hands on a bloody apron, a large bald man hurried out of a place called HIRSCHFELD'S MEATS, which was caddiecornered across East 79th from the little candystore. He dodged across East 79th as gracefully as a chorus girl. As he entered the little candystore, he knocked down the last of the seven men from the apartment building. The man from HIRSCHFELD'S MEATS hit the man from the apartment building broadside. Whooping, they both sprawled across the threshold of the little candystore.

Shrieking, six women and four men piled out of an apartment building that was next to the apartment building that was next to the little candystore. Two of the women wore bathrobes. The men all were tucking in their shirttails. They swarmed inside the little candystore just in time to knock down again the man who had been knocked down by the man from HIRSCHFELD'S MEATS. At the same time, a shrill yell came from inside the little candystore—probably from the barefoot man, if the truth were known.

Women with shoppingbags came running up Linwood and East 79th.

An automobile pulled to the curb behind the police car. A colored man jumped out.

By this time there were more people inside the little candystore than there was room. All sorts of sounds were being made. "Take it easy with my shirt!" yelled a voice from inside the little candystore. "Take it easy yourself!" yelled another voice. "Watch your big feet!" yelled a third.

Morris Bird III held tightly to the handle of NOSMIRC KAERTS. He still was moving forward, but his heart really wasn't in it. He wondered if maybe he should pull NOSMIRC KAERTS across the street and thus avoid the crush at the door of the little candystore. But no, he couldn't do this. The whole point of this walk was courage, and he could not be scared off by a little crushing and shoving and a few loud voices. How could you learn anything about courage if you avoided trouble the first time you ran into it? So Morris Bird III bit hard on his tongue, kept moving forward, straight toward the crush. Behind him, Sandra was making small piping noises. He did not look back. He did not want to see her face, and he did not want her to see his. "Excuse me," he said. "Excuse me. Uh, can I get through please?" Slowly he pulled the wagon between the people who were milling around the door. As he passed the door, he could not resist looking inside. The place was black with people, and behind the counter a small man with a Hitler mustache was waving his arms. His hair was all knotted and mussed. "Get in line!" he shouted. "Please everybody get in line!" Nobody paid a bit of attention to him. Everyone was shoving and grappling. Even the poor barefoot man was shoving and grappling. His teeth were exposed, and one of his elbows was planted in the midsection of the man from HIRSCHFELD'S MEATS. The man with the Hitler mustache looked around. He waved toward the two policemen, who were shoving and grappling just like everyone else. "Mr. Barnard! Mr. Coyne!" he yelled. "Please help me get these people in line!" The two policemen looked at him and shrugged and spread their arms. At this point, someone kicked Morris Bird III in the ankle. "Get this wagon out of the way!" a woman's voice yelled in his ear. He looked up. He blinked, gasped. So did June Weed. *The* June Weed. She was wearing a kimono, and her hands were on her hips, and her blond Permanented hair was all going this way and that.

EVENTUALLY THE POLICEMEN DID their duty. A line was formed. It took a lot of doing, but they were equal to it. They hollered and shoved, and after maybe ten minutes everyone was in a nice neat little line. Altogether, about fifty people were in this line. It spilled out of the little candystore and back down Linwood.

June Weed's place in the line was just outside the door. Morris Bird III and Sandra and the wagon were next to her. She hadn't stopped talking since bumping into them. It turned out she was living in an apartment building on East 79th just south of Linwood. She was married now, she told them, to a Sailor. She asked them how they had been. They told her they had been fine, just fine and dandy. She told them they certainly did *look* well, in such good health and all. She said nothing about their mother and father, nor did she say anything about the Oar incident. From time to time, she tried to pat down her hair. It didn't do much good. She smiled a lot, and Morris Bird III just bet she was sort of cold, what with only her kimono protecting her from the weather. She hugged her bosom as she talked, and her eyes never seemed to want to light for more than half a second on any one thing. For some reason, she did not ask them what they were doing away over here at Linwood and East 79th, especially on a school day. Morris Bird III couldn't understand why the question didn't occur to her, but he certainly wasn't complaining. With those two policemen so close at hand, he was stretching his luck simply standing there. But then what could he do? Run? If he ran, he would only call attention to himself. The policemen would catch him, and that would be that. He would be taken home. He would fail. So what he did was—he stood there and listened to June Weed and tried to be as inconspicuous as possible.

The voice of the man with the Hitler mustache issued from within the little candystore. "All right now, people! The limit is two to a customer!"

Groans from the line. June Weed's groans were among the loudest.

Sandra gave Morris Bird III a blank look.

He ignored her. He was too busy keeping his heart from popping out of his mouth.

June Weed was carrying an immense black patentleather purse. She fumbled inside it, produced a dollar. "Morris?"

"Yes?"

"I'll give you a quarter out of this if you go to the end of the line and buy for me a couple of—"

She was interrupted by a man who stood a few places back in the line. "That's against the law, blondie," he said.

June Weed glared back at him. "Mind your own business. And anyway, it's two to a *customer.* Nobody's said anything about how old the customer has to be."

"That's what you think," said the man. "The law specifically states that minors cannot buy—"

"Dry up!" shouted June Weed.

Morris Bird III looked around. He wished June Weed would stop calling attention to them. Any minute now someone would ask why he and Sandra weren't in school. When that happened . . .

The man was not frightened by June Weed's loud voice. "You're the one ought to dry up," he told her. "Corrupting little kids like that. You ought to be ashamed of yourself."

June Weed opened her mouth to holler something, but at that moment the two policemen emerged from the little candystore. They had stood in line like everyone else.

"You was going to say something?" said the man who had been heckling June Weed.

June Weed shut her mouth. She was breathing through her nose. The sound was about as pleasant as bad plumbing.

One of the policemen looked at June Weed. "Something wrong?"

"She wants the little kid to go to the end of the line for her," said the man who had been heckling June Weed.

"You creep," said June Weed under her breath.

"What?" said the first policeman.

"Nothing," said June Weed. "I didn't say nothing."

The second policeman spoke up. "You can't do that, lady."

"It's against the law ain't it?" said the heckler.

"That's right," said the second policeman.

June Weed stuck out her tongue at the heckler. "I hope you're really happy."

"I feel great," said the heckler, grinning.

The first policeman looked at Morris Bird III.

Morris Bird III looked at the sky, the street, the sidewalk, the houses. He looked everywhere but at the policeman.

"Sonny?" said the policeman.

"Mm?"

"I think you and your little sis here better run along."

Morris Bird III looked at June Weed, but June Weed was too busy glaring at the heckler.

"Mm," said Morris Bird III, nodding. He picked up the handle of NOSMIRC KAERTS and started pulling.

June Weed paid no attention to him.

Morris Bird III glanced back at Sandra. He said not a word. All she had to do was open her mouth. But she said not a word.

Tiddlelump, they crossed East 79th, continued west on Linwood. Morris Bird III tried to breathe as little as possible. He decided that under no circumstances would he look back. He kept waiting for a shout from June Weed, a shout that would go like this: Officers! Officers! Stop those kids! They're supposed to be in school!

Tiddlelump, heavily, and his arm was beginning to hurt. Overhead, birds squawked and argued. A Pepsi-Cola truck went past. Along this part of Linwood Avenue, the houses were set back farther from the streets. The lawns were larger, and some of them were still green. They smelled good.

It wasn't until they were more than a block away from the little candystore that Morris Bird III's heart sank back into its proper place. Once this happened, he allowed his breathing to get back to normal.

Sandra was humming to herself. It didn't sound like any tune he knew, or any tune at all. "Morris?"

"Yeah?"

"How come so many of those people had on their peejays?"

"I don't know. Maybe they work nights. War Plants."

"They make bombs and things, you mean?"

"Maybe."

"So why did they all run outside?"

"You don't know?"

"No."

"Some sister."

"Huh?"

"Doesn't even know what's going on in the world."

"So *tell* me," said Sandra, and she started to sniffle.

"All right. All right. Just don't bawl. It was cigarettes."

"Huh?"

"Cigarettes. They were buying cigarettes. There's a war on, remember?"

"Oh. Is that all?"

"Yes."

"And people like cigarettes that much?"

"Yes. There's not enough cigarettes to go around, so people have to stand in line."

"Oh," said Sandra, and she went back to her humming.

THE NEXT PART OF the route promised to be kind of fun. Or at least Morris Bird III thought so. Maybe it wouldn't mean much to Sandra, but too bad for her. She could hum, or stare at the sky, or do whatever she wanted. Up ahead, on the left, at the corner of Linwood and East

66th Street was League Park, and League Park was the greatest place in the world. It was the place where the Cleveland Indians played a good many of their home games. Morris Bird III was very enthusiastic about the Cleveland Indians. Therefore, he was very enthusiastic about League Park. It was a tall old ballpark, part concrete, part wooden. The wooden parts were painted green, and this green was greener than the greenest green Morris Bird III had ever seen. Moving forward, pulling on the handle of NOSMIRC KAERTS, he first came to League Park at the corner of Linwood and East 69th Street. This was where the cement bleachers began. The cement bleachers were out in left field. Home plate was at the East 66th end of the park, near Linwood. Which meant that you had to hit the ball almost *three blocks* if you wanted to hit a home run into those cement bleachers. This was enough to take a person's breath away, and it wasn't lost on Morris Bird III. In the past three years, he'd seen nine games at League Park, and the Indians had won seven of them. He had kept track. Mr. Wysocki, Suzanne's father, had taken him to these games. Mr. Wysocki was quite a knowledgeable baseball fan, but unfortunately he did not root for the Indians. He was what was known as an Indian Hater. He booed all the Indians, and he liked to speak at great length on the virtues and superiority of the New York Yankees. As for his booing, you could hear him for blocks. He was especially vigorous in his booing of the Indians' second baseman, a fellow named Ray Mack. *Hey, Mack!* Mr. Wysocki would shout. *You can't hit your way out of a paper bag!* One day, however, Ray Mack hit a home run into the distant left field cement bleachers, and Morris Bird III just yelled and whooped like anything. He wanted very much to say something to Mr. Wysocki about paper bags, but he supposed it wouldn't have been polite. Besides that, he didn't want to offend Mr. Wysocki. After all, an offended Mr. Wysocki might not have taken him to any more games. This would not have done. No sir. Not a bit. Morris Bird III's trips to League Park with Mr. Wysocki were even more exciting than the times when he was taken to Euclid Beach Park where the rolleycoasters were. Not that he had anything against rolleycoasters; it was just that he liked going to League Park better. The excitement began long before the game began, and even long before they arrived at the old ballpark. It

began the instant Morris Bird III got inside Mr. Wysocki's magnificent '36 Packard, the only car on Edmunds Avenue with a C sticker. It
was a majestic car. Mr. Wysocki was small and dark and he had no
thumb on his right hand. Morris Bird III did not know why Mr.
Wysocki had no thumb on his right hand. He'd never gotten up the
nerve to ask. Mr. Wysocki's missing thumb was like The Voice of
Cleveland & Northeastern Ohio's missing foot—terrible and mysterious. Still, Morris Bird III was fascinated by Mr. Wysocki's missing
thumb. He couldn't help it: he liked to sneak glances at the place where
the nub was. The skin there was all shiny. He'd never seen the place
where The Voice of Cleveland & Northeastern Ohio's foot had been
cut off, so he didn't know whether all stumps or nubs or whatever
were shiny, but it surely was interesting to think about. Several times
Mr. Wysocki caught Morris Bird III staring at the shiny nub, but
never was anything said. That was the kind of man Mr. Wysocki was.
Once, while driving to League Park, Mr. Wysocki smiled at Morris
Bird III and said: You know something? You're doing me a favor. I
mean that. With my boys away, I still got somebody to go to the games
with me. It's no good going to the games by myself. Doesn't mean
anything, you know what I mean? And then Mr. Wysocki smote Morris Bird III across the shoulder-blades, and Morris Bird III winced.
Good old Mr. Wysocki and his good old car. Each time they drove to
League Park, Mr. Wysocki shouted to Morris Bird III over the engine's roar. He shouted about the players they would see—players
whose names were Roy Cullenbine and Jim Bagby Jr. and Oris Hock-
ett and Chet Laabs and Nelson Potter and Johnny Niggeling and Ken
Keltner and George Case and Jeff Heath and Mickey Rocco and Nick
Etten and Snuffy Stirnweiss and Lou Boudreau and Don Gutteridge
and Al Hunnicut and Joe Heving and Chubby Dean, and he grunted
and made contemptuous sounds as he discussed most of them, calling
them Wartime Ballplayers, but yet he always finished by saying: Wartime Ballplayers or not, they're still *professionals*, and they play ball
better than you or I could ever dream of playing ball, which is something good to keep in your mind. So they're 4-F. So a lot of people are
4-F. Ah then, maybe you're wondering about something. Maybe you're
asking yourself: How can Mr. Wysocki defend them and call them

professionals and at the same time boo Ray Mack? A good question, and for it I have a good answer: Mr. Wysocki boos Ray Mack because everyone has to have someone to pick on. For me, it's Ray Mack. For you, maybe sometimes it's your little sister. You follow my meaning? And then Mr. Wysocki would chuckle, and Morris Bird III would stare out the window. After a time the bad feeling would go away. It usually went away as they approached the old ballpark. Driving south on East 66th Street from Hough Avenue, they passed knots and sprays of people, and naturally a thickness rose in Morris Bird III's chest, and he got to feeling that his blood was about to squirt from his ears. Shabby men with rolledup newspapers stood in the driveways of the homes that lined East 66th. They used the rolledup newspapers to motion passing cars into the driveways. *Parking Just Fifteen Cents!* they hollered, making swooping motions with the rolledup newspapers, flapping away for all the world like orchestra conductors. For some reason, these shabby men frightened Morris Bird III. Maybe this was because they were so shabby. Or maybe it was because their voices were so loud. Somehow he got the idea they would beat up on people who didn't park their cars in those driveways. But Mr. Wysocki never parked his car there. He had a friend who worked for the Davis Laundry & Dry Cleaning Co. at Linwood and East 66th, caddiecornered from League Park, and he always parked his '36 Packard in the lot at the rear of this place. Then he and Morris Bird III got out of the car and joined the knots and sprays of people walking toward the ballpark. It was at this point that Morris Bird III actually could hear the beating of his heart. Sights, noises, odors—all made it so that he almost wanted to cry. Who needed rolleycoasters? On entering the ballpark, there was this great smell of hotdogs and sweat and peanut shells. It was enough to make a person dizzy. After passing through the ticket gate, Mr. Wysocki always bought a scorecard for himself and a hotdog for Morris Bird III. They always had seats on the first base side of the field, just behind the Cleveland dugout. That way, Mr. Wysocki could boo Ray Mack and be fairly certain Ray Mack heard him. *Hey, Mack!* hollered Mr. Wysocki. *You couldn't hit a bull in the rump with a twobyfour!* Some days Mr. Wysocki used this accusation more often than he used the one that had to do with paper bags. Cupping his hands at the corners of his mouth, Mr. Wysocki booed Ray Mack with great vigor and good humor, hollered at the Cleveland Indians with just as much vigor and good humor, talked loudly and at great length on the unparalleled merits of the New York Yankees, and quite often the people who sat around him were heard to snicker. Sometimes they even laughed aloud. Morris Bird III could understand this. It stood to reason that people would enjoy seeing someone who was obviously having so much fun. As for Morris Bird III himself, *fun* wasn't really a strong enough word. To him, there was nothing beyond this. There couldn't have been. The world was only so large. Sitting there, looking out at the field and the grass and the players and the immense SHERWIN-WILLIAMS PAINTS COVER THE WORLD sign over the centerfield bleachers, staring at the great green wall out in right field, seeing all the white shirts and straw hats, listening to all the voices, Morris Bird III wriggled and twisted. From time to time Mr. Wysocki grinned at him, and once he said: Eat it up, boy. It only lasts so long, so eat it up now, before it goes away. Morris Bird III didn't quite know what Mr. Wysocki meant, but this didn't matter. He figured he'd know soon enough.

NOW, PULLING SANDRA IN NOSMIRC KAERTS, Morris Bird III passed inside the great black shadow cast by the old ballpark. Tiddlelump, and he wasn't feeling the tired place in his shoulder.

They passed a gate, and over this gate was a sign that said GENERAL ADMISSION 90¢. The gate was open. He stopped and looked inside. He saw a part of the field. It was covered by a tarpaulin. There had been rain at one of the games Mr. Wysocki had taken him to see, and the game had been delayed about half an hour. The ground crew had covered the field with the tarpaulin. Mr. Wysocki had called it tarpaulian.

"Tarpaulian," Morris Bird III said aloud.

"Huh?" said Sandra, frowning.

Morris Bird III made his voice nasal and loud. "Good afternoon, baseball fans," he said, "this is your ace sportscaster Fred Frick bringing you today's game between the Cleveland Indians and the New

York Yankees. The Yankees are, as you know, in last place. Well, fans, it's been looking like rain all day, and the tarpaulian has been over the—"

"I'm hungry," said Sandra.

"—field since morning. The Yankees naturally don't want to play this game. They are praying for more rain. You ought to see them. They're so scared to play this game that they're shimmying and shaking. No kidding. As a matter of fact, fans, in case you didn't know it, there's been talk that their name is going to be changed to the New York Slops. What I mean is—they're so bad that—"

"What are you talking about?" Sandra wanted to know.

"I'm Fred Frick," said Morris Bird III, nasal and loud.

"Who?"

"Fred Frick, ace baseball announcer."

"Mm," said Sandra, and her eyes were small and apprehensive.

Morris Bird III blinked at the field and the tarpaulin. He wished he had the nerve to go inside and take a look around. But that much nerve he didn't have. The nerve he did have he had to save for this journey with Sandra and NOSMIRC KAERTS. He couldn't afford to let any of it dribble away in side adventures.

Sighing, he tugged on the handle of NOSMIRC KAERTS. Tiddle-lump.

Fred Frick. A good name. *Sounded* like an ace baseball announcer's name. Fred Frick, a man among men. Fred Frick, holder of free passes to all the games.

He thought about the St. Louis Browns. The American League championship had been won by the St. Louis Browns this year. It was the Browns' first championship ever. He was happy for them. Next to the Indians, the St. Louis Browns were his favorite team. He liked the names of the Browns' players: Jackucki, Muncrief, Potter, Gutteridge, Zoldak, Mancuso, Hunnicut, Laabs. And so on and so forth. They were strange and fascinating names, the sort you didn't forget. Ah, the good old St. Louis Browns. Hooray for them. They had taken the championship away from the Yankees, and hooray, hooray.

"Tarpaulian," said Morris Bird III, and then he grinned.

No sounds from Sandra.

Grunting, he pulled NOSMIRC KAERTS and Sandra to the corner of Linwood and East 66th. Then, just to be on the safe side, he again consulted his map and compass. Yes, they still were on course. Now they would turn north—to the right. Fred Frick, a man among men, was seeing this thing through. With his customary skill and fortitude.

He dropped the compass back in his pocket, slipped the map back inside his shirt. He adjusted his Gun for a moment, making sure it was securely lodged between his belt and his stomach.

Then, just as he was buttoning his jacket, a colored man walked up to him, a big fat colored man with enormous lips. "Boy?"

Morris Bird III cleared his throat. "Mm?"

"I want to shake your hand."

"Mm?"

"Yessir, put her there," said the colored man, and out came his right hand. It was really more of a paw than a hand. Grinning, the colored man waited for Morris Bird III to grab hold.

Out came Morris Bird III's right hand. Slowly.

The colored man's paw closed over Morris Bird III's hand.

Morris Bird III was all set to wince.

But nothing happened. The colored man's hand was warm and soft. "Congratulations, boy," he said. "Congratulations. You all *right*."

"Mm?"

"Yessir. He's my candidate too."

"Oh," said Morris Bird III. "Oh."

"He's a good man. I'd vote for him if he runs sixty times. Fourth term, fifth term, sixtieth term—don't make no difference to *me*."

Morris Bird III looked down at the

ROOSEVELT

button on the front of his jacket. He nodded, smiled at the colored man.

The colored man released Morris Bird III's hand. "You just keep on thinkin straight," he said. "An keep one thing in mind. Remember that your time will come."

"Mm?" said Morris Bird III.

"To *vote* for him!" said the colored man, whooping. "When *you* grow up, don't *you* forget to vote for Mr. Roosevelt!" And then the colored man guffawed. It was all lips and teeth, and for some reason it put Morris Bird III in mind of marshmallows and warm butter.

Morris Bird III grinned. He looked back at Sandra, and she was grinning too.

"Take care now!" whooped the colored man, and he moved away. He walked in a sort of skip, and his guffaws hung in the air all around him.

Morris Bird III giggled. So did Sandra. Then, tiddlelump, they turned north on East 66th.

OVER ON MASSIE AVENUE, Naomi Bernstein glanced out the front window, saw her husband lying next to his rake. She knew right away that he was dead. Screaming, she stumbled outside. Several neighbors came running. By the time they got to her, she was sitting crosslegged on the lawn. Her late husband's head was in her lap. She was patting his cheeks. At East High, Harry Wrobleski, the nephew of Mrs. Barbara Sternad, sat in a studyhall and admired the legs of a girl named Judy Saum. He wondered if she would be going to the football game this afternoon. He hoped so. After a time, an ambulance came and took away the body of Leo Bernstein. The neighbors led Naomi Bernstein into her house. Someone fixed her a nice cup of tea. Meantime, another neighbor was trying to get in touch with the Bernstein's son, Irving, their only child. Irving was an attorney who specialized in personal injury suits. The neighbor telephoned Irving's office, but Irving wasn't in. He had gone to see a client whose name was Casimir Redlich. This Redlich was a former brakeman for the Baltimore & Ohio Railroad. He had lost both legs in an accident at work, and he and Irving Bernstein were suing the B & O for half a million dollars. At Mount Sinai Hospital, Miss Edna Daphne Frost had a nice chat with her friend Miss Katharine Arthur. She had brought Miss Arthur six yellow roses. Miss Arthur had been so pleased she had wept. Oh *you*, Miss Frost told Miss Arthur, for heaven's *sake*. Then, sniffling, they embraced each other.

• • •

THEY HAD MOVED, TIDDLELUMP, about half a block when Morris Bird III thought of the alarmclock. He told Sandra to keep an eye out for a clock in a store window. She asked him why. He told her he wanted to set the alarmclock. There was no sense taking along an alarmclock, he told her, if it didn't run. Oh, said Sandra, and she turned her head this way and that. He looked up and saw a yellow place in the sky. It was the first piece of sunshine that had appeared all day. Grandma had once told him it was good for people to look at the sky at least once a day. She said it helped them keep their *perspectives*, whatever *perspectives* were.

The houses that lined East 66th Street were mostly wooden and smaller than the houses on Linwood. Closer to the sidewalk, too, which meant they had smaller front yards. He didn't like this street as much as he'd liked Linwood. The houses seemed sort of spindly and tottery. The word that came to his mind was TIRED.

A cloud did away with the yellow place in the sky.

THE FOUR LIQUID GAS storage tanks, together with a "holder" tank (a large cylindrical structure that this day was about half full of natural gas, as opposed to liquefied gas, natural gas that always was held in reserve for quick emergency needs), were clustered atop a cliff overlooking Lake Erie. Five tanks in all, and they were flanked by the East Ohio Gas Co.'s liquefication plant, a large brick building that also contained a research laboratory. On East 66th Street, Vicki and Viola Oravec ran inside their home to fetch their jacks. They immediately returned outside and started playing. They had a tough mean rivalry going, and never mind the fact that they were just five. The transformation of natural gas into a liquid is rather difficult and complicated, since gas will not liquefy until its temperature is re-duced to 250 degrees below zero Fahrenheit. Thus, a lot of expensive refrigeration equipment is needed. But the East Ohio Gas Co. people did not mind the expense. Liquefied gas is not combustible—a rather significant safety factor. The East Ohio Gas Co. had no particular desire to blow up the city of Cleveland. Hence, the construction of the tanks and the liquefication plant. Bryan Oravec, the father of Vicki and Viola, was a bus driver for the Cleveland Transit System. He had four other children, but Vicki and Viola were his favorites. This was because they were so smart. They had just started kindergarten, but they knew how to count to ten. Bryan Oravec, whose education had ended in the fifth grade, brought candy to Vicki and Viola almost every night after work. They always ran to him with their arms and mouths open, and he never failed to tell them how proud they made him feel. When his wife complained that all the candy would ruin their teeth, he told her never mind. And anyway, his wife was the world's most notorious worrier and nag. They looked quite ominous, those five tanks, but they were not (with the exception of the "holder" tank and its partial load of gas in its natural state) dangerous. Lique-fied natural gas is not—repeat: *not*—combustible. The tanks had been there on that cliff overlooking Lake Erie for more than three years now, and the people who lived in the neighborhood weren't at all concerned. The noncombustibility of liquefied natural gas was a scientific *fact*, and so why *should* they have been concerned? Miss Edna Daphne Frost took her leave of Miss Arthur, went outside to her electric automobile and started home. Stanley Chaloupka saw the gas tanks every day from his bedroom. They partially obscured his view of Lake Erie. He paid no attention to them. At first they'd kind of scared him, but that had been last summer, and time had passed, and now he paid them no mind. He was more interested in looking at the lake, and the New York Central tracks that ran parallel to the lake and the Memorial Shoreway. He saw plenty of boats, and he saw plenty of trains, and *they* were what interested him, not some dumb old tanks that just sat there and did nothing. There the tanks were, right over there, just a block to the northwest of Stanley Chaloupka's bedroom window, at the place where East 62nd Street deadended at the edge of the cliff, and they bored him, and so he paid them no mind. Instead, he ate breadcrusts from his pockets and watched the boats and trains. The breadcrusts were delicious.

● ● ●

THERE WAS THIS TERRIBLE tired place in Morris Bird III's shoulder, the shoulder that was attached to the arm that was attached to the hand that was attached to the handle that was attached to NOSMIRC KAERTS, which was hauling Sandra and the alarmclock and the jar of Peter Pan Peanut Butter.

He figured he'd give Sandra about five minutes more. Then she could get out and walk for awhile. Wouldn't kill her.

Tiddlelump.

"Morris?" said Sandra.

"Huh?"

"That store across the street? See the store?"

He glanced across the street and saw a little candystore. It was similar to the little candystore where the people had rioted. "So?"

"It's got a clock in the window. You said—"

"Yeah, I know what I said." Morris Bird III stopped, dropped the wagon handle, turned back and took the alarmclock from Sandra. According to the clock in the window of the little candystore, the time was 1:31. He wound the alarmclock and set it. Then he handed it back to Sandra. "Don't drop it," he told her.

"You're very welcome," said Sandra.

"What?"

"You didn't say Thank You."

"Stop your complaining. Or maybe you want to get out and walk?"

"You're *mean*."

"What gave you the first clue?"

"I'm your *sister*."

"Well, that's not *my* fault."

Sandra's nose was wet. She wiped it with a mittened thumb. "You won't even tell me where we're *going*—"

"Aw, shut up," said Morris Bird III. He picked up the wagon handle and resumed his pulling.

Silence from Sandra.

Morris Bird III ground his teeth. He figured Sandra's five minutes were just about up. He opened his mouth to order her out. But no words came. Not a syllable. He closed his mouth, went back to grinding his teeth. He tried not to think of the terrible tired place in his shoulder. He switched hands, but this did no good. One shoulder was as tired as the other. With his free hand he squeezed the evil penknife. He thought back to the cigarette riot. One word from Sandra back there and the game would have been up. But she'd said nothing—to June Weed or the policemen or anyone else. She had been full of silence up to her eyeballs, and where was the understanding of it? Grimacing, Morris Bird III told himself so all right, *okay,* maybe he owed her something. Okay. *Okay.* Hurtful as he felt, he would allow her to stay in the wagon.

Tiddlelump. Tiddlelump.

NOSMIRC KAERTS, boo.

He opened his mouth. There was something he wanted to say. He tried to form the words, but no sounds came out.

Somewhere someone was playing the radio very loudly.

He closed his mouth, looked around. They came to the corner of East 66th Street and Wade Park Avenue. The radio sound was louder now.

Tiddlelump, they bounced across Wade Park and continued north. The radio sound came from a window over a hardware store. It was the sound of a voice.

"That's Daddy," said Sandra.

Morris Bird III nodded.

"*. . . and preliminary reports indicate that American troops are advancing easily against the Japanese garrison. In London, Prime Minister Churchill . . .*" said The Voice of Cleveland & Northeastern Ohio, and then it faded as, tiddlelump, they moved past the window.

"Daddy . . ." said Sandra.

"Sh."

"I want Daddy . . ."

The wagon handle was icy against Morris Bird III's hand. He said nothing.

Sandra sniffled.

"Sh," said Morris Bird III.

"Eeeee," said Sandra, softly. It was almost a sort of croon.

Morris Bird III kept pulling. Tiddlelump. The sound of The Voice of Cleveland & Northeastern Ohio faded out of earshot. He wiped at his eyes with the side of his free arm.

Sighing, Morris Bird III halted. He turned around. "Sandra?"

She would not look at him.

"Sandra."

She looked at him.

He rubbed his hands together. "Thank you. About the clock, I mean. And, uh, for keeping your mouth shut back there when we saw June Weed. I appreciate it. No fooling."

"I want Daddy . . ."

"No. We got to finish this thing."

"What thing?"

"This thing we're doing."

"But what *is* it?"

"Just trust me, okay?"

"Trust you?"

"Uh huh. It's real complicated."

"What's compicated mean?"

"Compl*i*cated. It means . . . uh, well, it means . . . uh, oh I don't know, hard to understand."

"Is compicated like when you get all stopped up and can't go to the bathroom?"

"No! It's compl*i*cated! It's got nothing to do with the bathroom!"

"Oh," said Sandra. "I want Daddy."

Morris Bird III let his lips flap. "No," he said, and his head moved from side to side, "not now. First we got to finish this thing. Just trust old Morris. Nothing bad's going to happen. I promise. Word of honor. We'll be back home tonight, and we'll be all in one piece. Word of honor." A hesitation, then: "And, uh, I mean it when I say thank you. Word of honor."

"Word of honor," said Sandra. "Okay."

Morris Bird III looked around. There were some more things he wanted to say, but he didn't know the words. He looked at a house that had a FOR SALE sign in the front yard. Then he looked at a parked Studebaker. Then he looked up at Grandma's sky. Then he looked at Sandra, and Sandra was swiping at her nose with a mitten. He looked at her for a long time. "Oh *boy*," he finally said, and then he turned and started pulling again. He didn't suppose Veronica Lake or Ulysses S. Grant or Mrs. Dallas or his grandmother would have thought much of him, but the words just wouldn't come. Sandra was, after all, only dumb old Sandra, and it wouldn't have meant anything to her if he'd spoken to her of love. So all right, so maybe his Conscience *was* giving him pain in his belly. She was just Sandra, and she didn't amount to a hill of beans, and she wouldn't have understood.

He decided he would let her stay in the wagon as long as she wanted.

He grinned. The air felt warmer.

"Morris?"

"Yeah?" He did not look back. It occurred to him that the terrible tired place in his shoulder wasn't quite so terrible now.

"You know what?" said Sandra.

"What?"

"This is kind of fun."

Morris Bird III blinked.

"About Daddy," said Sandra. "It's all right. What I mean—I'm going to try to make it . . . make it so I don't cry."

"Me too," said Morris Bird III.

"What?"

His face was warm. "Nothing. I didn't say a word."

"Okay," said Sandra, and then she started humming again.

THE FOOTBALL GAME BETWEEN East High and Central would be played at Thomas Edison Field, East 71st Street and Hough Avenue. East High was a prohibitive favorite, even though its team hadn't won a game all season. The reason: Central hadn't won a game since 1940. Harry Wrobleski really was looking forward to seeing this one. It was no fun watching your school's team lose week after week. Today things would be different, and Harry Wrobleski for one couldn't have been more delighted. Over in Casimir Redlich's place on East 63rd Street, the telephone rang. He hollered to his wife that he would answer it. He laid aside his trumpet, wheeled himself to the telephone, lifted the receiver. It was the Bernstein neighbor. No, Irving Bernstein hadn't arrived yet. What? Irving's father had died? Sure. Sure. Naturally. Casimir Redlich would give him the news as soon as he arrived. Heart attack? Ah, too bad. Casimir Redlich told the neighbor to convey his condolences to Mrs. Bernstein. Then he hung up. He shook his head. A shame, a terrible shame. He wheeled himself to the front window and looked outside. No sign yet of Irving Bernstein. Liquefied natural gas is not—repeat: *not*—combustible. But of course there is one catch. If liquefied natural gas somehow escapes into the atmosphere (because of a leaky tank, for instance), the warmer temperature causes it to vaporize and revert to its natural state. As a vapor, it is rather spooky, and after a time all that is required is one spark. Dickie Fristoe and Allie Sandwick, the two nasty little Norwood Road bullies who detested Miss Edna Daphne Frost, decided to cut school that afternoon. They strolled into Grbec's Variety Store on St. Clair Avenue and stole a deflated football when the proprietor wasn't looking. They sprinted across the street to a filling station and inflated the football. They clapped each other on the back and went looking for a place where they could play catch.

"MERCATOR TARPAULIAN," SAID MORRIS BIRD III, grinning at the sky.

"Huh?" said Sandra.

"Onward, ever onward," said Morris Bird III, pulling.

"Oh," said Sandra.

Morris Bird III kept grinning at the sky. It was a dirty gray old sky, but so what? He sniffed the fine odor of leaves. All things considered, his shoulders (and the rest of him, too) felt pretty good. Tiddlelump.

SOMETHING WOULD HAPPEN TODAY. Mrs. Imogene Brookes (a rare beauty if there ever was one, a woman of immense passions and appetites who really didn't belong there in Shaker Heights living out her years in a succession of blank matronly conditioned activities and responses) just *knew* it. She didn't know how she knew it, but she *knew* it. Somehow she and her optician, her beloved G. Henderson LeFevre, would put events into motion. Casimir Redlich wheeled himself to the table where he had set down his trumpet. He wet his lips, returned to the *Fra Diavolo*. Before going to work thirtysix years ago for the B & O, he'd seriously considered trying to make his living as a musician, but the kids had come too fast (six of them, all grown and married now), and his wife had convinced him that his future lay in working like a dog for the railroad. Well, what could he have expected? He and Helen hadn't been off the boat very long, and a job with the railroad had been a big thing. Steady and all that. You didn't turn down a job with the railroad. Mrs. Brookes spent the morning quietly. She bathed, did her nails, read a rather foolish short story in *The New Yorker*, held a desultory discussion of the war news with her maid, a large middleaged Negro woman named Muriel Hatfield. The children (Karen, four; Mark, two) played quietly and were no particular bother. For lunch they all had chicken croquettes. They were excellent. Muriel Hatfield was very good when it came to chicken. Even little Mark, who was a fussy eater, had seconds. Shortly after lunch Mrs. Brookes went upstairs and—for want of something better to do—took another bath. At East High School, Harry Wrobleski overheard Judy Saum tell a girlfriend she was going to the game this afternoon. Dickie Fristoe and Allie Sandwick played catch in a schoolyard at Superior Avenue and East 66th Street. It was a Catholic school, and so they didn't worry about the truant officer. Mrs. Barbara Sternad scrubbed her kitchen floor. Casimir Redlich kept looking out the window for Irving Bernstein. Miss Edna Daphne Frost stopped at the Fisher Foods store at Hough Avenue and East 93rd Street and bought a tomato and a box of Kellogg's All-Bran. Helen Redlich told her husband she had to go by Grbec's Variety Store and buy a couple of sponges. He nodded, told her about Irving Bernstein's poor father. Aw, said Helen Redlich, such a shame. She put on her coat and a babushka and went out. Once out on the porch, she smelled something funny. She sniffed. She could not define the smell. Finally she shrugged, sighed, came off the porch and forgot all about the smell. About two hundred yards away, one of the gas tanks had sprung a leak. The liquid trickled out to East 62nd Street and slowly slid along the gutter. In a little while, it would start to vaporize.

• • •

THEN CAME THE INCIDENT of Sandra and the two little girls and the jacks.

As far as Morris Bird III was concerned, jacks was the most foolish game in the world. Not only that, but how was anyone in his right mind supposed to understand it, let alone want to *play* it? It was played by silly girls, and it was played with great concentration and solemnity. The girls who played it were almost always silent. He supposed this was something, though. Anytime you could get girls to be silent . . .

Here was his understanding of the game:

Jacks were little sixpointed starshaped hickies. Ten of them were used in a game. A rubber ball also was used. A player bounced the ball with one hand, picked up jacks with the other. Or maybe with the same hand. Or something.

At any rate, the player had to pick up the jacks at *exactly the same time* as he was bouncing the ball. He did it in sequence, first one jack, then two, then three, and so forth and so on, all the way up to ten.

Then, once having reached ten, the player did the sequence in reverse order all the way back down to one. On this sequence, however, there was something added. The player not only bounced the ball and picked up the jacks; he had to say "Cart," whatever that meant. Why "Cart"? A good question. Morris Bird III did not have the answer. Maybe, for all he knew, there *was* no answer.

The winner of the game was the player who went through both sequences without either a) missing the ball, b) picking up the wrong number of jacks, or c) forgetting to say "Cart" during the descent from ten jacks to one.

Some game.

A game for stupid idiots.

A game for girls.

Little girls.

Little girls like Sandra. Little girls like the two little girls they encountered there on East 66th Street.

Morris Bird III and Sandra and NOSMIRC KAERTS were about half a block south of Superior Avenue when they encountered the two little girls. They were about five years of age, and they appeared to be twins. They sat crosslegged on the sidewalk. They wore red stocking-caps. They were so intent on bouncing their ball and picking up their jacks that they didn't see Morris Bird III and Sandra, nor did they hear the tiddlelump of the wagon.

But Sandra saw them. "I want to play," she said, squealing.

Morris Bird III decided the best thing was to ignore her. The terrible tired place in his shoulder was returning. He grimaced, bore down on the two little girls. They sat squarely in his path. "One side," he said when he was just about on top of them.

They looked up at him, but they did not move.

He stopped. "One side," he said.

"I want to *play*," said Sandra.

He said nothing to Sandra. Instead he nudged one of the little girls with a toe. "Move," he said.

The little girl looked right through him. "You want to play?" she said to Sandra.

"Uh huh," said Sandra, and she climbed out of the wagon.

"Get back in the wagon," Morris Bird III told her.

Sandra walked to him and placed her hands on her hips. "I see something you don't."

"Huh?"

"Look up ahead. Other side of the street."

He looked. Across the street, up near the corner of Superior, a car was parked. It had a word painted on its side, and that word was POLICE.

"All I have to do is scream," said Sandra. "Just one scream."

"But you said you were going to be good."

"That was then. Now is now."

He made fists.

"He looks mad," said one of the girls.

"He always looks mad," said Sandra.

"I'm Vicki," the girl said.

"I'm Viola," the other girl said.

"I'm Sandra," said Sandra, seating herself on the sidewalk.

"We're five," said Vicki. "We're twins."

"I'm six, and I'm in the first grade," said Sandra.

"You want to go first?" said Vicki.

"Okay?" said Sandra. She looked up at Morris Bird III.

"You're asking *me*, your highness?" said Morris Bird III.

Sandra glanced at the car that said POLICE. "No. I guess not. I guess I can do what I want."

"He your brother?" Vicki asked Sandra.

"Yes."

"We got a brother like him," said Viola.

"Lot of people got brothers like him, I bet," said Sandra. She bounced the ball, scooped up a jack.

Morris Bird III leaned forward and squeezed his knees.

"Morris?" said Sandra, bouncing the ball and picking up two jacks.

"Yeah?"

"Just one game—that's all. Then we can go."

"Oh."

"I mean it. I promise."

"Cross your heart?"

"Yes."

"Hope to die?"

"Yes."

"So do it."

"All right," said Sandra. She crossed her heart. "Hope to die."

Morris Bird III nodded, sat down on the edge of NOSMIRC KAERTS. As long as the car that said POLICE was parked so close by, he didn't see what else he could do.

"I play the tambourine in rhythm band," said Vicki.

"I play the drumsticks," said Viola.

"We only go to school half a day," said Vicki. "We get to play all afternoon."

"We can count to ten," said Viola. "Our daddy says we're real smart."

"I can spell my name," said Sandra, bouncing the ball and picking up three jacks. "It's S-A-N-D-R-A. I have a little card, and my name's written on it, and every morning I hang it around my neck. And I have a big box of Crayola crayons. I can spell Crayola too. It's C-R-A-Y-O-L-A."

"Big deal," said Morris Bird III under his breath.

• • •

MRS. BARBARA STERNAD SAT down and had a cigarette. Then she went into a bedroom and took a kerchief from a bureau drawer. Her husband had sent her this kerchief from England. It had the word LONDON written across it in a large Olde Englishy scroll. It was colored red, white and blue, and it was decorated with representations of the Tower of London, St. Paul's, Trafalgar Square, Waterloo Bridge and Westminster Abbey. Carefully she tied it around her head. There was no sense getting dust in her hair. She was rather a goodlooking young woman, tall and slender with reddish hair and a nice shape, and she saw nothing wrong with a little honest vanity. So what if she did sort of baby herself? Ralph had always been proud of the way she looked; she wasn't about to let herself go to pot while he was away. The Bernstein neighbor again telephoned Casimir Redlich. No, no sign yet of Irving. Yes, he would be told as soon as he arrived. Mrs. Imogene Brookes gently soaped herself in her tub. She always was gentle with her body. Its measurements were 35-22-35, and she didn't want to disturb anything. She was humming, and her head was full of visions of her passionate optician, her wonderful G. Henderson LeFevre. She wondered what he was doing. Probably fitting some silly woman with a silly pair of glasses. Whoever the woman was, Imogene Brookes *despised* her. She despised anyone who took up G. Henderson LeFevre's time. A year ago, she would have been shocked and outraged if anyone had suggested to her that she would be having an affair and enjoying it. But a year ago was a year ago. Times changed. Now she was entrapped in a dreadful situation, and the awful part of it was—she was enjoying it. It was uncomfortable and it was preposterous, but she'd never enjoyed anything more. Never.

SANDRA WON THE GAME of jacks. Grinning, she climbed back into NOS-MIRC KAERTS with no protest.

"Is your highness ready?" Morris Bird III asked her.

"Yes," said Sandra.

Sighing, Morris Bird III picked up the handle. The game had taken about ten minutes. He supposed it could have been worse. The car that said POLICE still was parked up by the corner.

Sandra settled back with a sort of grinning queenly dignity. She had taken off her mittens while playing the game. Now she put them back on—and on the proper hands.

Vicki and Viola stood up and smiled at her.

Sandra lifted a regal mittened hand. "Ta ta," she said.

Ta ta? Grunting, Morris Bird III pulled the wagon forward.

"Bye bye," said Vicki.

"Bye bye," said Viola.

Ta ta: oh for corn's sake. Another grunt came from Morris Bird III as la de da, tiddlelump, he pulled Lady Sylvia Frothingham, rawther and hip hip and all that, north toward Superior Avenue. The muscles in his shoulder were a little more relaxed. He supposed the rest had done him some good.

"Morris?"

"Yeah?"

"They weren't very good."

"Mm."

"They let me catch the ball with a different hand."

"Huh?"

"You're supposed to catch the ball with the same hand you pick up the jacks with. They didn't know that."

"Oh."

"Where we going?"

"No. Stop asking me that."

"I'll scream."

"You promised you wouldn't."

"That was when we were playing jacks. Now is now."

He kept pulling, didn't look back. He wished his face weren't so warm. "You're a cheat. Sandra Bird's a dirty cheat."

"Huh?"

Aha! He *had* her! He *knew* he had her! No one in his right mind wanted to be called a cheat, not even Sandra. Some of the warmth went out of his face. He spoke deliberately. "Go on," he said. "Go on and scream. Get the policemen over here."

"Huh?"

"Sure. You go on and do that little thing. Go ahead and tell on me. And, while you're at it, I guess I'll just have to tell on you too. I'll tell the policemen about how you cheated those girls. I'll tell them about how you used two hands. Huh. *Two hands.* Sandra Bird is a dirty cheat. Two hands for dirty cheats. SANDRA BIRD'S A DIRTY CHEAT, TA TA TA, TA TA, TA TA. SANDRA BIRD'S A DIRTY CHEAT. SANDRA BIRD USES TWO HANDS, TA TIDDLETY TA. I bet the policemen'd be real inter—"

". . . no," said Sandra. Small voice.

"So then you be quiet."

". . . yes," said Sandra. Small voice.

Morris Bird III breathed deeply, thrust his free hand into a pants pocket, curled his fingers around the evil penknife. The air tasted good. Tiddlelump. Head high, he pulled NOSMIRC KAERTS past the car that said POLICE. Nothing happened. Sandra was silent as a stone. Tiddlelump, and Morris Bird III decided it wouldn't disturb anything if he grinned. So he grinned, and sure enough, nothing was disturbed.

Mrs. Imogene Brookes emerged from the tub, dried herself, drained the tub, brushed her teeth, went into her bedroom and lay down. Harry Wrobleski and a buddy named Al Panetta left East High and started walking toward Thomas Edison Field and the football game. Harry Wrobleski bet a quarter on East High, giving Al Panetta Central and twenty points. Miss Edna Daphne Frost's electric automobile moved northwest at about seven miles an hour. It was on Addison Road, headed toward Superior Avenue. Casimir Redlich sat at his front window and played his trumpet and kept an eye out for Irving Bernstein. Mrs. Barbara Sternad sniffed, looked up from her dusting and frowned. For a moment there she had thought she had smelled gas. But then the odor, or whatever it had been, went away. It had probably been her imagination. Her kitchen stove was electric, and the house was heated by a coal furnace. Shrugging, she resumed her dusting. Outside on East 62nd Street, more of the liquefied natural gas was in the gutter. It was sluggish, and it was just starting to vaporize. Mrs. Brookes closed her eyes, and there was the face of G. Henderson LeFevre, the LeFevre in her blood. Ah, such a face. Narrow, with a receding hairline and eyes set too close together, the face of G. Henderson LeFevre clamored with rabbity little apprehensions. Which meant that her love for him was ridiculous. Which made that love no less real. Which would have caused her, had she been in her right mind, to laugh. But she wasn't in her right mind. He was quite tall and thin, and his shoulders were rounded, and he wore rimless spectacles that in no way concealed the fact that he blinked too much, but oh *dear*, appearances were so deceiving. She loved him. Truly she did. She had to. If she didn't, what did that *make* her? Oh dear. Such a dreadful thought.

WELL, IT DIDN'T FIGURE that there would be any more delays.

Morris Bird III knew a little about The Law of Averages. According to The Law of Averages, the chances were dim that there would be any more cigarette riots or games of jacks to hold him up.

He tugged. They were approaching the corner of East 66th Street and Superior Avenue. East 66th ended there. According to his map, they would take a short dogleg west to East 65th Street, then continue north. He had committed this part of the route to memory, so he had no need to go through all the unbuttoning that was necessary if he wanted to look at the map.

He thought for a moment of the picture of Veronica Lake that was inside the map. All things considered, he supposed there was a chance she would have been proud of him. Ah, but hold on. This was too soon to be thinking of something like that. There was a lot of distance yet to be covered. No sense ruining everything by counting chickens before they were in the pot, or however the saying went.

Tiddlelump.

They came to the corner and waited for the light to change. A streetcar went past. It said SUPERIOR THROUGH. Across the street, two boys were playing catch with a football in a schoolyard. A colored woman walked past him and smiled. He supposed it was because of his

ROOSEVELT

button. Then the light changed. Tiddlelump, NOSMIRC KAERTS bounced off the curb. Tiddlelump, NOSMIRC KAERTS bounced over the streetcar tracks. Tiddlelump, NOSMIRC KAERTS was pulled up and over the opposite curb, Morris Bird III grunting. From Sandra there came not a sound. In the schoolyard, the two boys with the football were yelling and laughing. Another streetcar went past. It was going in the opposite direction. It said SUPERIOR PUBLIC SQUARE. Morris Bird III turned west toward East 65th. Tiddlelump. The football came bouncing up behind him and hit him on a leg. Sandra gave a small shriek. Morris Bird III dropped the handle of NOSMIRC KAERTS, bent down and picked up the football.

One of the boys came running out of the schoolyard. He was maybe twenty yards away. "Hey, kid!" he yelled. "Toss it back!"

"Okay!" hollered Morris Bird III. Holding the ball at arm's length, he stepped clear of the wagon. It was a good ball, almost new from the looks of it. He dropped it to the sidewalk. *Pfump!* It was a great dropkick. Maybe the greatest dropkick of his career.

"Hey!" hollered the boy. He began drifting back. Eye on the ball, he circled under it.

Then came the wind.

Spiraling majestically, the ball floated out over Superior Avenue.

"Hey!" shouted the boy, and he staggered out into the street after it.

The ball descended.

A truck headed straight toward the boy, but he saw it in time. He scurried back out of the street. This was a dump truck, and it was full of coal. The words CITY ICE & FUEL CO. were written on its sides.

The football landed in the coal.

Morris Bird III waved at the driver to stop.

So did the boy.

The truck did not stop. The football had apparently dug itself into the coal. The whole shooting match moved away—football, coal, truck and all.

The boy made a high mewing sound.

Morris Bird III stared at him.

"*Uh* oh," said Sandra.

AT THOMAS EDISON FIELD, the East High and Central High football teams were loosening up. All the Central players were colored. In all, Central had less than a dozen white pupils. The East High side of the field was crowded. Since this was a game East figured to win, a lot of kids had showed up. Harry Wrobleski and Al Panetta sat in the top row of the stands. Harry kept looking around for Judy Saum. Over on East 62nd Street, Harry's aunt, Mrs. Sternad, received a telephone call from a Mrs. Francine Dzurek. Francine was an old school chum, and she liked to call and chat. Some of the liquefied natural gas trickled through a number of catchbasins into the sewer system. *Hello, Central!* hollered the East High cheering section. *Hello, Central! East says hello!* Then everyone clapped and whooped, including Harry Wrobleski. Miss Edna Daphne Frost's electric automobile was headed west on Superior Avenue toward the traffic light at the corner of East 66th Street. Francine Dzurek had a baby girl named Mary Beth, eleven months old. It seemed Mary Beth had a rash on her little bottom. Mrs. Dzurek told Mrs. Sternad all about it. Then she talked about the war news, and wasn't it *wonderful* that General MacArthur had landed in the Philippines? Oh yes, said Mrs. Sternad, oh yes indeed. Sighing, she cradled the receiver against a shoulder and stared at the ceiling. Out in Shaker Heights, Mrs. Imogene Brookes lay in her bed and wrestled with the larger issues in her life. Namely, her anxieties over G. Henderson LeFevre, the passionate optician. She wondered if maybe they were connected somehow with the times, *the war* and *nervousness* and so forth. To look at her, one never would have suspected. She knew this. She knew she had a pretty good view of herself as others saw her. People saw a happy mother of two (Karen, four; Mark, two), a fine young lady who lived in a fine house in a fine neighborhood in a fine suburb with a fine husband who made a fine living. All very fine, of course, but what if you had nothing more exciting to do with your time than play bridge and attend Red Cross first aid classes and take desultory baths? Imogene Brookes was a fine bridge player, but there was only so much bridge could do for a person. Last night she'd played duplicate downtown at Hotel Carter. Her partner had been a rather stupid woman named Sally Oates, and this Sally Oates had left her in a ridiculous contract of five spades instead of carrying on to six no trump, and the resultant poor score had caused them to come in second instead of first, and where was the excitement in *that?* Aggravation, yes, but *excitement?* No. Never. Excitement was love. Excitement was the high sweet drama of this war. Excitement was the taking of chances. Here, within the dimensions of her life, Imogene Brookes was—and had been for longer than she wanted to remember—vegetating. She didn't want to be a vegetable. Who in full possession of his faculties did? All over the world people were dying, and what was Imogene Brookes doing? She was taking desultory baths. Life was horrid. Life was dreary. Life was enough to make her scream. *Her* life, that is. Judy Saum and two other girls seated themselves three rows in front of Harry Wrobleski.

"OH *MY*," SAID SANDRA.

Morris Bird III looked around. He opened his mouth, but no sounds came out. The CITY ICE & FUEL CO. truck was several blocks away and getting smaller by the second. The boy who had been chasing the football was joined by his friend. They advanced toward Morris Bird III. Sandra started to weep. Morris Bird III stared across the schoolyard and for some reason studied the school windows. They were decorated with paper jackolanterns and such. The children who attended this school clearly believed in preparing early for Halloween. The two boys were shouting shrill words that he couldn't quite make out. He looked back over a shoulder. The CITY ICE & FUEL CO. truck was out of sight. He picked up the handle of NOSMIRC KAERTS and started to run. Tiddlelump. His chest hurt, and so did the tired places in both his shoulders. He was able to hear the boys' shoes slap against the sidewalk behind him. Sandra whooped and shrieked. Five more seconds maybe, and he knew they would catch him. His knees hurt. His *knees*. He stumbled, threw out his free arm to keep his balance. And then someone was pulling the wagon backwards. "EEEEE!" went Sandra. The reverse pull made Morris Bird III lose his grip on the handle of NOSMIRC KAERTS. Flailing, he flew forward, then fell flat on his face. He rolled over, tried to get up. The boys were tipping over the wagon. Screaming, Sandra fell out. The alarmclock and the jar of Peter Pan Peanut Butter went with her. They rolled into the gutter. One of the boys came at Morris Bird III. "EEEEE!" went Sandra. The boy's right hand was curled in a fist. Morris Bird III put his hands over his head and tried to roll himself into a ball. Then along came a lady in a funny car.

FRANCINE DZUREK TALKED TO Barbara Sternad on the telephone for about fifteen minutes. After hanging up, Barbara Sternad made a hollow puffing noise, shook her head, went into the kitchen and fixed herself a cup of coffee. Oh that Francine. She *meant* well and all *that*, but how much of her blabber was a person supposed to put up with? Shaking her head again, Barbara Sternad blew on her coffee to make it cool faster. Some of her hair had come loose from under her LONDON babushka. She tucked it back. The liquefied natural gas was flowing quite freely now, and here and there were wisps of vapor. Casimir Redlich continued his vigil for Irving Bernstein. He had put aside his trumpet. His lips were sore. As East and Central concluded their warmups, Harry Wrobleski kept his eyes on Judy Saum. Mrs. Brookes sat up in bed, made a fist of her right hand, pounded it into the open palm of her left hand. Yes, she said to herself, tonight I'll tell Tom. No matter what. No matter even if the world ends, I *will* tell him. Gasping, she lay back. She wondered if she would have the nerve. Her resolve had come on her so suddenly that she'd not had time to prepare herself for it. She wondered if perhaps *this* was the thing her intuition had told her would happen today. She closed her eyes, rubbed fists against the lids. She was being melodramatic, and she knew she was being melodramatic. Which did about as much good as tossing a feather into the wind. Grimacing, she told herself: Be realistic. Act your age. Stop losing yourself in foolishness. You'll never tell Tom until something comes along to help you. Some event you don't know

anything about. An Act of God or something like that. You can slap
your palm until it's black and blue, and a lot of good that will do. By
and of yourself, you'll accomplish nothing. You need a push from the
outside. Your good manners demand it. Certainly, fear holds you back
from acting on your own. But so do your manners. Just to walk up to
Tom and *tell* him—no, you'll never be able to do that. It would be too
rude. You have a certain concept of yourself to protect. You cannot
destroy it by being gross. Moaning, Mrs. Brookes rolled over and
pressed her face against her pillow. She wished she could flush out her
mind. There was such a thing as thinking a problem to death—which
was what she was doing right now. Her thinking was fatuous and
empty, and if she could only just shut everything *off*. Ah, Tom. Poor
dear Tom. He had such a clean jaw. In profile, he looked something
like Dick Tracy. Such a clean jaw the world had never seen. The only
trouble was—he kept ruining the effect by opening his mouth. So
poor dear Tom nothing. So she *was* betraying him. He deserved the
betrayal. For nine years she had been married to Jack Armstrong The
All-American Boy. Nine years, and they were like nine centuries, and
how much more of it could she be expected to endure? He was tall and
handsome, was this Thomas Calder Brookes, and naturally he was a
Yale man, and naturally he had a fine position in a bank. Yes. Naturally. It had to be a bank. She was a proper young matron with a
properly accredited prosperous young husband, and when they went
places together they looked like a couple of movie stars, but what was
that sound she kept hearing? Wasn't it the sound of Life? Wasn't it the
sound of The World? Wasn't it the sound of The War and Great Events
and History Being Made and People Taking Risks? What did her life
with Thomas Calder Brookes have to do with any of these things? (So
all right. So maybe G. Henderson LeFevre, the passionate optician,
didn't promise to be much of an improvement. But at least he was passionate. At least she loved him. In her situation, she couldn't afford to
be too choosy. The truth was—if Bela Lugosi had offered her a way
out, she wouldn't have hesitated for a moment.) As for Tom, why of
course he had attempted to enlist at the outbreak of the war. But he
had a heart murmur, and he had been classified 4-F. A *heart murmur*.
Oh how terrific. How romantic. Jack Armstrong The All-American

Boy had this big fat *heart murmur.* So now he was fighting the war in the Estate Planning Department of the National City Bank. He was thirtyfour years old, but he might as well have been seventy. Wills. Codicils. Executors. Trust Funds. Ugh. And oh did he ever carry the *trappings* of his life! Such a Republican the world had never seen. Whenever he talked, his words had to do with Roosevelt and Sidney Hillman and the CIO and how they were involved in some sort of gigantic conspiracy that would turn the nation communist. Not that Imogene Brookes cared for Roosevelt or Sidney Hillman or the CIO (she didn't), but people *did* discuss other things. Love, for instance. And warmth. This was how they showed they had blood in their veins. The men seized the women, and things happened, and those things were what living was all about. G. Henderson LeFevre knew this, but Thomas Calder Brookes didn't and never would, and this was why one of these days there would be some changes made. And really, when you came right down to it, would Tom be ruined? Hardly. He was, after all, a Yale man. And his jaw was clean. He would Bear Up. He would Carry On. He would be A Brick Through The Whole Bloody Mess. People, especially women people, would admire him for his courage, his quiet acceptance of his melancholy fate, and within a year or two some eager and almost aging Bryn Mawr virgin (slightly horse-faced perhaps, with short blond hair, a whinny and a fondness for camelshair coats) would drag him, not particularly kicking and screaming, into a comfortable second marriage. As for the children (Karen, four; Mark, two), generous visitation arrangements would be made. Tom was too much of a bloody gentleman to do anything else. As for Marva LeFevre, the less said about *her,* honeychile, the better. Marva LeFevre was a female oaf. Really. An *oaf.* Imogene Brookes had never heard the word oaf used to describe a woman, but it surely did describe Marva. The woman was half an inch under six feet tall, and she weighed close to two hundred pounds, and she was so blond and had such a big mouth that she was forever reminding people of about fourteen Mae Wests. When she coughed, it was like an explosion in a coal mine. When she laughed, bits and dribbles of her flesh went in about 7,139½ directions. She made a great fuss of telling people how much she loved her husband, and she didn't care who knew it, and you could just bet your Aunt Maud's paisley shawl on *that*, honeychile. She was never anything but loud in proclaiming her love for G. Henderson LeFevre, honeychile, sugar bun, and there was a dark fat defiance in her eyes whenever she spoke of him. She was frightening, but at the same time she was preposterous, and Imogene Brookes didn't know whether to cringe or laugh. Marva LeFevre was carnivorous and absurd, and Imogene Brookes hadn't the slightest idea how to deal with her. Imogene Brookes never had encountered such a woman. As a beauty, Imogene Brookes had never had anything to do with Marva LeFevre types. People held beauties at arm's length. Which made beauties different. Which gave them no way of understanding how the Marva LeFevres functioned. Oh, and so help her this was true, sometimes Imogene Brookes wished she weren't *quite* such a beauty. If she were only a little less beautiful, then maybe more men would have treated her like a human being instead of a piece of lifeless alabaster or whatever. *Lifeless alabaster!* Oh for heaven's sake! Giggling, Imogene Brookes hugged her pillow to her stomach. She supposed this was why she'd been drawn to G. Henderson LeFevre. It had begun last year at a party at Polly Vickery's. It was the night G. Henderson LeFevre (admittedly more than a bit tipsy) went to the sofa where Imogene Brookes was, seated himself next to her, thoughtfully dropped a hand on her knee, grinned, then leaned to her and whispered the most *horrid* suggestion she'd ever heard. A week later they met in Room 1409 of a most respectable downtown hotel. He was a revelation. In no way did he treat her as though she were about to break. On the contrary, and her response was clear and loud and obvious. They had been meeting in that room at least once a week ever since. Now he was renting it by the month. They both had keys. (She kept hers hidden under the runner on the fifth step from the bottom of the stairs that led to the attic. She had removed and thrown away the big hotel thingamajiggy that said DROP IN ANY MAILBOX WE GUARANTEE POSTAGE.) It was that simple, and that lovely. He wasn't in awe of her. Not a bit. He loved her because she was a *woman*. There was nothing he would not do to show his love. Ah, how delicious. Hallelujah. Praise the Lord. Praise Him who made people to take precedence over alabaster. And praise excitement. Praise the grabbing up of life and the living of it. Smiling, Imogene Brookes remembered from college her Marvell, dear Marvell, and aloud she said: *Now, therefore, while the youthful hue . . . Sits on thy skin like morning dew . . . And while thy willing soul transpires . . . At every pore with instant fires . . . Now let us sport us while we may . . . And now, like amorous birds of prey . . . Rather at once our time devour . . . Than languish in his slowchapped power . . . Let us roll all our strength and all . . . Our sweetness up into one ball . . . And tear our pleasures with rough strife . . . Through the iron gates of life . . . Thus, though we cannot make our sun stand still . . . Yet we will make him run.* And then aloud she said: Oh *poo.* And then she closed her eyes and silently addressed the Lord. The words came out PLEASE, TIME'S AWASTING.

THE LADY WAS VERY old and she was dressed all in black and she was brandishing an umbrella and she scrambled out of the funny car like Wrath. She was very tall.

She whacked one of the boys on the head with the umbrella. The boy whooped. Then she speared the other boy with the point of the umbrella. "Dickie Fristoe! Allie Sandwick!" she hollered. "You two stop that! You stop that *right now!*" The speared boy staggered back. The whacked boy was holding his head. Then, abruptly, his hands over his stomach, the speared boy sat down. The lady bent over Sandra. "There, there," she said. "It's all right." She patted Sandra's head. Sandra's face was a pink knot. She was coughing and snorting. Her nose ran. "Blow your nose," said the lady. Then she turned to Morris Bird III, who was just taking his hands away from his head. "You too," she said. He uncurled himself and stood up. Sure enough, his nose *was* running. He took his handkerchief from a jacket pocket and blew. Hard. Sandra also was blowing. And hard too. The speared boy lurched to his feet. He looked at the whacked boy and the whacked boy looked at him. The whacked boy was sniffling. He wiped at his nose with a sleeve. Morris Bird III rubbed wetness from his eyes and waited to see what would happen next. His throat was scratchy. He cleared it. He looked around and studied the lady's funny car. It was taller and blacker than she was, and it appeared to have been built in about The Year One. Then the two boys began addressing the tall black lady very loudly, both of them talking at once, telling her about the football and Morris Bird III's dumb showoffy dropkick and the CITY ICE & FUEL CO. truck. Morris Bird III looked at Sandra, and Sandra looked at him (she had finished blowing her nose), and he got to wishing there was an open manhole nearby. If there had been, he gladly would have hurled himself, *and* Sandra, *and* NOSMIRC KAERTS, *and* the alarmclock, *and* the jar of Peter Pan Peanut Butter, down into the sewer waters with all the slime and stink and guck. But there wasn't an open manhole to be seen, so he had to stand there and get his breath back and listen to those boys. A number of people had gathered. One of them, an old man, pointed to Morris Bird III's

ROOSEVELT

button and wondered aloud if maybe politics had caused the fight. A plump woman giggled at this, whereupon the tall black lady glared at the plump woman and told her nothing was funny. Then the tall black lady's attention returned to the two boys. She was breathing a little heavily, but otherwise she was giving nothing away. The boys talked for some time, and then gradually they ran out of words. They kept glaring at Morris Bird III, who had backed away, maneuvering himself sort of behind the tall black lady. Sandra made a succession of small keening noises, but otherwise she was no trouble. When the two boys had finished talking, the tall black lady gave them a heavy look and said, nodding toward Morris Bird III: "Do you honestly think he *deliberately* kicked the ball into that truck?"

"Aw, why don't you mind your own business?" said the whacked boy.

He shouldn't have said that. Whick! Out came the tall black lady's umbrella, spearing the whacked boy in the stomach.

"Uf," said the whacked boy.

"You keep a civil tongue in your head, Dickie Fristoe," said the tall black lady.

"I paid for that football!" said Dickie Fristoe. "I bought and paid for it!" He rubbed his stomach, looked at his companion.

His companion was still rubbing his stomach. With his free hand, he pointed at Morris Bird III. "What are we supposed to do—kiss him?"

"Nobody was speaking to you, Allie Sandwick," said the tall black lady. Then, to Dickie Fristoe: "Do you know how to use the telephone?"

"Huh?"

"Don't say huh. Say I beg your pardon. Stop acting like such a churl."

"Churl? What's that?"

"Never mind. Let's return to my original question—namely, do you know how to use the telephone?"

"The telephone?" said Dickie Fristoe.

"Yes. And I'll thank you to stop repeating everything I say."

Dickie Fristoe glared at the sidewalk. "I know how to use the telephone."

"Good," said the tall black lady. "Splendid. So suppose you go find yourself a telephone. Call the City Ice & Fuel Co. and make inquiries. Ask if anyone's found a football."

For want of something better to do Morris Bird III bent over NOS-MIRC KAERTS and pulled it upright. He retrieved the alarmclock and the jar of Peter Pan Peanut Butter from the gutter. He gave them to Sandra. Sniffling, she sat down in the wagon.

The tall black lady looked at him.

Morris Bird III picked up the handle of NOSMIRC KAERTS.

"Just. Hold. On," said the tall black lady.

Obediently, Morris Bird III dropped the handle. He shrugged, looked at Grandma's sky.

The tall black lady turned back to the boy whose name was Dickie Fristoe. "Go on. Make your telephone call."

"That won't do no good."

"*Any* good. And you let me decide what's good and what's not good. You telephone the City Ice & Fuel Co. people. If you get no satisfaction, I'll tell you what you do. Telephone me. My number is listed in the book."

"And what're *you* going to do?"

The other boy, the one whose name was Allie Sandwick, spoke up. "You going to buy us a new football?"

"Never mind what I'm going to do," said the tall black lady. "Whatever I *do* do, it probably will be too much. Such brave cowards you two are, picking on a boy half your size and a little girl who obviously couldn't hurt a fly." The tall black lady's voice was stern, clipped, colder than the wind. "Perhaps *I* should be the one to do the telephoning. Perhaps I should telephone your parents. Would you like me to telephone them?"

Silence from Dickie Fristoe and Allie Sandwick.

"Well?"

Reluctantly they shook their heads no.

"All right then. Go make your call."

Dickie Fristoe pointed at Morris Bird III. "And what about him?"

"I'll take care of him," said the tall black lady.

Morris Bird III drew back. Silence from Sandra.

Dickie Fristoe and Allie Sandwick moved away. The crowd broke up. Dickie Fristoe and Allie Sandwick were talking and waving their arms. The loudness of their voices increased in direct proportion to the distance they put between themselves and the tall black lady. Then they disappeared around a corner, and their voices faded out of earshot.

The tall black lady looked down at Morris Bird III.

Morris Bird III felt as though he were standing in the shadow of a great tree. The only thing was—he'd never known of any trees that had an odor of facepowder.

The tall black lady had pale blue eyes. "You didn't do a very smart thing, did you?"

". . . no."

"Are you sorry you did it?"

". . . yes."

"Will you ever do it again?"

". . . no."

"Do you think I should tell your parents?"

". . . no."

"And why not?"

". . . I don't know."

"If those boys can't get back their football, should I buy them a new one?"

". . . I don't know," said Morris Bird III, and his eyes stung.

"Do you have the money to buy them a new football?"

He stuffed a hand in a pocket and fingered his 57 cents. ". . . no."

"Then, if anybody buys them a new football, I'm elected. Correct?"

". . . yes," said Morris Bird III, and he kept his fingers tight on the 57 cents. He didn't want to jingle.

The tall black lady's voice was gentle. "I have another question."

". . . yes?"

"Tell me, why aren't you in school?"

JUDY SAUM LOOKED BACK at Harry Wrobleski and smiled. She wondered if maybe she would have to hit him on the head with a plank before he got the hint. The East High rooters started a cheer. Helen Redlich examined the sponges at Grbec's Variety Store. She couldn't find the kind she wanted, so she decided to walk to St. Clair Avenue and East 55th Street, where there was a hardware store. Mrs. Imogene Brookes sat up, smoothed back her hair, picked up her bedside telephone and called G. Henderson LeFevre at his office. When he came on the line, she cleared her throat and said: I'm going to tell Tom tonight. That means you'll have to tell Marva. Do you understand? She hung up before G. Henderson LeFevre could answer. Trembling, she lay back.

MORRIS BIRD III DID the only thing he could have done—he told the tall black lady the truth. All of it. The first few words were difficult, but then they came easily. He told the tall black lady about Stanley Chaloupka. He told her about Mrs. Dallas, about Grandma, about Veronica Lake, about old Ulysses S. Grant, about Suzanne Wysocki, about Logan MacMurray, about Hank Moore, about that filthy crook of a Teddy Karam, about NOSMIRC KAERTS, about Sandra, about the cigarette riot, even about Vicki and Viola and the game of jacks. The only thing he didn't tell her about was the 57 cents in his pocket. He used his arms to help the words along. They were especially handy when he told the tall black lady about the spelling competition Stanley Chaloupka had thrown to Dolores Bovasso. The words came quickly, and sometimes they stumbled over each other, and the tall black lady smiled as she listened.

Sandra didn't smile, though. Sandra just sat there with her mouth open. From time to time she hit the roof of her mouth with her tongue, but she said not a single solitary word.

He told the tall black lady about his Unexcused Absence this afternoon. He spoke to her of the Cleveland Museum of Art. He told her he didn't care about *anything*—just as long as he made it to 670 East 63rd. Shaking his head, his eyes still stinging, he described the salami sandwich incident, the Loew's Stillman incident. He even told her about the speedometer he'd once believed was in his belly.

All the tall black lady did was smile.

When he finished telling all of it, he blinked at her. A streetcar went past. A colored man walked by. This was a very old colored man. He had a cane. Morris Bird III looked at Grandma's sky. Off somewhere was a sound of leaves. He looked at Sandra. Her mouth was still open. He looked at the funny car. For a car that probably had been built in The Year One, it was in good condition. It was shiny, and it had no scratches or nicks, and it blotted out a good part of the sky.

The tall black lady spoke. "I suppose you want me to let you continue this journey of yours."

Morris Bird III nodded.

"All right," said the tall black lady.

He looked at her.

She chuckled. It had a fine thick tone. "I mean it. I really do. I would be the last person in the world to stand in the way of a practical education." Another fine thick chuckle from the tall black lady. "Young man, I think you're in control of the situation. I think you'll survive. And I think the experience will do you a great deal of good." A wink, then: "Perhaps you'd never guess it from looking at me, ah hah, hah, but I used to be a schoolteacher. Does that surprise you?"

"No," said Morris Bird III.

This time the tall black lady did not chuckle. She laughed. Her head went back, and she showed a great many teeth. "Why you rascal you!"

Morris Bird III smiled.

"Ah, you have a fine smile," said the tall black lady. Then, bringing her laughter under control, she said: "Perhaps I'm doing the wrong thing, but I think I can leave you to your own devices. I have very little doubt that you'll make it to your destination. As for school, well, that's something you'll have to face up to on Monday. I have an idea you'll be brave enough for it. There's just one more question I'd like to ask you, though. Uh, today, or tonight or whenever, how are you going to go home?"

Morris Bird III scratched his head. "I don't know. I didn't think about that."

"Tell me this—does your friend's mother have an automobile?"

"Yes."

"Then promise me you'll ask her to drive you home."

"I promise."

"Would you like to know a secret?"

"Yes."

"The Art Museum always bored *me* too." With these words, the tall black lady again laughed. Then she shook hands with Morris Bird III. Her glove was scratchy. Morris Bird III also laughed. So did Sandra. Then the tall black lady shook hands with Sandra. "You take good care of your brother," she said. She got into her funny car, waved at them, then drove away. The funny car hummed. It turned north on East 65th Street and then passed out of sight.

Morris Bird III picked up the handle of NOSMIRC KAERTS. Tiddlelump.

CASIMIR REDLICH WONDERED WHAT was keeping Irving Bernstein. East High won the toss of the coin. Harry Wrobleski kept his eyes on the back of Judy Saum's head. Had she smiled back at him? No. What a dumb thought. Why should she have smiled back at *him*? Before getting back to her housework, Mrs. Barbara Sternad had a second cup of coffee and reread her husband's letter. The Brookes telephone rang about thirty seconds after Imogene had hung up on G. Henderson LeFevre. Grinning, she picked up the receiver and said: It's your nickel, darling. A laugh from her husband. Hey, Tom Brookes said, aren't *we* frisky today! Imogene Brookes just about fell out of bed.

TIDDLELUMP, THEY TURNED THE corner and headed north on East 65th Street. Sandra hadn't said a word. Grinning, Morris Bird III pulled NOSMIRC KAERTS at a good clip. He couldn't understand why he felt so much better, but he wasn't about to fight it. He'd heard people speak of Confession being good for The Soul, and he supposed maybe this was it. He supposed maybe he'd needed to tell someone. He supposed maybe the tall black lady was the best person he could have found to Confess to. And anyway, he owed her that much. She had saved him from Dickie Fristoe and Allie Sandwick hadn't she? If it hadn't been for her, everything would have been ruined. And, if this weren't enough, the tall black lady had called his attention to a big oversight—it had never occurred to him how he (along with Sandra now, and NOSMIRC KAERTS) would return home. Ah, but the tall black lady had solved this problem for him. He would impose on Mrs. Chaloupka. She wouldn't mind. She was a nice lady. He remembered how good she was about laughing.

He whistled through the openings between his teeth. Sandra was humming. He glanced back at her, but she said nothing. Now she knew where they were going, and at least part of the why of it. He wondered when she would say something. Oh well, there was no sense rushing it. If there was one thing he didn't need right now, it was an argument.

He heard starlings and sparrows and bluejays. Most people disliked starlings and sparrows and bluejays, but not Morris Bird III. He kind of admired them. They stuck it out through the winter didn't they? They didn't believe in fleeing from cold winds. There was something very fine about this. Something that had to do with courage and determination and doing a thing no matter what.

"Huh," he said aloud, and he decided he was being sort of stupid.

East 65th Street was narrow, and most of its houses were narrow too. They were tall and gray, and all around them were odors of burning leaves and other dry things. Tiddlelump, he wiped at his eyes. Tiddlelump, he remembered that he'd bawled a little when those two boys had come after him. Tiddlelump, so who cared? Tiddlelump, that had been then, and now was now, and a person learned things.

Tiddlelump, they crossed a street called Schade, and tiddlelump, they crossed a street called Edna, and tiddlelump, they crossed a street called Bonna. At the corner of Bonna, East 65th Street veered to the northwest and for some reason changed its name to Norwood Road. That was Cleveland for you; streets were forever veering and changing their names. But this didn't throw Morris Bird III. He'd already noted the change on his map. All he had to do was proceed straight ahead on Norwood; it led directly to St. Clair Avenue. Once they arrived at St. Clair Avenue, they were practically within spitting distance of Stanley Chaloupka's place.

It wouldn't be long now.

Prepare yourself, Atlantic & Pacific Railroad. Here comes The Great Engineer.

IT TURNED OUT TOM BROOKES had wanted to ask Imogene if they could have the Adamses over for dinner next Saturday. Sam and Geraldine Adams were rather dull and stupid, but Sam *was* Tom's boss, and occasionally you did have to invite him and his wife. And besides, Sam liked Imogene a great deal, always made a great fuss about how pretty she was. Tom knew this, but it didn't bother him a bit. Sam was almost thirty years older than Imogene. And anyway, Imogene could be trusted, wasn't that so? Laughing, Tom Brookes said: So is it all right if we have them? Imogene made a face at the walls. Of *course*, she said. Whatever you say. Tom thanked her, told her he had to run, blew her a kiss, hung up. Imogene hugged herself for a moment, then broke the connection, waited for a dial tone, put in another call to G. Henderson LeFavre.

● ● ●

SANDRA WAS THE FIRST to see the funny car. "Look," she said, pointing. It was the first word she'd uttered since his talk with the tall black lady back there on Superior Avenue.

He looked toward where she was pointing.

The funny car was parked in a driveway next to an old brown house.

Tiddlelump, Morris Bird III slowed down, then stopped.

He had an idea.

It had come to him zip, just like that.

He dropped the handle of NOSMIRC KAERTS. "Be right back," he told Sandra. "There's something I got to do."

"Huh?" said Sandra.

"Never mind," said Morris Bird III. He strode up the narrow brick walk to the old brown house. *Strode.* He climbed the porch steps and rang the doorbell.

The tall black lady opened the door. Her dress was every bit as black as her coat had been. "Well, look who's here," she said. She looked past Morris Bird III's shoulder and waved at Sandra.

Sandra waved back.

"And what can I do for you?" said the tall black lady to Morris Bird III.

Morris Bird III shuffled his feet this way and that. He stared at them as though maybe they held the secret of what everything was all about.

"Do you have to Go?" she asked him.

He shook his head no.

"Then what is it? Tell that cat to let go of your tongue."

Morris Bird III nodded. He thrust a hand into a pants pocket and fumbled around. After a time he got his fingers around two quarters. "I lied," he said. The hand came out of the pocket and he held out the two quarters.

"Lied?"

"You asked me did I have any money to pay for the football. I said no. I lied."

"Oh . . ."

"So take the money. Please take the money."

The tall black lady sniffled. A handkerchief came from one of her sleeves.

Morris Bird III frowned at her.

No, Mr. LeFevre wasn't in, the girl told Imogene Brookes. He'd just left for his home. He'd told the girl he didn't feel very well. His appointments for the rest of the afternoon had all been canceled. Imogene Brookes thanked the girl and hung up. Hey, how about that! He was on his way home! That meant he'd probably gotten up enough courage to tell his wife! Smiling, Imogene Brookes got out of bed, walked to her vanity, sat down and began combing her hair. Hey you, she said to her reflection, stop that purring. You have some telling of your own to do, and don't you forget it.

I'm sorry," said the tall black lady, wiping her eyes. "I must have picked up some sort of allergy."

"Oh," said Morris Bird III. He was still holding the money.

"You want me to take the money?"

"Yes."

"But what if they get the football back from the City Ice & Fuel Co. people?"

"They won't."

The tall black lady nodded. "No. You're right. They won't." She tucked her handkerchief back into the sleeve. Then she took the two quarters from Morris Bird III.

He turned to leave.

"Just a minute," said the tall black lady.

He turned back to her.

"I don't even know your name," she said.

"Oh. It's Bird. Morris Bird III."

"The *Third*! My goodness."

He nodded.

"I'm Edna Frost," said the tall black lady. "Edna *Daphne* Frost no less. *Daphne*. Such a name. I'm afraid I don't look much like a Daphne."

"You look like a Daphne to me," said Morris Bird III.

The tall black lady smiled. "Well, thank you, Morris. Thank you very much." She extended a hand. "Well, good luck." A hesitation, then: "Oh, if by some chance, the boys *do* get back their football from the City Ice & Fuel Co. people, where do I send you your money?"

"Edmunds Avenue. Nine-one-oh-six. The address is in the telephone book. Under my father's name—Morris Bird II. It's the only Morris Bird II in the book."

"Yes," said Miss Edna Daphne Frost. "I wouldn't be surprised."

Morris Bird III shook hands with her.

"Morris?"

He released her hand. "Yes?"

"Promise me something?"

"What's that?"

"If you should run into difficulties, telephone me? My name's in the book too. Frost, Edna D. I'll come get you and take you home. I expect you've never been for a ride in an electric automobile have you?"

"An electric automobile? Is that the car in the driveway?"

"Yes."

"No, I've never been for a ride in one."

"Will you call me? Not that I expect you'll *have* to, but just in case. Is that agreeable to you?"

"Yes," said Morris Bird III.

"Thank you," said Miss Edna Daphne Frost. She nodded toward Sandra out there in NOSMIRC KAERTS. "What's your little sister's name?"

"Sandra."

"Ah. Sandra. A pretty name."

"Mm," said Morris Bird III. He supposed it was time to make another try at getting away. He nodded at Miss Edna Daphne Frost, moved off the porch.

This time she did not try to stop him. She stood there at the door and waved. "Good luck!" she shouted. "Be careful!"

Morris Bird III nodded, waved at her. So did Sandra.

Miss Edna Daphne Frost had her handkerchief out again. Noisily she blew her nose.

Morris Bird III picked up the handle of NOSMIRC KAERTS, and tiddlelump. "Onward," he said. "Onward, ever onward."

"You bet," said Sandra.

AFTER LEAVING HIS ROSE BUILDING office, G. Henderson LeFevre walked to the hotel where he maintained the room for his meetings with Imogene Brookes. As soon as he entered the room, he took off his coat and shoes and lay down. He looked all around the room, but all he saw was the face of poor Marva. After a time, he picked up the telephone. He asked for room service, ordered a bottle of Early Times. Room service didn't have Early Times. The war, you know. He finally had to settle for Ancient Age. Which was good enough. And appropriate, considering the way he felt.

"MORRIS?"

"Yes?"

"I like Stanley Chaloupka too."

"Huh?"

"Yes. I do. I know he's your friend and all that, but I don't care. I like him anyway."

"Oh. Well. I'm sure he'll be glad to hear that."

"Morris?"

"Yes?"

"This trip . . ."

"What about it?"

"I'm glad about it. That's all."

"Glad about it?"

"Yes. It's fun. I like seeing people I haven't seen for a long time. It's almost like seeing new people."

"Sure."

"And that lady."

"What about her?"

"She was nice."

"Uh huh."

"Morris?"

"*Yes*?"

"I got to Go."

THE NEIGHBORHOOD THAT ADJOINED the East Ohio Gas Co.'s storage tanks and liquefication plant was stable, neat, drab and noisy. Slovenians lived there, many Slovenians. And Serbs. And Croats. And Lithuanians. And Czechs. And Ukrainians. And even a few Hungarians and Poles. The Slovenians were the definite majority, however. The neighborhood was famous because of them. The Cleveland mayor, a fellow named Frank J. Lausche, had been born there. And, in this year of 1944, he was the Democratic candidate for governor of Ohio. This made nearly everyone in the neighborhood proud. Everywhere you went, you saw LAUSCHE signs. They were especially prominent along St. Clair Avenue, which was the neighborhood's main artery. It was this St. Clair Avenue that was responsible for a great deal of the noise. It was an Official Truck Route. What with the war and all, it trembled and banged night and day with a clamor of immense tractortrailers heading to and from such eastern points as Ashtabula, Conneaut, Erie and Buffalo. These trucks, plus the regular vehicular traffic, plus the streetcar line that ran down the middle of St. Clair, made it one of the busiest streets in the city. It certainly had to be one of the loudest. Both sides of St. Clair, extending east from East 55th Street to East 79th Street, were crowded with a vast rickety swarm of small business establishments. Most of them were housed in flimsy frame buildings. The homes in the neighborhood, most of them owner-occupied, were also of frame construction. North of St. Clair, fingering off toward Lake Erie and the plant and the tanks, the streets (East 61st, 62nd, 63rd, 64th and so on) were lined with these frame dwellings. They were neat and undistinguished, but the people who lived in them had great pride of possession. They had lived in them ever since coming to this country, and ownership was important to them. These were not lazy people. The men worked hard (and drank hard too; there were many saloons along St. Clair Avenue, and none of them was hurting for business), and they were big eaters, good Catholics, good Democrats, raised large families, had homely wives and pretty daughters, kept their wives pregnant and got their daughters married early. Most of the children in this neighborhood attended Willson Junior High and East High School, and many of the boys were excellent sandlot baseball players. Some of them even turned professional. (Even Mayor Lausche had once played professional baseball. Thirty years before, he had performed without any particular distinction at third base for Duluth.) But the neighborhood's largest athletic reputation did not come from baseball. It came from the sport of bowling. A good percentage of the nation's really accomplished bowlers, both amateur and professional, came from Cleveland, and many of them lived in this neighborhood along St. Clair Avenue. In this neighborhood, there were two paths to financial success. One, you could open a saloon. Two, you could open a bowling alley. Especially now, what with the war and all and rationing. The men of the neighborhood were mostly factory workers, and they were earning more money than they'd ever dreamed of. The big word was Overtime. With all this good money rolling in, naturally the people had to spend it. Even the frugal homeowners in this neighborhood. Sure, they saved some of it, but still there was so much left over, and so the people spent a great deal of their time in the saloons and the bowling alleys. For the first time in their lives, these people could afford to be both thrifty and profligate. It was quite a feeling, and they cherished it. After the war, they would have a fine creamy future. So all right, maybe the neighborhood *was* drab. And no one denied that it was noisy. But, the thing was—its residents had nothing to be ashamed of. Most of them owned their own homes. They had been in this country, some of them, forty years or more, and they no longer were strangers (not with their Frank Lausche running for governor!), and they were doing quite well, thank you very much. They were Citizens and Taxpayers, and so what if their names *were* Lausche and Grdina and Grbec and Blabolil and Nagy and Sternad and Redlich and Vasilauskas and Chaloupka and Oravec and Kovacic? They paid their bills; they socked away some of their money; they had a good time with the rest of it; they played baseball; they bowled; their daughters were pretty; they attended Mass regularly; they voted about 85% Democratic; they wholeheartedly existed as *Americans,* and hardly anyone was foolish enough to question this. On this 20th day of October in the year 1944, as the vapor spread out from those tanks there at the end of East 62nd Street on the cliff overlooking Lake Erie, as it trickled along the gutters and into the sewers, as it proceeded slowly and spookily, moving through the neighborhood, making people sniff and frown and idly wonder where the funny smell was coming from, if you'd been walking through this neighborhood, your surroundings would have struck you as being a bit stolid and nondescript, and you certainly would not have been excited. This simply was not the sort of community to get people worked up. It was *there,* and its thereness was about all you could say for it.

"WHY DIDN'T YOU SAY something when we were back at that lady's house?"

"I didn't have to Go then."

"Can you wait until we get to St. Clair?"

"How far's St. Clair?"

"About a block. As soon as we get there, I'll take you to a gas station or something."

"Okay."

AT ABOUT 2:30 OR SO, just as the East-Central football game was beginning, Stanley Chaloupka arrived home from school. Harry Wrobleski stared at the back of Judy Saum's head. Miss Edna Daphne Frost went into her bathroom and washed her face and hands. She was smiling, and her eyes were moist. G. Henderson LeFevre tore open the seal on the bottle of Ancient Age. He dropped two ice cubes into a glass, filled the rest of the glass with whisky. Casimir Redlich was beginning to worry about Irving Bernstein. Mrs. Imogene Brookes was having trouble with her breath. The passionate optician was on his way home! This could mean only one thing—her telephone call had caused him to get up the nerve to tell his wife. Ah, how about that! Yay! Whoopee! Praise God!

● ● ●

TIDDLELUMP, THEY HURRIED NORTH on Norwood Road toward St. Clair Avenue. Sandra was letting out small pinched sounds. Tiddlelump, they bounced across a street called Glass Avenue, and a block ahead was St. Clair. "Won't be long now," he said.

A squeak from Sandra.

A PIECE OF RYE bread was in one of Stanley Chaloupka's pockets. He took it out, sat down on the front steps of the little frame house at 670 East 63rd Street and began to eat. He chewed slowly. The weather wasn't particularly cold, and it was comfortable just sitting there. He hoped his buddy Morris Bird III had remembered. He didn't want to think how he'd feel if Morris Bird III had forgotten. Oh, but that was stupid. Morris Bird III wasn't the sort to forget something so important. The bread was a little stale, but this was the way Stanley Chaloupka liked it. Chewy bread was the best kind. If people thought he was crazy because he liked stale bread, let them. They didn't know what they were missing. It had been a long time since he'd worried about what people thought of him. He would survive. He had survived so far, and he would keep on surviving. He had his Atlantic & Pacific Railroad, and he had the view of the boats and the trains from his bedroom window, and he had great pride in his father's important position at that camp in Georgia, and he'd never deliberately tried to hurt anyone, and so what if people *didn't* understand why he was the way he was. He would stay out of their way. He grinned his big blank grin, bestowing it on the houses across the street, on the sky, on all faraway trains and engineers and freighters and captains, on the birds, on the street and the neighborhood and the high swaying old streetcars that lurched up and down St. Clair Avenue, and he felt better than he had felt in months. His buddy was coming. His good dear old friend. The engineer on the Extra runs of the Atlantic & Pacific Railroad. Ah, life was good, and a person had a right to grin. Stanley Chaloupka swallowed the last of his bread, looked up the street toward St. Clair. Morris Bird III would be coming from that direction. A little later, Stanley Chaloupka's mother opened the door behind him. She told him she had fixed some sandwiches for him and Morris Bird III. She asked him did he have any idea how Morris Bird III was coming. No, said Stanley Chaloupka. Well, said Mrs. Chaloupka, it's quite a long trip by bus and streetcar or whatever. Stanley Chaloupka nodded. It's nice to have a friend who's willing to travel such a long distance, said Mrs. Chaloupka. Yes, said Stanley Chaloupka. He thanked his mother for making the sandwiches. Then he asked her how his grandmother was feeling. Mrs. Eva Szucs suffered from chronic heartburn, and she belched a great deal. This morning she'd been quite sick to her stomach. She's lying down, Mrs. Chaloupka told her son. You and Morris try to be as quiet as you can, all right? Stanley Chaloupka nodded. I'll be quiet, he said. Ah, said his mother, smiling, as if I had to ask *you* to be *quiet*. She went back inside the house. Stanley Chaloupka again turned his gaze up the street toward St. Clair. Something . . . some sort of vague odor . . . made him frown for a moment. But, whatever it was, it went away quickly. He grinned. He grinned widely. He grinned at everything.

St. Clair Avenue! It wouldn't be long now!

Tiddlelump, and Morris Bird III dragged NOSMIRC KAERTS around the corner. This was a right turn, and now they were on St. Clair Avenue. East 63rd Street was just one block ahead. They had almost made it. A turn north on East 63rd Street, a short walk, and then they would be at Stanley Chaloupka's home.

But first, though, he had to find someplace where Sandra could Go.

He looked around for a gas station. There was one behind him, but it was about two or three blocks away.

Sandra made an ominous sound.

He looked ahead. The street was lined with narrow wooden buildings. Tiddlelump, he hurried forward, past Grbec's Variety Store and a place called Food Lunch Beer and a place called Zarecky's 5¢ 10¢ and 25¢ and a place called John's Barber Shop, and then they were in front of a place called Olga's House of Beauty, and he stopped the wagon, turned to Sandra and said: "Go."

She was out of the wagon in about half of a half of a second. She dashed inside Olga's House of Beauty, and then Morris Bird III heard a muffled sound of shrieks and laughter. He seated himself on the edge of NOSMIRC KAERTS and began wondering if her Going consisted of #1 or #2. Oh well, it felt good to sit down for a moment. He didn't deny it—he was kind of pooped. It had been kind of that kind of a day.

G. HENDERSON LEFEVRE LAY on the bed and listened to the sounds of the city and worked on his second drink. His face was warm, but he still saw the face of poor Marva. East High and Central High played through a scoreless first quarter. Judy Saum wondered what she could do to let that stupid Harry Wrobleski know *she* was interested too. Mrs. Brookes went to her closet, dragged out a suitcase and began packing. Tom would be home in about two hours, and she would tell him as soon as he arrived. Irving Bernstein was wearing a new hat. It was a bowler, the first bowler he'd ever owned. He was a thinnish fellow, and the man at the hat store had told him the bowler would make him look more robust. Now, as he drove out St. Clair Avenue toward Casimir Redlich's place, Irving Bernstein kept glancing at himself in the rearview mirror. He didn't quite know whether he liked his new hat. Then he decided he had better like it. It had cost too much for him not to have liked it. Mrs. Barbara Sternad smoked a cigarette and thought about her husband. She sighed. She knew she should have started already with her vacuuming. Ah, but there was time. With Ralph in England, she had nothing *but* time. She patted her hair, adjusted her LONDON kerchief. As she packed, Mrs. Brookes kept looking out the window for sign of G. Henderson LeFevre. He would be coming soon now. He would march next door and tell his wife, and then Imogene Brookes would tell Tom, and then the future would be nothing but marshmallows and chocolate sauce. Casimir Redlich picked up his trumpet and resumed his work with the *Fra Diavolo*. G. Henderson LeFevre grinned at the ceiling and told himself: COURAGE, BOY. SHOW THE WORLD THE STUFF YOU'RE MADE OF. Irving Bernstein parked his car in front of Casimir Redlich's place. He tucked his briefcase under an arm, got out of the car. He adjusted his new hat, cleared his throat, marched up the sidewalk, climbed the porch steps, rang the Redlich doorbell. He had to ring it twice before its sound penetrated the sound of Redlich's trumpet.

SANDRA WAS SMILING WHEN she emerged from OLGA'S HOUSE OF BEAUTY. She took her seat in the wagon and said: "Thank you."

"Sure," said Morris Bird III. He stood up, grabbed the wagon handle and started pulling. Tiddlelump.

"A nice lady helped me," said Sandra.

"Great."

"My skirt got all wudged up, and her name was Renée."

"Mm."

"She had the prettiest red hair you ever seen."

"Great. Fine. Big deal."

"They all giggled, and they all were real nice. The ladies in that place, I mean. Some of them had their heads in big Things."

"Mm."

"They giggled real good. They seemed real happy."

"Uh huh," said Morris Bird III.

They passed an old lady who wore a babushka. She smiled at them. The sun had become quite warm. Morris Bird III unbuckled the chin-strap of his cap. Then they were at the corner of East 63rd Street. They turned, waited for a break in the St. Clair traffic. Then, tiddlelump, they clattered across St. Clair. They headed north on East 63rd. Up ahead, on the left, was a cluster of gas tanks. Tiddlelump, and allofa-sudden Morris Bird III's sensitive smeller detected something peculiar. He blinked. Maybe he was seeing things, but not far in front of him, maybe two or three dozen yards, there was a kind of fog. It was thin and smeary, and it hung close to the gutter. "Huh," he said.

"What?" said Sandra.

"Nothing."

CASIMIR REDLICH WHEELED HIMSELF to the front door, opened it and said: Irving my friend, I'm afraid your father has dropped dead. Irving

Bernstein opened and closed his mouth several times, then asked Casimir Redlich to repeat what he'd just said. Nodding, Casimir Redlich repeated it. Thank you, said Irving Bernstein when Casimir Redlich had finished, thank you very *muhhhhhch*. The last word came out in a sort of wail. Then Irving Bernstein began to keen. He turned and staggered off Casimir Redlich's front porch. His keening was shrill. He lurched to his car and got inside. In sliding into the front seat, he knocked off his hat. It fell to the floor, and he didn't bother with it.

A MAN IN A strange hat came running off a porch. He was crying like a child, only louder. He jumped into an automobile. It leaped away from the curb. He turned around in someone's driveway, only the car's wheels missed the driveway and plowed a furrow in the grass. The tires made shrieky noises. So did the gears. The car backed out into the street, then headed south toward St. Clair.

"What's wrong with him?" said Sandra.

"How should I know?" said Morris Bird III, squinting and sniffing.

Sandra didn't say anything.

The sun really was warm. Morris Bird III took off his cap, handed it back to Sandra. "Here," he said. "Hold this."

Sandra nodded, dropped the cap in her lap with the alarmclock and the jar of Peter Pan Peanut Butter.

Still sniffing, Morris Bird III began checking house numbers. They practically were on top of the fog now, and the smell of it had become stronger. On the left was a 712, then a 694, and then he heard somebody yelling. He squinted ahead.

Stanley Chaloupka was standing on his front porch and waving his arms. "Bird!" he yelled. He was maybe half a block up the street.

"Chaloupka!" hollered Morris Bird III. "Stanley Chaloupka!"

"I smell something funny," said Sandra.

"Never mind that," said Morris Bird III. He began running forward. A few yards more, a few seconds more, and it all would be over. Tiddlelump went the wagon, careening. Sandra shrieked. Morris Bird III grinned. He ran toward good old Stanley Chaloupka, and he

heard birds, and then up jumped a huge hot orange ball, a great big
fat whoosh of a

CASIMIR REDLICH KNEW HE had been maybe too abrupt with poor Irving
Bernstein, but what would have been gained by beating around the
bush? No matter how you sliced such news, it was bound to come as a
shock. The way Casimir Redlich saw it, he hadn't really had much of
a choice. He wheeled himself into the front room. He was just plac-
ing his trumpet to his lips when he was blown through the front of
his house. The next thing he knew, he was sitting in the middle of the
street. His shirt was on fire, and he was still holding his trumpet. He
beat at his shirt and looked around. His house was gone. His mouth
was open, and he did believe he was screaming, but he could hear
nothing. Up the street, Stanley Chaloupka was enveloped in a smear
of flame and incinerated on the spot. So was his mother, who had
been standing in the kitchen. His grandmother, Mrs. Eva Szucs, was
crushed to death by a roofbeam that fell across her bed and cut her in
two. Over in the Hall of Armor of the Museum of Art, a Mrs. Helene K.
Dallas was berating a boy named Theodore Karam for allegedly at-
taching (with the aid of chewing gum) a note saying SEROLOD
OSSAVOB SKNITS on the back of the coat worn by a girl named
Dolores Bovasso. Not that Mrs. Dallas particularly disagreed with
the boy's judgment, but discipline was discipline. At 713 East 62nd
Street, Mrs. Barbara Sternad had no sooner plugged in her vacuum
cleaner when all the walls of her house turned pink. My Lord, she
told herself, I've shortcircuited the house. Then her pink walls fell in.
They were followed by orange flame, and she screamed. She shut her
eyes, but not before the flames had seared her eyeballs. At Thomas
Edison Field, a good two miles away, all the players and spectators
looked up. They could feel the heat. Hey, said Harry Wrobleski to his
friend Al Panetta, that must be some fire. Al Panetta nodded. Necks
were craned. Harry Wrobleski estimated that the fire was about two
blocks away, maybe three. Probably somebody's furnace blew up, said
Al Panetta. The explosion had come from one of the spherical tanks
at the East Ohio Gas Co. liquefication plant. It made a sound that was

not so much a boom as a great hollow *whumm*, something like the sound a gas oven gives off when you light it. Only of course this was a much larger *whumm*. It created a yellow and orange balloon of flame that shot both up and out. Its height was about two thousand feet, and it could be seen twenty miles away. Mrs. Imogene Brookes turned on her bedside radio. What she needed was some nice calming music. She had already packed her lingerie and toilet articles. She began folding some blouses. Mrs. Sternad had been blinded. Her dress was on fire. Flaming boards fell on her. Shrieking, she staggered out into her front yard. She fell, rolled on the grass. Her vision was crimson. She beat at the flames with the sides of her arms. All over the neighborhood, houses were exploding. Walls fell away, and people and furniture came flying. Automobile tires blew up. Birds were fried. Some of them hung blackly from utility wires. The air seethed with wisps and puffs of fire. Flames ran along the gutters and down into the sewers, and then manhole covers exploded. G. Henderson Le-Fevre went to work on his third drink. A moment before, he'd heard a thud, but he'd paid it no mind. The paint on cars and buildings burst into flames from the heat. The roof flew off the liquefication plant, and all the cars in the parking lot were melted. All the people inside the liquefication plant were either roasted or torn into slivers or both. Windows were broken five miles away, and the heat could be felt within a radius of three miles. On one small street (Lake Court, just west of East 55th Street), eighteen of nineteen houses were flattened within a minute. Grass caught fire. Sidewalks melted, and so did streets. Casimir Redlich sat in the middle of East 63rd Street and kept beating his flaming shirt. DIRTY NAZIS! he shouted. DIRTY RAT NAZIS! An announcer interrupted Mrs. Brookes' nice music to report an explosion had rocked the East Side. Oh, so *that* had been the thump she'd heard a couple of minutes ago. The announcer urged everyone to stay tuned to that station for further details. With Mrs. Dallas holding him by a shoulder so he couldn't get away, Theodore Karam apologized to Dolores Bovasso. And, naturally, Dolores Bovasso had to smirk. All the dishes fell off the shelves in Miss Edna Daphne Frost's diningroom. My stars! she said, running in from the kitchen to find out what on *earth* had happened. Rows of houses, or what was left of them, were burning on both sides of East 61st, 62nd, 63rd and 64th Streets north of St. Clair Avenue. A flying manhole cover knocked down three pedestrians at St. Clair and East 64th. The afternoon papers were right on their final edition deadlines, and the best they could do was run bulletins saying that some sort of mysterious explosion and fire had caused great havoc in the St. Clair-Norwood area. Don't for a moment think that those afternoon paper people weren't disgusted. Why was it that all the good stories seemed to break on the one morning paper's time? Didn't hardly seem fair. Rolling on the grass, making mewing noises, tearing at her dress, Mrs. Sternad finally managed to extinguish the fire in her dress. But she couldn't see anything, and so she didn't know which way to run. G. Henderson LeFevre began hiccoughing. He held his breath. Even though she didn't know which way to run, Mrs. Sternad knew she had to get away from wherever she was. Wailing, she scrambled to her feet and staggered across the street—straight toward a burning house. Casimir Redlich's arms were quite strong. After putting out the fire in his shirt, he started dragging himself south toward St. Clair. He did not let go of his trumpet. The heat had bent the street-car tracks out of shape on St. Clair. The wisps and puffs of fire flew everywhere. More manhole covers went up. At the liquefication plant, the other tanks still hadn't gone, but they *could* go at any second. Everywhere were fried birds.

MORRIS BIRD III WAS knocked flat on his back. NOSMIRC KAERTS tipped over, and Sandra fell out. Her coat caught fire. She whooped. Streaks of flame shot over their heads. A shower of glass, all shards and crystals, fell on them. Morris Bird III didn't know whether to try to stand up or what. Some of the glass cut his forehead. He did not particularly feel the cuts. Sandra was kicking and shrieking. Her shoulders were on fire, and so was one of her sleeves. He crawled to where she lay. She beat at him with her fists. "Stop that!" he yelled. He began unbuttoning her coat. The buttons were hot. One of them had just about melted. He hesitated. His head felt hot. He reached up and touched it. His hair was on fire. Quickly he rubbed his hair with a sleeve of his jacket. The fire up there went out. He gently rubbed his head, felt a couple of baldspots. Now Sandra was drooling. He returned to his work with her buttons. The burning places had made her coat stink. Its lower buttons were completely melted. He grunted and tugged, was unable to get the melted buttons undone. Then he thought of his Uncle Alan's evil penknife. He took it from his pocket and opened one of its evil blades. Quickly he cut the coat off Sandra. He pulled it away from her shoulders and threw it out into the street. One of her arms was all pink and blistered. She rubbed it and screamed. The jar of Peter Pan Peanut Butter lay next to her. So did the alarmclock, but its face had been smashed. Morris Bird III's cap, which he'd given her to hold, was nowhere to be seen. A car blew up. Pieces of metal came flying toward them. Morris Bird III rolled over on his stomach and put his hands over his head. Sandra kept yelling. Something struck him on the rear end. He felt something rip, but he didn't feel any pain. He rolled over. Sandra was sitting crosslegged. Her arm wasn't pink anymore; it was red. He sat up, scrootched himself to her. He reached for the jar of Peter Pan Peanut Butter. It was hot, but he managed to hang on to it. He grabbed hold of the top and tried to twist it off. Nothing happened. He grunted, applied more pressure. Still nothing happened. Sandra's legs shot out. She started kicking. She banged her heels against the sidewalk, and no sounds came from her except screams. Morris Bird III struggled with the Peter Pan Peanut Butter jar top. If he ever got it loose, he might be able to help Sandra. Some time ago he'd burned a hand on a radiator, and his grandmother had rubbed butter on it. The butter had made most of the sting go away. He didn't know whether *peanut* butter had the same effect, but he didn't think he had much to lose if he gave it a try. Unh. Unh. *Unh.* He grunted, bit his tongue. Nothing happened. Then he again remembered the evil penknife. He had dropped it on the sidewalk beside him. He opened another of its evil blades. This blade was shorter, and it had a little scootchy thing at its end for the opening of cans. Grimacing, he applied it to the Peter Pan Peanut Butter jar top. He wondered what had happened to Stanley Chaloupka. Sandra was licking her arm. She still was kicking and screaming, but she also was licking. Then—WHONG!—the top flew off. Morris Bird III used his fingers to scoop out a handful of peanut butter. He smeared it on Sandra's red arm. She blinked at him, kept kicking and screaming. "This'll make it feel better!" he hollered. He had no way of knowing if she heard him. He decided maybe it was time he tried to stand up. First he got to his knees. He shook his head like a dog coming out of the water. Then, slowly, he stood up. He looked down at Sandra. She had stopped kicking, and now she was bawling instead of screaming. She was staring at her arm. Then she began licking it again. "Stop that!" hollered Morris Bird III. She looked up at him. Then she nodded. "It feel better?" he asked her, hollering. She nodded. "Good!" hollered Morris Bird III, and then he bent down and righted NOSMIRC KAERTS. One of its rubber tires had split, but otherwise it was in pretty good condition. He wondered what had happened to Stanley Chaloupka. He looked toward Stanley Chaloupka's house, but the house wasn't there anymore. Nothing was there but a pile of burning junk. He looked elsewhere. Lawns were on fire. Telephone poles were on fire. And everywhere were all these dead birds. He looked at Sandra. Well, at least there weren't any dead Birds. Not yet anyway. Out in the street, not much was left of her coat. He looked toward the gas tanks, and for the first time it occurred to him how warm he was. The tanks were surrounded by flames, and the flames rose in immense rhythmic gusts. They made huge hollow sounds: *whumm* and *whumm* and *whumm*. The heat made it hard for him to breathe. Then a great big fat man came running down the middle of the street. Blood was shooting from his nose in a great spray. He staggered, fell, screamed. He got to his feet, pressed his hands to his nose, resumed running. The blood came through his fingers. He ran straight past Morris Bird III and Sandra. He was shrieking something about someone named Mildred. It was impossible to make out his exact words. Morris Bird III looked at the flames and listened to the *whumm* and *whumm* and *whumm*, and then he decided it was time he and Sandra got out of there. He wondered what had happened to Stanley Chaloupka. His face stung. He took off his jacket, threw it in the wagon. He was sweating. He looked toward St. Clair Avenue. The way seemed clear. The street was lined with burning houses, but there still was an open path between them. Morris Bird III squinted. He caught a glimpse of the big fat man who had the bloody nose. The big fat man was almost to St. Clair. Well, if the big fat man could make it, so could Morris Bird III and Sandra. And NOSMIRC KAERTS. There was no question but what they had to take along NOSMIRC KAERTS. Teddy Karam had rented NOSMIRC KAERTS in good faith. They owed it to him. It would be returned. Grimacing again, Morris Bird III bent down and pulled Sandra to her feet. She was staring at the peanut butter on her arm, but most of her bawling had ceased. She still was bawling a *little*, but she was Sandra, and a person had to make allowances. He led Sandra with one hand, pulled NOSMIRC KAERTS with the other. They moved slowly, and Morris Bird III kept an eye out for flying things. Then a burning wire fell across the street. Part of it landed on top of a parked car. The car turned pink. Morris Bird III knocked Sandra down, threw himself on top of her. This was what people in the movies did when there was an enemy air raid, and he figured it was a pretty smart thing to do. The burning wire crackled and snapped. Then the car's tires began exploding. One by one, bang and bang and bang and bang. Then the car itself went up. Morris Bird III pressed his face against his sister's neck. Something scorched the back of his head. His hair was on fire again. "AHHHHH!" he yelled. He rolled over, rubbed his head back and forth on the sidewalk. The fire went out. He felt his head, and now he had four or five more baldspots. He was crying. Sandra was shaking and gasping. He rubbed the baldspots with peanut butter. He tried to stop crying. He swallowed, fought for air. After a time, he managed to stop crying. The peanut butter didn't feel half bad.

THE PAIN FROM HER seared eyeballs made Mrs. Barbara Sternad weep and scream. She stumbled into a burning automobile, again setting her dress on fire. She fell down and rolled over and over, tearing off most of what was left of her clothes. G. Henderson LeFevre had his fourth drink. His hiccoughs were gone. He was singing to the ceiling, and his belly was warm. Mrs. Sternad's body was covered with blisters and scratches and welts and great blackish burnt places. The only air she could feel was hot air, which of course made her pain worse. Muriel Hatfield came upstairs to Mrs. Brookes' room and asked Mrs. Brookes what she wanted fixed for dinner. I don't care, said Mrs. Brookes. All right, said Muriel, I expect I'll whip up some macaroni and cheese then. Mrs. Sternad tried to crawl on her hands and knees, but her knees were burnt too badly. She had to stand up. It wasn't easy. On her way out of Mrs. Brookes' room, Muriel Hatfield saw the open suitcase. You goin somewhere? she wanted to know. Yes, said Mrs. Brookes. Oh, said Muriel. With that, she left the room. Imogene Brookes shook her head, asked herself what was keeping her passionate optician. Mrs. Sternad held her arms stiffly in front of herself like a blind woman. She walked straight into a burning wall, pressing her palms against it. She whooped, flapped her palms, did a little dance. One of her shoes flew off. This made her barefoot. (The other shoe had been torn from her foot by the explosion.) Dancing and flapping, she stepped on a burning board. She shrieked, then began hopping. She heard footsteps and shouts. PLEASE! she screamed. PLEASE SOMEBODY STOP AND HELP ME PLEASE PLEASE PLEASE! No one stopped. PLEASE! she screamed. I CAN'T SEE! No one stopped. She fell down. She rubbed her face against what felt like sidewalk. She rubbed with such force that she tore a good deal of skin off her cheeks and forehead and nose. Everything between East 55th and East 67th north of St. Clair was on fire. Mayor Lausche was on his way there in a police car. He had canceled all his campaign appearances. The heat was so intense that no one could get within half a block of the scene of the explosion. Casimir Redlich crawled as best he could. A great big fat man ran past him, and this great big fat man's face was gushing blood, and he was screaming something about someone named Mildred. It was impossible to make out his exact words. Some of his blood spattered Casimir Redlich. Downtown, in the main office of the East Ohio Gas Co., officials told reporters they didn't have the slightest idea what had happened. They said they would have to keep checking. From East 55th to East 67th, every storewindow along St. Clair was knocked out. Within half an hour of the explosion, thirty of Cleveland's forty firefighting companies were either at the scene or on their way. One fire truck almost ran down Casimir Redlich. He had to roll into the gutter to avoid it. He waved his trumpet at the driver, gave the fellow a piece of his mind. Cleveland Fire Chief James E. Granger arrived and took personal control of operations. More than a hundred buildings had already been destroyed by either the explosion or the fires. No one had any way of knowing if there would be any more explosions. Only one of the tanks had gone up, and there were three others, plus the "holder" tank. NINETYNINE BOTTLES OF BEER ON THE WALL! NINETYNINE BOTTLES OF BEER! sang G. Henderson LeFevre. IF ONE OF THOSE BOTTLES SHOULD HAPPEN TO FALL, NINETYEIGHT BOTTLES OF BEER ON THE WALL! Grinning, he kept at the song. NINETYEIGHT BOTTLES OF BEER ON THE WALL! NINETYEIGHT BOTTLES OF BEER! IF ONE OF THOSE BOTTLES SHOULD HAPPEN TO FALL, NINETYSEVEN BOTTLES OF BEER ON THE WALL! At Thomas Edison Field, East High was dominating play, but still hadn't scored. The spectators there still could see the fire. They craned their necks and paid as much attention to it as they did to the game. Sure is some fire, said Al Panetta. You think maybe East High blew up? Harry Wrobleski asked him. Naw, said Al, we're not that lucky. They both laughed. Still, the fire was coming sort of from the direction of East High (north of the field, about a mile away, at East 82nd Street and Decker Avenue), and it didn't hurt to hope. But aw nuts, if you stopped to consider it, the fire wasn't really coming from East High. If you used your head, you could see that. East High was north all right, but it was too far to the east. No, whatever was burning, it wasn't East High. Then everybody stood up. The East High fullback, Jim Roberts, had just burst through the middle of the Central line for thirty yards. Imogene Brookes sat on the edge of her bed and tried to figure out what had happened. Willson Junior High School, at East 55th Street and Luther Avenue, just southwest of the disaster area, was designated by Mayor Lausche as an emergency relief and medical center. One hundred trainees from a local Navy school, including a riot squad, were dispatched to the disaster area. So were some forty MPs and SPs, plus four hundred coast-guardsmen, two thousand sailors from various other naval installations, two hundred policemen, thirtyfive doctors, twenty nurses and several dozen Red Cross volunteers. East High scored a touchdown. No one stopped to help Mrs. Sternad. EIGHTYTWO BOTTLES OF BEER ON THE WALL! EIGHTYTWO BOTTLES OF BEER! sang G. Henderson LeFevre. IF ONE OF THOSE BOTTLES WOULD HAPPEN TO FALL, EIGHTYONE WOTTLES OF WEER ON THE BALL! Mrs. Sternad was crawling now, and never mind her burnt hands and knees. She had no idea *where* she was crawling. She couldn't understand why she hadn't passed out. She could taste the blood from the cuts on her face. She crawled across stones and grass and splintered boards. Then her hands and knees gave way. She lay facedown and did not move. She held her breath, made a face, tried to resume crawling. But her hands and knees weren't up to it. She wondered if all her clothes had been burned off. She hoped she was decent. She cried. She cried like a small child, keening, gulping her breath. Then a hand touched her on a shoulder. It's okay, someone said. Help me, said Mrs. Sternad. Help me. Please. My eyes, they're so hot, and I can't see anything. Please help me. And then Mrs. Sternad reached forward. She was shaking all over. Please, she said. Please. Please. And the voice said: Okay. It was a very young voice. And then something was being rubbed on her eyes and the other burnt places—on her arms, her shoulders, her legs, her upper chest. The hand that did the rubbing was small and gentle. Thank you, said Mrs. Sternad. Thank you. Thank you. God bless you. And then she sniffed. She was smelling something peculiar. When she realized what it was, she began to laugh. Her mouth became cavernous, and she laughed until her throat was sore. She decided she had gone out of her mind. No doubt about it. Otherwise she wouldn't have been smelling peanut butter.

MORRIS BIRD III WEPT. He didn't want to weep. He had wept enough today, and enough was *enough*. But right now what was he supposed to do? This lady, this poor burnt lady: he'd never seen anyone who was such a poor blistered mess. Oh well, at least she was laughing now. Her laughter probably covered the sound of his weeping.

Sniffing, he gently applied the peanut butter to her burnt places. He supposed her laughter was a sign that she had gone out of her mind. He supposed pain had that effect sometimes. He wiped at his nose. Her laughter scared him, but at least she wasn't hearing him weep. This was what he had to keep in mind. At least she wasn't hearing him making a big boohoo disgrace of himself. In a situation such as this one, a person had to count his blessings. He hoped he was doing her some good. He was glad he had found her. Maybe, if he helped her, he would be able to make up for his lies to Grandma. And all the other things he owed. This poor burnt lady . . . he hoped God would let him do her some good. She had come crawling through an opening in a fence. For some reason, he had glanced in that direction at just the right time. He and Sandra and NOSMIRC KAERTS had gone perhaps half the distance back down East 63rd Street toward St. Clair Avenue. The fence had been to his right, separating the East 63rd back yards from the back yards on the next street—probably, unless he missed his guess, East 62nd. He'd had no reason to glance in that direction, which meant that maybe God had turned his head that way. That was the way God operated sometimes. At any rate, as soon as Morris Bird III saw her, he went to her. He told Sandra to wait there by NOSMIRC KAERTS, grabbed the jar of Peter Pan Peanut Butter, ran to the place where the burnt lady lay. Most of her clothes had been either burnt off or torn off. A kerchief was tied around her head. It said LONDON, and it had pictures of buildings and churches and such. He rubbed peanut butter on all the burnt places he could find. The kerchief had protected her hair. It was good hair, a fine deep red. Very pretty hair. He had no way of knowing if the rest of her had been pretty. Too much of it was burnt or cut. After he finished applying the peanut butter, he stood over her with his hands on his hips and let her laugh herself out. Finally, and now she was weeping a little, she asked him if she really was smelling peanut butter. He told her yes, and then he told her why. "Oh," she said, and then she began to tremble. He took a deep breath. He wasn't crying anymore. He told her he was willing to try to help her up. He told her they had to get out of there. She nodded, sat up. He bent over her, wrapped his arms around her middle, began to tug. Moaning, she lurched to her feet. But she lost her balance, fell forward, knocking him down, flopped on top of him. The wind was knocked out of him. She smelled like hot meat. He felt as though something was trying to rip open his chest. The burnt lady trembled and screamed. Finally he was able to wriggle out from under her. He swallowed air, and all of it was hot. He wondered what had happened to Stanley Chaloupka. *Whumm* and *whumm* and *whumm* went the great fire over by the gas tanks. He stood up, asked the burnt lady if she wanted to give it another try. She kept trembling and screaming. He repeated the question. Finally she nodded. It wasn't much of a nod, and he was just barely able to make it out. He squatted behind her and lifted her shoulders. When he had her sitting upright, he moved around in front of her and seized her by her wrists. He tugged. Gritting his teeth, he tugged until he felt his insides were about to pop out. The burnt lady was trying to help him. She was trying to use her legs for leverage. "ONE! TWO! THREE!" he hollered, and then allofa-sudden she was on her feet. He braced himself, caught her when she fell forward. She moaned. He took deep gulping breaths. Then they moved forward. She limped, but she managed to keep her balance. "Just you hang on," he told her. She nodded. They moved slowly. He let her lean just about all her weight on him. They lurched toward Sandra and NOSMIRC KAERTS. He didn't know how much breath he had left to call on. He figured all he could do was hope for the best. His baldspots stung a little, and he did all he could to ignore them. The burnt lady was soft against him. Her moans weren't as loud now as they had been. When they arrived where Sandra was waiting, he had just about run out of breath. Sandra was crying. He told her to Godalmighty shut up. He decided the best thing would be to put the burnt lady in the wagon. He sat her down on the edge of the wagon. She began sliding forward. He leaned against her to keep her from falling off her perch. A fire engine went past. A tremendous stink was coming from all the things that were burning. Gingerly he touched his baldspots. The burnt lady bent double and threw up. Sandra screamed. Morris Bird III slapped the burnt lady on the back. He didn't know whether this did any good, but he didn't think it did any harm. The burnt lady's knees gave way. She slid farther forward, tipping the wagon to one side. He braced her with an arm, pushed her back. The wagon settled back on all four of its wheels. Sandra was still screaming. Again he told her to shut up. He wondered what had happened to Stanley Chaloupka. Then he put his mouth close to the burnt lady's ear and told her she was sitting on the edge of a wagon. "Look," he said, "we might as well put you in the wagon and give you a ride. So slide back. Just slide back real slow and easy, okay?" The burnt lady nodded. Gently he pushed her. She began to cough and gag. She shoved him away, bent double and threw up again. She threw up until nothing was left. He looked away. Sandra was gasping. Then, when the burnt lady was through, he started pushing again. This time he got her into the wagon. Her rump slid down inside and her legs flew up. She was sitting sideways, but that would have to do. He didn't want to take the chance of tipping over the wagon by trying to get her turned facing forward. Her head was against her chest, and the top part of her was bent forward almost double. The LONDON kerchief had loosened a little, and some of her hair had fallen over her eyes. Several thick strands were stuck to her face and eyes because of the peanut butter. He braced her, studied her for a moment, then beckoned to Sandra. He told Sandra to walk alongside the wagon and brace the burnt lady. That way, the wagon wouldn't tip over, and the burnt lady wouldn't fall out. Sandra drew back and told him she couldn't do it. He told her she sure *could* do it. He told her she *better* do it. Sandra's eyes were just about white. All right, she told him, she'd try. She came to him. He told her to hold the burnt lady by the shoulder. Sandra nodded, reached out and took hold of the burnt lady's shoulder. "You got her?" said Morris Bird III. Sandra nodded. "Okay," said Morris Bird III, and he released his own grip on the burnt lady. "Now don't let go," he told Sandra. A nod from Sandra, who was biting her tongue. The burnt lady swayed a little, but Sandra managed to keep her from falling out of the wagon. Sandra looked down, saw what the burnt lady had thrown up. Sandra made a face. Morris Bird III told her not to *look* at it for crying out loud. Sandra nodded, looked away. Morris Bird III's baldspots stung worse. The jar of Peter Pan Peanut Butter was in a pants pocket. He pulled it out. It was empty. "AHHHHH NUTS!" he yelled, and he threw it away. Then he spat on his hands, lifted the handle of NOS-MIRC KAERTS and started to pull.

ABOUT ALL THE FIREMEN could do was shake their heads. If the rest of the tanks went, they went; if they didn't, they didn't. The matter was entirely in the hands of the Almighty. The tanks were surrounded by flames and smoke and searing impossible heat, and the firemen had to be satisfied with trying to bring all the subsidiary fires under control—the burning homes and automobiles, for instance, and the fallen live wires and all the grass fires. They fought these subsidiary fires and kept themselves prepared for whatever decision the Almighty might make. Late in the second quarter, East High scored another touchdown. The score at the half was East 12, Central 0. Harry Wrobleski gave his pal Al Panetta a good ribbing. You think your twenty points are going to stand up? he wanted to know. Al shrugged, said nothing. Harry got to wishing the bet had been for more than a quarter. Out in Shaker Heights, Imogene Brookes' telephone rang. She ran to answer it. Actually ran. Mayor Lausche conferred with officials of the East Ohio Gas Co., and they told him they had no way of knowing whether the remaining tanks would go. Imogene Brookes figured her caller *had* to be G. Henderson LeFevre. He had been delayed—that was all. Now he was home, and he had told Marva, and everything was all right. But the caller wasn't G. Henderson LeFevre. It was a Mrs. Dwight F. Carleton. Imogene dear, said Mrs. Carleton, we need people to help out in the disaster area. Imogene Brookes frowned at the receiver. Mrs. Dwight F. Carleton was head of the Red Cross unit to which Imogene belonged. Disaster area? Was the woman talking about that explosion or what? She asked Mrs. Carleton what did she mean. There's been a terrible disaster over by St. Clair and East 55th, said Mrs. Carleton. It's supposed to be perfectly dreadful. I understand the entire neighborhood has gone up. Mrs. Brookes sat down on the edge of the bed. Oh, she said. Two suitcases were packed. She looked at them. They held all the clothes she would take with her for now. Hello? said Mrs. Carleton. Imogene, are you still there? Imogene Brookes cleared her throat. Yes, I'm still here. Uh, excuse me for a second. Imogene Brookes stood up, placed the receiver on the bed, walked to the front window and looked out. By craning her neck, she was able to peek into Marva LeFevre's front room. Marva was sitting there. She was reading the paper. G. Henderson LeFevre was *not* home yet, the swine. Shuddering, Imogene Brookes walked back to the bed. She picked up the receiver. Thank you, she said, I thought I heard one of the children crying. Mrs. Carleton told her to think nothing of it. Now then, said Mrs. Carleton, can you be there in half an hour or so? We're supposed to report to Willson Junior High School. I understand it's a little south of St. Clair on East 55th. We're to be put on refugee duty, Mrs. Brookes frowned at the word *refugee*. Somehow it didn't seem the right word. *Refugees?* This was *Cleveland*, not *Rotterdam* for heaven's sake. Oh well, it didn't matter. She couldn't go. She had to see to this business of G. Henderson LeFevre. She had to find out what had happened to him. She spoke. Uh, well, Janice, no, I'm afraid I can't. You see there's no one here to take care of the children, and . . . Her voice petered out. Oh, said Mrs. Carleton. Well then. All right. Yes. I understand. Uh, goodbye. And Mrs. Carleton hung up. Imogene Brookes stared at the receiver. She supposed Janice Carleton was angry with her. Well, that couldn't be helped. And anyway, who cared? What difference did it make? Imogene Brookes was trading in her life for a new one, and in the new one it didn't matter the slightest *what* Janice Carleton thought. There would be no room for Janice Carleton. Janice Carleton would no longer exist. The only thing was—where was G. Henderson LeFevre? Sighing, Imogene Brookes hung up. She walked to the window and stared out. After a time, she went downstairs. The firemen were grateful that the wind was blowing to the northeast. Had it been blowing in the opposite direction, the fire undoubtedly would have spread over at least twice the area. Imogene Brookes' telephone rang again. This time it was Marva LeFevre, and she was weeping.

AFTER PULLING NOSMIRC KAERTS a few feet, Morris Bird III had to stop and lick his hands. The peanut butter had made them sticky. He licked away all of it, and it tasted awful. It had become mixed in with too much dirt and sweat. He looked around, told Sandra to keep hanging on to the poor burnt lady. Sandra nodded. The LONDON kerchief was slipping down over the burnt lady's face. He told Sandra to pull it back. She obeyed. The burnt lady's face was smeared with equal amounts of peanut butter and blood. Morris Bird III sighed, turned, started pulling again. Tiddlelump. He wondered what had happened to Stanley Chaloupka. The *whumm* and *whumm* and *whumm* of the fire had not diminished. But, over this huge sound, he heard a giggle. He frowned, hesitated, turned around. "You say something?" he asked Sandra. She shook her head no. There was nothing particularly unusual on her face. "You giggle?" he asked her. Again she shook her head no. She was hanging on tightly to the burnt lady. He looked at her closely. As far as he could tell, her face was its usual blank nothing. Sure, she *looked* a little peculiar, what with the peanut butter smeared on her arm, but then he didn't suppose *he* looked like much of a bargain either. Then he saw that she was shaking a little. He asked her if she was cold. Her head went up and down. He pointed to the wagon. The burnt lady was sitting on part of Morris Bird III's jacket, but Sandra managed to pull it out. Morris Bird III braced the burnt lady while Sandra put on the jacket. It covered her like a horseblanket, and she had to roll up the sleeves. Boy, did she ever look like something that had escaped from the Booby Farm. "Thank you," she said. "You're very welcome," said Morris Bird III. Then Sandra again grabbed hold of the burnt lady, and Morris Bird III resumed his pulling. Ah, boy, this was getting to be *work*. The wagon tiddlelumped reluctantly over bits of glass, pieces of boards, hunks of metal, and he hollered back at Sandra to push a little too, if she could. He felt no appreciable lightening of the load, but then he supposed Sandra had her hands full just keeping the burnt lady from falling out of the wagon. He wondered what had happened to Stanley Chaloupka. He kept his eyes on the pavement directly in front of him. He held his breath, grunted, felt redness come into his face. He was pulling with both arms now, and the tiredness was evenly distributed in both his shoulders. Tiddlelump tiddlelump WHUMP BUMP BANG tiddlelump TIDDLELUMP went the wagon over the bits of glass and pieces of board and hunks of metal. Again he thought he heard a giggle. This time, though, he didn't stop or look back. He tugged NOSMIRC KAERTS in spurts, and the burnt lady wasn't nearly as light as maybe she looked. The poor burnt lady. Never in his life had he seen a lady with so few clothes on. Ahhh, this was no time to be thinking about something like *that*. He flapped his lips and told himself he was a dumbhead. Now, all around him, people were materializing. None of them stopped to help him. None of them even paid any attention to him. He heard another giggle. Grunting, he didn't look back. He kept concentrating on the sidewalk. From time to time he looked up and watched some of the people, but most of the time he concentrated on the sidewalk. Most of the people were angry and bawling. Their clothes were torn, and their faces were smudged. Many of them were bleeding. Those who could run were running; those who couldn't were trying. Two men carried a third man who apparently had a broken leg. An old lady wheeled several suitcases and a birdcage in an old babycarriage. A parrot was in the birdcage. It was making argumentative sounds. Another lady ran past, much younger than the babycarriage lady. She was wearing a green bathrobe. Tiddlelump tiddlelump WHUMP BUMP BANG tiddlelump TIDDLELUMP. A man ran past. He was barefoot. He wore nothing but an undershirt and a pair of trousers. He was holding one side of his face and moaning. For some reason, Morris Bird III was reminded of the barefoot man who had participated in the cigarette riot. *Again* he thought he heard a giggle. This time he looked back. Sandra's face was averted. He frowned. This was no time for people to be giggling. Oh well. He'd have a word with her later. He wondered what had happened to Stanley Chaloupka. Somewhere a child was shrieking. Now what good did *that* do? He wanted to holler to the shrieking child to shut up, but he didn't know where the sound was coming from. There were too many other sounds, which made it impossible to locate one particular one. Everything stank. Unh. Whoo. Some load. He wiped sweat off his face with the back of an arm. His baldspots stung. He didn't see the legless man until he was practically on top of him. The legless man lay near the gutter, and he was hugging a trumpet. "Boy!" he shouted. *"You there! Boy!"* he was pointing at Morris Bird III, and hot dog, wouldn't you know it. "Come here!" hollered the legless man. Sighing, Morris Bird III dropped the handle of NOSMIRC KAERTS and went to where the legless man lay. He squatted beside the legless man. "I need help," said the legless man. "I got no legs." Morris Bird III nodded. "Yes," he said. A small grin from the legless man. "Yeah. Well. I guess you can see that," he said. "Uh huh," said Morris Bird III. Then the legless man began shouting things about all the people who had run past him without stopping to help him. He called them pigs. He called them all sorts of other names— most of which Morris Bird III didn't catch because of the noise and all. He figured he wasn't missing much. What he wanted to do was tell the legless man there would be time enough for a discussion of the situation *after*. Finally, after running out of names and breath, the legless man sat up. He nodded toward NOSMIRC KAERTS. Sandra still stood there, and she still was bracing the burnt lady. "You bring the wagon here, boy!" hollered the legless man. "You can give me a ride!" Morris Bird III stared at him. "But what about the lady?" he wanted to know. "There's enough room for both of us," said the legless man. He nodded down to where his legs had been. "I don't take up so much room anymore," he said. Morris Bird III frowned. He had to admit there *was* some room in the wagon. "But what about the weight?" he asked the legless man. "I can't pull all that weight." Smiling, the legless man reached out and seized Morris Bird III by a wrist. He squeezed, and it was like iron. "Don't worry about that," he said. "I'll use my arms to push. I got strong arms. Very strong arms." Hastily Morris Bird III nodded. The legless man released his wrist. He rubbed the wrist. Iron all right, and no fooling. He went to NOSMIRC KAERTS and pulled it out into the street. Sandra hung on tightly to the burnt lady. Tiddlelump, and then they were next to where the legless man lay. Morris Bird III bent down to help the legless man, but he was waved away. "I don't need any help," said the legless man. "All you got to do is hold my trumpet." He gave Morris Bird III the trumpet. Sandra hung onto the burnt lady and made wheezing sounds. The legless man pulled himself upright, or as upright as he could get. Then he maneuvered himself until his head was resting against the side of the wagon. He reached up, pushed the burnt lady as far to the rear of the wagon as she would go. He told Sandra to keep a tight grip on the burnt lady. Sandra nodded, hung on. The burnt lady's legs flopped.

Grunting, the legless man rested his elbows inside the wagon. "*Now* then," he said, and with a great gasp he lifted himself up and in. Breathing hard, he scrunched himself around until he was facing forward. His back was pressed against the burnt lady's side. "I told you I got strong arms," he said to Morris Bird III. "Now give me my trumpet." Morris Bird III gave him the trumpet. "Okay," said the legless man, "we can go now. Hi ho, Silver." He dropped his arms over the sides of the wagon. "You pull. I'll push," he said. "We'll make it." A nod from Morris Bird III. He picked up the wagon handle, turned and began pulling. Behind him, the legless man was grunting. He looked back over a shoulder, and Sandra still had hold of the burnt lady. The legless man was using his arms. NOSMIRC KAERTS moved. It actually really & truly *moved*. "Hi ho, Silver," said the legless man, pushing and snorting. Morris Bird III used both arms for his pulling. He was bent forward like the oldest pack mule in the world. He wondered if maybe his spine would snap. He kept pulling. He pulled so hard he closed his eyes. Unh. Oh. Ah. Whoo. "That's it, boy!" shouted the legless man. "Pull!" Oh boy. Big deal. The man was saying pull. How about that? Morris Bird III flapped his lips. He heard sirens, and the stink was worse. He wondered what had happened to Stanley Chaloupka. His eyes watered, and never mind that they were closed. He opened them, wiped them with a shirtsleeve. Behind him, the legless man kept grunting away. He did not bother to look back. There was nothing behind him that he hadn't seen too much of already as it was. You'd have thought that someone else maybe could have stopped to help the legless man. Boy, how unfair could a situation *get?* Unh. Oh. Ah. Just a little tiny *wagon*, and how come allofasudden Morris Bird III had gone into the ambulance business?

BOBO SKEEWOTTENTOTTLE ALLAH SHHHHH! hollered Harry Wrobleski and the rest of the East High rooters. BOBO SKEEWOTTENTOTTLE ALLAH SHHHHH! YAY, EAST! Their team had just scored its third touchdown, and now the score was East 18, Central 0. So what if East *had* missed all three of the points after! Who cared! Sure, had East made the three points after, the twenty points Harry had given Al Panetta would have been wiped out, but there was nothing really to worry about. East surely would score another touchdown. And anyway, who cared about a lousy quarter? The important thing was that East High was on its way to a *victory*. There were plenty of quarters around. There were few East High victories. It didn't seem like much of a price to pay. The colored boys from Central lined up rather disconsolately to receive the kickoff, and everyone knew why. If they couldn't beat East High, they couldn't beat *anyone*, and no wonder they hadn't won a game since only Methuselah knew when. Harry Wrobleski laughed, and so did Al Panetta, and then they got to talking again about the big fire over there wherever it was. Manhole covers were still exploding. There was no telling how far the gas in the sewer system had spread. Miss Edna Daphne Frost had her radio on. She stood at her side door and looked out at the flames. She could see them quite clearly. They rose well above the buildings that lay between her home and the place the explosion had taken place. She wondered if she should go there and lend assistance. But no, that was ridiculous. She was seventy years old, and she would only be in the way. She *was*, though, terribly worried about that little boy and his sister. Outside her door, the air was thick and dark with ashes and small anonymous swirling things. She went into the kitchen, put on some water for a pot of tea (her stove was electric, not gas), then took a broom, went into the diningroom and swept up all her poor broken dishes. FORTYFOUR BOTTLSH OF BEER ON THE WALL! sang G. Henderson LeFevre. FORTYFOUR BOTTLSH OF BEER! IF ONE OF THOSHE BOTTLSH HOULD HAPPEN HOO WALL, FORTYTHEE BOTTLSH OF BEER ON THE FALL! By this time, police and firemen were estimating that about ten thousand persons would be made homeless by the explosion and all the fires. Mayor Lausche was seriously considering evacuating the entire surrounding area—about two square miles. Everyone watched the unexploded tanks. No one knew what would happen. If the unexploded tanks went, the fires would spread Lord knew how fast or how far. As it was, the little flying wisps and puffs of flame were still setting the small subsidiary fires. *Whumm* and *whumm* and *whumm* went the great orange fire at the liquefication plant, and how long could the other tanks be expected to resist all that heat? The smoke from this main fire had become a good deal thicker, hampering visibility, making it even more difficult for the firemen to get close enough to use their hoses. Added to the terrific heat, the smoke made the situation intolerable for the firemen. About all they could do was stand at a safe distance and watch. And the main fire wasn't the only problem. The sewer explosions had undermined most of the streets. On St. Clair Avenue, a fire truck literally fell through the pavement, vanishing from view. None of the men aboard it was hurt, but it had to be abandoned. The men scrambled from the hole, looked down at their truck, scratched their heads, cursed, walked away. St. Clair Avenue was a complete mess. Broken glass was everywhere. So were fire hoses. So were abandoned trucks and automobiles, even a couple of abandoned streetcars. And then of course there were all the abandoned people. St. Clair Avenue swarmed with them. No one seemed to know quite what had happened. Shielding their faces from the heat, they walked aimlessly, shouted back and forth to each other, buttoned the policemen and the firemen and the MPs and the SPs and the coastguardsmen and the sailors and asked them for God's sake what had happened. And all the policemen and the firemen and the MPs and the SPs and the coastguardsmen and the sailors could do was shrug and ask the people to keep moving, folks; *please* keep moving; walk over to Willson School; that's where you'll find help. But, with all those aimless people wandering about, and with the policemen and the firemen and the MPs and the SPs and the coastguardsmen and the sailors themselves not sure what was happening (at a time like this, who can ever find anyone in authority? who can ever find anyone who *knows?*), with fire trucks and ambulances and jeeps and various other official vehicles picking their way through the ruined littered streets, with the high mad sound of so many people doing so much shouting (and wailing too), with all those voices cutting across each other so mindlessly, thicker than the smoke and infinitely more confusing, St. Clair Avenue and its adjacent streets were an enormous squirming chaos; they were a battlefield (only no one knew who the enemy was and when he would attack again), and no one could understand any of it. Only anger and grief could be understood, and they had nothing to do with reasons.

Falling wires, screams, fried birds, explosions, burning houses, flying manhole covers—everyone milled and shoved, and no one knew the why of anything, not even the people in authority. All *they* knew for sure was that they didn't want to think of what would happen if there was another explosion. Naturally enough, Imogene Brookes thought she knew why Marva LeFevre was weeping. Obviously, G. Henderson LeFevre had arrived home and had told the poor woman he was leaving her. So now Imogene supposed she would have to put up with some abuse from Marva. Well, what harm did it do? The woman would feel better for venting her spleen. (A good figure of speech, that. Nice and gutsy and raw.) The way Imogene saw it, she certainly owed Marva *that* much. So, smiling, she held the receiver a little away from her ear and waited for Marva's weeping to subside. Finally Marva spoke. Her voice was moist, and it was punctuated by little snorts. First she apologized for bothering Imogene, and of course this remark made Imogene frown. Then Marva made a loud nose-blowing sound, cleared her throat and asked Imogene would she mind doing a favor for a friend. Imogene sat down. Whatever was coming, she figured she was better off sitting down to receive it. Then Marva began weeping again. It seemed that Marva's mother had been taken ill. Marva had tried to get in touch with her husband, but he'd left his office for the day, and she didn't have the slightest idea where he'd gone. He should have been home some time ago, she told Imogene. Maybe for all I know he's doin some shoppin. My birthday's in a couple of weeks you know. Well, anyway, my Mommy is sick in bed. My sister Hortense called me just now from Rochester, an she told me Mommy's in the hospital with the pneumonia. Rochester—Hortense lives in Rochester, an Mommy's been visitin her. Hortense's married to a Yankee named Andrews, an this Andrews is an officer of the traction company. *Well* to make a long story short, I tried to get a plane, but there's no planes available, an so I called the New York Central, an there's a train leavin the East Cleveland station in fortyfive minutes. You suppose you could drive me there? I called the cab company, but some little snip at the other end of the line told me there was at least a one hour's wait—so do you mind? I mean, I'd be very grateful. Imogene Brookes pressed her forehead against a palm and told Marva no, it was no imposition. Could Marva be ready in ten minutes? Yes, said Marva, I'm already packed. I'll leave a note for that husband of mine an then I'll be all ready to go. Fine, said Imogene. See you in ten minutes. She hung up. Her tears were salty. She stood up. BALONEY! she said. She ran upstairs and changed into her Red Cross uniform. She called Muriel. When Muriel came into the bedroom, Imogene told her to unpack the suitcases. It's the explosion, she said. I'm needed there. Then she told Muriel to mind the children (Karen, four; Mark, two) until Tom got home. She also told Muriel to tell Tom not to worry. Muriel nodded to all this, began unpacking the suitcases. Quickly Imogene combed her hair, inspected her makeup. She slipped into a coat, ran downstairs and out of the house. The children (Karen, four; Mark, two) were playing in the basement. She hollered down to them to be good, then ran out of the house and across the lawn to Marva LeFevre's place. Marva was just coming out her front door. It was quite a sight. All that flesh, and two suitcases, and a fur coat, and a hat with an honest to the Lord *peacock feather*. Be right with you! shouted Imogene Brookes. She ran to her driveway, backed out her '41 Mercury. She was an exceptionally poor driver. In backing out of the driveway, she dislodged a large round whitewashed stone, one of two that served as ornaments flanking the driveway where it met the street. The car's undercarriage scraped over the stone, and Imogene had to wince. Finally, though, she got the car out into the street. She backed until she was in front of Marva LeFevre's front walk. Marva came running. Everything went every which way. She opened the door and hurled her two suitcases into the back seat. Imogene shuddered for the upholstery. Then, wheezing, Marva slid in next to her. She slammed the door as though she were trying to teach it a lesson. She was wearing too much perfume. She always wore too much perfume. The day never went by but what she wore too much perfume. Imogene shifted gears, and the car shot forward in a great leap. Marva talked all the way to the East Cleveland station. She supposed the train would be full of servicemen (servicemen were always goin and comin; you wondered why some of them couldn't for land's sake stay *put*), and she supposed there wouldn't be a diner, but ah well, it was only six hours, and six hours without food weren't goin to kill her. *Hardly*. Ha ha.

Some joke. Oh some people had such a sense of humor you could fall down and have a heart attack from laughing. Then, chuckling, Marva said she would try to be brave. She said she would try to keep any of the servicemen from pickin her up. She had heard on the radio about the disaster, and so she asked Imogene did the Red Cross uniform mean Imogene was goin there to give succor to the injured, or whatever one did when one was sent somewhere by the Red Cross? And Imogene said yes, she was indeed going to the disaster area, but she'd probably do nothing more exciting than serve coffee and doughnuts. And Marva said oh well, at least Imogene would be able to *share* in the *excitement*. And Imogene nodded. Yes, she said, the excitement. And Marva said: That husband of mine, you tell him I love him hear? And Imogene said: Yes. And Marva said: Keep an eye on him for me huh? He can't hardly fend for himself very much. And Imogene said: I'll keep an eye on him. And Marva said: You're a true friend. And Imogene said: You're very kind to say that. And Marva said: I say it because I *mean* it. I know a friend when I see one. We were lucky when we moved next door to youall. And Imogene said: Mm. And Marva said: My Mommy. My poor Mommy. And Imogene said: I'm sure she'll be just fine. And Marva said: Friends. It's good to have friends. And Imogene said: Yes. You have a point there. Biting her lower lip, she passed a truck on the right, then made a left turn. The truck driver honked, but poo on him. Then she made a right turn, and they were at the station. Marva leaned over and kissed Imogene, who summoned all her hidden reserves of strength and actually managed to smile. Then Marva piled out of the car in a swirl of fur and peacock feather. She smiled back, waved for a porter. Presently an elderly colored man appeared. He wore a uniform that had been clean back in about 1888. Now it looked as though it had been dipped in baked beans and Worcestershire sauce. Marva shouted several paragraphs to the elderly colored man. He nodded, opened the back door of Imogene's car, pulled out the two suitcases. Marva again waved, disappeared inside the station with her superannuated friend. He was staggering a little, and Imogene wasn't so callous that she didn't feel sorry for him. Before starting the engine, she opened her window to let out some of Marva's perfume. She thought about G. Henderson LeFevre. She thought about Marva's poor old Mommy. Well, this was the Act of God she'd been expecting all day. This and the disaster, that explosion or whatever it was. But they were the wrong *kind* of Acts of God. Now G. Henderson LeFevre wouldn't be able to tell Marva. Which meant Imogene Brookes wouldn't tell Tom. And so now Imogene Brookes was wearing her Red Cross uniform. And so now she would go serve coffee or doughnuts or whatever. Well, why not? What else was there to do? Oh that G. Henderson LeFevre was a pluperfect *swine*. Where had he disappeared to? How much of a coward could one man be? Then a policeman came along and brought Imogene out of it. He was quite a handsome policeman, and he had a nice smile. Lady, he said, these are troublous times. We don't want to make them worse. So do everybody a favor and get this conveyance of yours out of the Loading Zone? Okay?

THERE WERE SO MANY sounds—the *whumm* and *whumm* and *whumm* of the great orange fire behind them, the shriek of firesirens, the tinkle and crunch of broken glass, the whip and slap of the flames that were working on what was left of the frame houses along this street, the thick whuffling smeary rolling windblown hishhh of smoke and tiny gritty flying things—that Morris Bird III really & truly couldn't figure out why he was hearing giggles behind him. He kept looking back, but the legless man's face was always straight, and so was Sandra's. Huh. It sure did, as people such as Walter Brennan were forever saying, beat all. If Morris Bird III had had a free hand, he would have scratched his head. But he had no free hand. He was using both of them for the pulling of NOSMIRC KAERTS. This was the thing he had to concentrate on. First things came first. Later he would conduct a thorough investigation of the giggling. Later was soon enough. Right now he was in the ambulance business, and he had to get all these people out of here. The legless man kept pushing with his strong arms, but this didn't make up for all of the added weight. No indeed. The rest of the added weight had to be taken care of by Morris Bird III, old pack mule Morris Bird III, the Charles Atlas of Edmunds Avenue. Hah! A person could almost laugh. But Morris Bird III couldn't spare the energy. He grunted, and his breath came thinly in reluctant little squeaks through the openings between his teeth. He kept his eyes on the pavement, and tiddlelump. He wondered what had happened to Stanley Chaloupka. Then he heard a great splintery crash. The legless man hollered something. He looked up. A burning tree had fallen across the street. All its branches were on fire. They would have to go around it. This meant detouring to the sidewalk. He stopped, dropped the wagon handle, rubbed his hands together. St. Clair Avenue was about a hundred yards beyond the burning tree. A number of trucks and automobiles were scattered across the intersection. He could see a dozen or so people running around, more or less like chickens with their heads cut off. Once he got to the corner, maybe some of those people would help him. Provided they stopped running around long enough. He turned to Sandra and the legless man, told them how he proposed to make the detour. They nodded. Then he told Sandra to hang on tight to the burnt lady. The legless man flexed his muscles, grinned and said: "I'm ready whenever you are, boy." Morris Bird III spat on his hands, rubbed them together, turned, picked up the wagon handle. The heat from the burning tree was really something. He hadn't realized it until just now. He began pulling. The worst part was the inclined driveway that led up to the sidewalk. Both he and the legless man really had to wheeze. Sandra used both arms to prop the burnt lady. Morris Bird III angled the wagon onto a lawn in order to get around the burning tree. The flames were loud. They smelled raw. His chest and belly hurt. Once around the tree, he pulled the wagon back into the street. It was safer in the street, farther from the burning houses. He breathed slowly, deeply. This made it so his chest didn't hurt quite so badly. And then *again* he heard the giggles. He looked back, and this time he caught the legless man grinning. He dropped the handle. "What's so funny?" he wanted to know. He was sort of wanting to cry. The legless man blinked, kept grinning, pointed to Morris Bird III's middle. Morris Bird III looked down. He saw nothing but his stomach. "No! Not your front! Your backside! Your old buttsky! Feel it!" Frowning, Morris Bird III felt the seat of his pants. There wasn't any.

● ● ●

EARLY IN THE FOURTH quarter, East High went over for another touchdown, bringing the score up to 24-0. Harry Wrobleski gave Al Panetta the business about the twenty points. Al grinned, shrugged, said the loss of a lousy quarter wouldn't be the end of the world. Then they got to talking about Jim Roberts, the East High fullback. This fellow had scored two of his team's touchdowns, and it was the considered judgment of Harry Wrobleski and Al Panetta that he was the best fullback in the city, even if the team was pretty awful. As the teams lined up for another kickoff, Harry Wrobleski frowned in the direction of the fire. He frowned, wondered how far away it really was. He got to thinking about his Aunt Barbara. Her home (and *his* too now, ever since the day last year his parents were killed when their car skidded on a patch of wet pavement and climbed up a light pole) was in the general direction of the fire—but ah *nuts*, it was too far away. He'd been able to feel the heat from *this* fire. Their home was what? two miles away? Yeah, a good two miles. The fire hadn't been invented that sent heat that far. No, she was okay. He was dumb for worrying. It was past 4:30, and so far no more tanks had gone up. Still, the firemen were unable to get close to the liquefication plant. They concentrated on the smaller fires and waited to see what would happen. The policemen and the MPs and the SPs and the coastguardsmen and the sailors were detailed to aid the homeless and protect stores from looting. There still was a great deal of confusion. The various official agencies had trouble keeping in touch with each other. Several radio stations had sent mobile units to the scene, and finally a number of these units were commandeered by the authorities. The hospitals were filling up, and about twentyfive bodies had already been taken to the Cuyahoga County Morgue. Most of these bodies were unidentified. Several of them were so badly burnt that their sex could not immediately be determined. Elsewhere in the city, an immense cobweb of rumors was spreading. Nazi bomber saboteurs had blown up the lakefront. Nazi bombers had bombed it. The entire East Side was on fire. The Army Corps of Engineers had been called in to dynamite St. Clair Avenue to prevent the spread of the fire. The explosion had released poison gases. A thousand persons were dead, and the poison gases were killing dozens more by the minute. Mayor Lausche was dead. Streets were exploding. Corpses were piled ten deep. Ah, they were splendid rumors, all of them, properly hyperbolic and chilling. TWENNYSIX HOTTLES OF FEAR ON THE WALL! sang G. Henderson LeFevre. TWENNYSIX HOTTLES OF FEAR! IF ONE OF THOSE HOTTLES TOULD HAPPEN TO BALL, TWENNYFORE NO FI TWENNYFI HOTTLES OF FEAR ON THE WALL! Over on Massie Avenue, Irving Bernstein comforted his mother and mused on the imponderables of fate. He sat at her bedside and held her hand and thought about his father's death and the explosion. If his father hadn't died, Irving Bernstein surely would have been killed in that explosion. Really now, who could understand anything? Irving Bernstein's face was damp, and his tears were coming for more than one reason. He wished he could sort them out. He supposed later would be time enough. Mrs. Elizabeth H. Jones, 9106 Edmunds Avenue, telephoned police to report her grandson and granddaughter missing. Her hands were moist, and she kept having to go to the bathroom. Willie Crosby, a driver for the City Ice & Fuel Co. delivered a load of coal to the home of Herman Richlak, 1845 East 69th Street. As the coal clattered down the chute from the truck to the Richlak basement, Crosby saw something that looked like a football. He snatched it from the clattering coal, and sure enough, it *was* a football. Now then, if this wasn't the great mystery of the age, Willie Crosby didn't know what was. Grinning and shaking his head, Willie Crosby dusted off the football, tossed it on the seat of the truck cab. He would take it home tonight to his son, whose name was Roosevelt and who was ten and who ran like nothing you ever saw. Mrs. Imogene Brookes couldn't find a parking place anywhere near Willson Junior High. She had to leave her car on a dinky little street called Harlem Court—a good two blocks from the school. *Harlem Court.* Great heavens. Some name. She looked around very carefully before she got out of the car. She saw no one. Quickly she got out. After making sure all the doors were locked, she walked toward the school. A colored man grinned at her. Maybe he was grinning at her because of her Red Cross uniform, and then again maybe he wasn't. She hurried across East 55th Street and entered the school. It had that awful School smell. It reminded her of chalkdust and Artgum erasers and girls with pimples on their foreheads. A teacher, a small grayhaired chattering woman whose name Imogene Brookes didn't catch, showed her to the gym. She decided she wouldn't think about G. Henderson LeFevre or Marva LeFevre's poor sainted mother or any of *that*. She hoped she would be given something to do. Anything. NEWS FLASH: She *needed* something to do. Anything. At Thomas Edison Field, Judy Saum glared back at Harry Wrobleski and decided to write him off as a total loss. Miss Edna Daphne Frost sat stiffly in the sturdy old straightbacked chair her maternal grandfather (Bertram Tompkins, 1821–1904) had brought with him from Middlesex in 1838. She rubbed her eyes. She had wept enough today. But why had the little boy lied? He'd seemed like such an honest chap. His story certainly had been plausible, and she'd believed every word of it. And, after forty years in The System, she thought she was a good judge of stories told by small boys. So why had he lied about his name? She'd wanted to telephone his parents to find out if they'd heard from him, but the name wasn't in the telephone book. It listed not a single Morris Byrd, on Edmunds Avenue or anywhere else. Sighing, Miss Edna Daphne Frost listened to sirens and blinked at her lap.

NOTHING COVERED MORRIS BIRD III's old buttsky. Absolutely not a thing. Cautiously he patted it, but all he felt was flesh. His face was warm. Not only was the seat of his pants gone, so was the seat of his undershorts. He was sure glad people didn't catch pneumonia down there. Boy, it certainly had to be quite a sight for the Passing Parade. Drawing a deep breath, Morris Bird III clapped his hands over his old buttsky and tried to decide whether to whistle or wind his watch (he had no watch) or fall through the pavement or sprout wings and fly to the moon or what. Now the heat from the great fire was like a cool breeze in comparison with the immense thumping redness that had come into his face. If his old buttsky were half as red as his face was, he was The World's First Walking Taillight. Oh haw haw. How funny. Morris Bird III, Mr. Lightning Bug. Haw haw. A person could die. Still holding his hands over his old buttsky, he walked to Sandra and told her to give him back his jacket. She told him he was an Indian Giver. He told her never mind that. She told him she would be cold without the jacket. He told her tough. The legless man spoke up, telling Morris Bird III that at a time like this people were too busy to care if part of a person's bottom was hanging out. Morris Bird III looked at the legless man and told him it wasn't his bottom. Sandra told Morris Bird III she wouldn't prop up the burnt lady anymore if he took his jacket. And anyway, said Sandra, what good would the jacket do? It was his *bottom* that was exposed, not his *top*. He told her he wanted to tie the jacket around his middle. So come on, he said, either you take it off or I take it off for you. The legless man spoke up. He nodded toward the burnt lady, suggested that Morris Bird III borrow the kerchief that was around her head, the LONDON kerchief. It was a large kerchief, and it could easily be wrapped around Morris Bird's hips so that his old buttsky was covered. Morris Bird III looked at the burnt lady. For all he knew, she was dead. Frowning, he moved toward her. He didn't particularly want to touch her. Her legs were pale and skinny, and her torn dress hung low in front. Real low. Most of the LONDON kerchief had slipped down over her nose. She sure had pretty hair. He touched one of her shoulders. He felt a tiny shuddering movement. Well, at least she was alive. The legless man nodded and said, "Go ahead, boy. Take it." The poor burnt lady smelled awful. Holding his breath, Morris Bird III bent over her and untied the kerchief. The burnt lady had done a lot of rolling in the dirt, and the kerchief wasn't a bit clean. But, as the fellow had been known to say, any port in a storm. You just couldn't leave your old buttsky out for all the Passing Parade to see. Morris Bird III supposed he should be grateful to the legless man. Now he wouldn't have to endure one of Sandra's weepy temper snits. She could keep the jacket. She could wear it until she fell over dead, for all Morris Bird III cared. He wondered what had happened to Stanley Chaloupka. He opened the kerchief and started wrapping it around his waist. "Hold on," said the legless man. "You let me help you." Nodding, Morris backed in front of the legless man. Grunting, the legless man wrapped it around Morris Bird III's waist so that the part that said LONDON was directly over the exposed buttsky. He left a corner of the kerchief free. It hung almost to the ground. "Now," said the legless man, "you take that corner and pull it forward between your legs and tie it in front of you. Then you'll be like Tarzan.

You'll have your own loincloth. Go on. Do it." Morris Bird III obeyed, and sure enough, he had his own loincloth. He also had a diaper, but he preferred to think of it as a loincloth. After all, when you watched Tarzan movies, you didn't think of Johnny Weissmuller as swinging from tree to tree in a dumb *diaper*. It was a *loincloth*, and no one thought anything about it. After tying the end of the kerchief as tightly as he knew how, Morris Bird III thanked the legless man for the idea. "Forget it," said the legless man. He put his trumpet to his lips, blew a high note. "Forward!" he hollered. Morris Bird III grinned, bent over (testing his diaper—*loincloth* rather—to make sure it held), picked up the handle of NOSMIRC KAERTS. Then, again using both hands, he faced forward and began pulling. The legless man pushed. Sandra braced the burnt lady. Tiddlelump. "This lady your mommy?" shouted the legless man. "No!" shouted Morris Bird III. "Who is she?" shouted the legless man. "I don't know!" shouted Morris Bird III. "You mean you just helped her because she needed help?" shouted the legless man. "Yes!" shouted Morris Bird III, and he wished the legless man would save his energy for his pushing. "Hey! You're quite a boy, you know that?" shouted the legless man. Morris Bird III didn't bother to answer. His chest and stomach were beginning to give him pain again. His breath was like things that hadn't bothered to trim their toenails. "This lady is burnt bad!" shouted the legless man. "You maybe saved her life! You think of that?" Morris Bird III said nothing. He just kept pulling. The legless man was a nice enough old fellow, but he certainly was full of a lot of hot air. The wagon tiddlelumped over a cluster of wires, then crunched through a pile of broken glass. Morris Bird III could have pulled the wagon *around* the cluster of wires and the pile of broken glass, but he was too tired. He didn't waste whatever energy he had left. He kept his eyes on the pavement. He kicked charred boards out of the way. And anonymous pieces of metal. The pieces of metal were so burnt and twisted that it was just about impossible to tell where they had come from. Cars, he supposed. And stoves, refrigerators, bedsprings, radios, anything that was around. He began counting bricks in the pavement. He counted them by twos. The counting was quicker that way. He was up to a hundred before he knew it. He decided it wasn't much fun counting bricks. He looked up.

They didn't have much farther to go. A policeman was standing at the corner of East 63rd and St. Clair. He was the only person there who was simply standing. The others were still running around like chickens with their heads cut off. The policeman pointed at Morris Bird and hollered something. Morris Bird III couldn't make out the words. The diaper—*loincloth*—had become a little binding, but he didn't bother to adjust it. The handle of NOSMIRC KAERTS was cutting into his palms, and his legs were shaky, and his baldspots stung, and his spine felt as though someone were pounding it sideways with a rolling pin, and whatever the policeman wanted could wait until Morris Bird III, *and* NOSMIRC KAERTS, *and* Sandra, *and* the burnt lady, *and* the legless man, arrived at the corner. Morris Bird III gasped, and his tongue hung out, and what he wanted to tell the policeman was: Don't shoot the pianoplayer; he's doing the best he can. And so he returned his attention to the pavement. When the policeman touched him on a shoulder, he just about jumped out of his skin. He dropped the handle of NOSMIRC KAERTS and looked up. "Hey, boy," said the policeman, "it's okay. Everything's fine." He patted Morris Bird III's shoulder and then he made a real good try at a smile. He was a skinny policeman, and his face was red. There was a smudge across his forehead, and one of his shirtsleeves was torn. He looked past Morris Bird III, shook his head and made a clucking sound. "What do we got here?" he wanted to know, nodding toward Sandra and the burnt lady and the legless man. He went to the legless man and squatted. They talked. The legless man waved his trumpet and kept pointing in the general direction of Morris Bird III. From time to time, the policeman nodded. Sandra still hung on to the burnt lady. Morris Bird III looked around. He had no idea what would happen next, didn't particularly care. He was too tired to care. He hugged his chest, rubbed his cut palms together, stretched, got some of the cricks out of his spine. He saw fire trucks and fire trucks. He saw hoses and hoses. He saw sailors. He saw automobiles scattered all over the street. He saw glass. Displays had been blown out of storewindows. Just up the street was a litter of oranges. They lay on the pavement in front of a derailed streetcar. A sailor who wore a white helmet (the letters on it were SP) walked out into the street and picked up one of the oranges.

He wiped it against his funny floppy pants, then bit into it and began to suck. This was St. Clair Avenue, and Morris Bird III was grateful to be seeing St. Clair Avenue again, but he certainly wasn't what you'd have called worked up. There was too much mess, and nothing looked very safe. Up the street, barely a block away, there was a gigantic hole in the pavement. Two firemen walked past. He heard one of them say something about there being a fire truck down in that gigantic hole. He didn't like the looks of any of this. He wondered how much farther he would have to pull NOSMIRC KAERTS before he found a place that was safe. He stared down at his hands. They were shaking. He stuffed them into his pockets. They still shook. He made fists. The thing he wanted to do was hug somebody. Just about anybody. Hon-est. The policeman completed his conversation with the legless man. He straightened, walked to Morris Bird III and said: "Young fellow, you take that right hand of yours out of your pocket. I want to shake it." Morris Bird III looked up at the policeman. Behind the policeman, the legless man was grinning. "Go on, boy," said the legless man. "Do like the policeman says." Morris Bird III made a hollow noise, with-drew the hand from the pocket. He'd certainly done a great deal of handshaking today. First that colored man, then Miss Edna Daphne Frost, now this policeman. He held out the hand, and the policeman grabbed it. The policeman sure did have a lot of teeth. He nodded back toward the legless man and said: "Your friend has told me all about you. You just ought to be pretty proud of yourself, and don't let anybody tell you no different." Then the legless man spoke up. "I told the policeman you're just about the finest boy I've ever known. I told him you're a great boy. *Great.* That's the word I used. I told him, I said: Officer, this boy is the greatest thing since sliced bread. This boy is going to grow into a real man. I told the policeman, I said: The things this boy done, only a *great* boy could of done them." Morris Bird III listened closely to all this, couldn't really make much of it. *The greatest thing since sliced bread?* What was *that* supposed to mean? Did it have anything to do with Mrs. Dallas and old Ulysses S. Grant and the lonely unbending bravery of a Hank Moore? What had Morris Bird III done that nobody else would have done? He couldn't think of a thing. He shook the policeman's hand, smiled a little, tried to keep his eyes averted. Then along came a truck with a big red cross on its side. The policeman waved it to a stop. Two men in white suits and a lady in a gray uniform got out of the truck. They went to the burnt lady and bent over her. Sandra still hung on to the burnt lady. They motioned her back. She looked at Morris Bird III. "It's okay," he told her. She nodded, stepped back. One of the whitesuited men returned to the truck. When he came back, he was carrying a stretcher. He set it down beside NOSMIRC KAERTS. He and the other whitesuited man lifted the burnt lady, eased her onto the stretcher. "It's peanut butter isn't it?" said the first whitesuited man. "It ain't axle grease," said the second. They laughed. So did the policeman. So did the legless man. Even Sandra laughed. Morris Bird III stared at Grandma's sky. Well, what would *they* have done? It's great to criticize when a thing is *done*, but what about when it's *happening?* How come no one's ever around? The two whitesuited men lifted the stretcher and carried it to the truck. They slid it into the rear of the truck. One of them stayed back there with the burnt lady. The other returned. He was carrying another stretcher. The lady in the gray uniform knelt next to the legless man. "Is that woman any relative of yours?" she asked the legless man. "No," said the legless man. "Is she the mother of these children?" she said. "They say no," said the legless man. "Then . . . uh, what I mean is . . . where did she *come* from?" said the lady in the gray uniform. "They found her. They brought her along. They found her, and they put peanut butter on her wounds, and they loaded her on the wagon. What they did was—they saved her life," said the legless man. "My goodness," said the lady in the gray uniform. "Yes. I know what you mean," said the legless man. The whitesuited man unfolded the second stretcher. "All right, old settler," he said the legless man. He and the policeman lifted the legless man onto the stretcher. The legless man held his trumpet to his chest. After he was settled on the stretcher, he motioned to Morris Bird III. "Come here," he said. Morris Bird III went to the legless man, knelt beside him. The legless man reached up, seized the back of Morris Bird III's neck. "Thank you," he said. "You are a great boy." Then he pulled down Morris Bird III's head and kissed him on the forehead. Morris Bird III wouldn't have been more surprised if the legless man had burst into song. Nodding, the legless man released Morris Bird III. The stretcher was carried away. Then a fire truck came careening toward them. It made a wide turn off St. Clair onto East 63rd. They all jumped back. Sandra ran to Morris Bird III, and he hugged her. The fire truck hit NOSMIRC KAERTS squarely broadside. CLONG! and NOSMIRC KAERTS took off. Was it a bird? Was it a plane? No! It was NOSMIRC KAERTS! It flew end over end and hit a telephone pole sideways. The impact loosened two of the wheels. On they flew. When they hit the pavement, they kept rolling. They maybe rolled half the length of a football field. Several firemen were hanging onto the truck. They looked back, but of course the truck did not stop. Both sides of NOSMIRC KAERTS were stove in. It was so much junk. Still hugging Sandra, Morris Bird III took a few steps toward the ruined NOSMIRC KAERTS. Then he sat down, right there in the middle of the street. He dragged Sandra with him. It all had fallen in on him. Whump, just like that. Morris Bird III wept. So did Sandra. You could tell she felt the same way.

FIRE CHIEF GRANGER MADE a preliminary damage estimate of five million dollars. At Thomas Edison Field, Central scored a touchdown. The score was now East 24, Central 6. Harry Wrobleski glared at the East High coach. This fellow's name was Gregory Conly, and he was running in his substitutes. Thanks to this Gregory Conly, Harry Wrobleski probably would lose his quarter. With the substitutes playing it would take a miracle for East to score another touchdown, which meant that the twenty points Harry Wrobleski had spotted Al Panetta were too many. *Two* too many, and how come East High had no one who could kick an extra point? Well, that wasn't a difficult question to answer. You had to score touchdowns in order to get experience kicking extra points. G. Henderson LeFevre got all the way down to eleven bottles of beer on the wall, then passed out. At Willson Junior High, the homeless were being assigned billets in nearby schools, churches and other public buildings. There was a severe shortage of cots and bedding. Doctors and nurses were stationed all over the neighborhood. The great fire at the liquefication plant did not diminish, but

neither did it spread. Mayor Lausche decided to have the entire neighborhood evacuated. At the same time, the East Ohio Gas Co. requested
all its East Side customers not to turn on their gas. The reasons for
this request were pretty clear. What with all that free gas down in the
sewers . . . well, you didn't need a road map. Mrs. Brookes' prediction
came true: Mrs. Carleton put her to work serving coffee and doughnuts to all the people who were streaming into Willson Junior High.
Mrs. Sternad regained consciousness in the ambulance that was taking her to Mount Sinai Hospital. She opened her eyes, blinked. They
stung, and they were quite wet, but she could see. She could see! Right
away she began to cry. Then she screamed. There, lying next to her,
was a man who had *no legs!* She screamed and screamed. Sh, said the
man. Smiling, he patted one of her hands. She kept screaming. The
final score was East 24, Central 6. Everyone on the East High side of
the field gave a great cheer. Grinning, Harry Wrobleski forked over
the quarter to Al Panetta. The East High players ran grinning off the
field. Even the sadsack substitutes were grinning. The world was a
horizon of grins. Harry Wrobleski and Al Panetta were walking out
the main gate when the second explosion came. Again they could feel
the heat. It was about 5 o'clock. My God, said Al Panetta. Nearby,
several girls screamed. At the scene, though, this second explosion
wasn't as bad as the firemen had feared. It was loud enough, but it did
not cause the fires to spread. Casimir Redlich and his wife were re-
united in the Mount Sinai emergency room. Mrs. Redlich had been
cut by flying glass. They embraced, and for a time neither of them
were able to say anything. At Willson Junior High, all sorts of ragged
and forlorn people lined up for Mrs. Brookes' coffee and doughnuts.
Still, a number of men did smile at her, and one even told her how
strongly she resembled that movie girl Loretta Young. Mrs. Brookes
thanked the man, asked him please to move on so he wouldn't hold up
the line. Sure honey, said the man, looking her up and down as though
she perhaps were a slice of sirloin butt. Grinning, he moved on. Sighing, Imogene shook her head, poured a cup of coffee for a little old
lady who wore an orange babushka. Harry Wrobleski told Al Panetta
not to spend the quarter all in one place. They parted at the corner of
Hough Avenue and East 71st Street. Harry and a mob of East and

Central pupils boarded a westbound Hough trackless trolley. At East 55th Street, he transferred to a northbound streetcar. Normally, this streetcar went all the way to St. Clair Avenue. Looking at all the people who were lined up for her coffee and doughnuts, Imogene Brookes got to thinking about the Siege of Warsaw. Certainly most of these people would have been perfectly at home in Warsaw. Why did so many of the women have to wear these absurd babushkas? A person would have thought that the emergency would have made them *forget* their babushkas. Such flat faces and tiny ears. The Face of Mother Poland. Ah, but wait a minute. Someone had told her this afternoon that most of these people were Slovenians. Oh well. Poles, Slovenians—what was the difference. Wasn't Slovenia a part of Poland? Or was that Slovakia? Wait now. That country in Europe, wasn't it called Yugoslovakia? Yugoslovenia? Oh *fudge*. All the people in the streetcar were talking about The Awful Explosion. Harry Wrobleski asked a man where The Awful Explosion had taken place. Somewhere up off St. Clair and 55th, said the man. Oh my God, said Harry Wrobleski. At Superior Avenue, the conductor announced that they had reached the temporary end of the line. St. Clair is all tore up because of the explosion, he said, and the police aren't allowing the cars north of here. The streetcar emptied. Harry Wrobleski began running north. He was just about crying. East 55th Street was darker here, much darker. It was full of smoke, and from time to time, Harry Wrobleski had to cough. His chest hurt, and he was having trouble seeing. He gasped and staggered, and through his head ran a string of words, and they went like this: AUNT BARBARA. AUNT BARBARA. AUNT BARBARA. I WAS AT THE FOOTBALL GAME. I SAT THERE FOR TWO HOURS AND I YELLED AND HOLLERED AND I DIDN'T KNOW WHAT WAS HAPPENING. I DIDN'T. I DIDN'T. IF I'D OF KNOWN WHAT WAS HAPPENING, I WOULD OF COME HOME. AUNT BARBARA, YOU'RE NOT DEAD. THERE'S BEEN ENOUGH DYING. MY POP AND MY OLD LADY ARE DEAD, AND ISN'T THAT ENOUGH DYING? IF YOU'RE DEAD, THEN WHERE DO I GO? WHAT HAPPENS TO ME? PLEASE AUNT BARBARA, PLEASE DON'T BE DEAD. Once, for some idiotic reason, Harry Wrobleski got to thinking that maybe next spring he would go out for the East High track team. As he was sprinting across St. Clair Avenue, with the heat from the great fire slapping at his face and chest, he ran straight into the side of an ambulance. He bounced back, lost his balance and fell down. Groggily, he tried to stand. But he wasn't quick enough. Another ambulance ran over both his legs, breaking them. The sound was audible. Two small children came up to Mrs. Brookes and asked her for doughnuts. The older one, a boy, was holding the hand of the younger one, a girl and probably his sister. A kerchief was wrapped around the boy's waist like a loincloth or perhaps a diaper. The girl wore a jacket—clearly her brother's—and it was about fiftyeight sizes too large for her. One of her arms was bandaged. So were various parts of the boy's head. The top of his head. Patches. Mrs. Brookes gave each of the children two doughnuts and paper cups full of milk. They thanked her, and then they walked away. She had to smile. The word LONDON was printed on the part of the kerchief that covered the boy's bottom, and a simply *dreadful* pun had occurred to her. She winced, and under her breath she began to hum *The Londonderry Air.* In acknowledgment, of course, of the boy's LONDON *derrière.* She shuddered, shook her head, cut off her humming, poured a cup of coffee for a plump woman with a bandaged left ear. The two children sat down on the floor next to a wall. They munched and sipped. Mrs. Brookes thought of her own children (Karen, four; Mark, two), and she got to wondering what they were up to. The doctor's name was Rimmel, and he was very gentle with Mrs. Sternad's burns. She lay in a ward in Mount Sinai Hospital, and a lot of people in this ward were doing a lot of moaning, but Mrs. Sternad made no sounds. She felt no particular pain. She remembered all the pain she'd felt back when she'd had to do all that crawling. She asked Dr. Rimmel what had happened to it. We've given you some sedation, he told her. Then he asked her about the peanut butter. Who had smeared her with it? She said she didn't quite remember. She told the doctor it seemed to her she'd encountered a little boy (or maybe a little girl). At any rate, maybe the little boy (or little girl) had done the smearing. You want to know something? she said. What's that? said the doctor. That peanut butter—it made some of the pain go away, she said. I wouldn't be surprised, said the doctor. Then Mrs. Sternad got

"Okay," said Morris Bird III. He was sitting on the extreme right. Sandra was squeezed in the middle. His diaper—*loincloth*—was too tight, but he didn't have the room to adjust himself.

They were headed south on East 55th Street. They had just stopped for the light at Superior Avenue. "Straight ahead?" said the pretty Red Cross lady.

"Yes," said Morris Bird III. A few minutes ago he'd consulted his map, and he had the route down good. "You keep on going until you get to Hough Avenue. Then you make a left turn."

"Thank you," said the pretty Red Cross lady.

"You're welcome."

The light changed. The pretty Red Cross lady ground the gears, but the station wagon still managed to move forward. "Mrs. Carleton told me your name is Morris. Is that right?"

"Yes."

"And what do people call you?"

"Morris."

"Oh. I thought maybe it was Morry. Sometimes names are shortened."

"Oh."

"And your sister? What's her name?"

"Sandra."

"Does she speak?"

"What?"

"Does she speak? She hasn't said anything yet."

"Say something," Morris Bird III told his sister.

"Hi," said Sandra.

"Hi yourself, Sandra," said the pretty Red Cross lady, smiling. Then, to Morris Bird III: "You'll have to tell me when we get to Hough Avenue."

"I will."

"I live in Shaker Heights, and I don't get to this part of the city very often."

"Oh."

Sandra spoke up. "We had a wagon," she said, "and it got busted."

"I'm sorry," said the pretty Red Cross lady.

"It wasn't even *our* wagon," said Sandra.

"Oh. That *is* too bad," said the pretty Red Cross lady.

"It was Teddy Karam's wagon. He says things backwards."

"Well," said the pretty Red Cross lady, "what do you know about that."

"I'll pay him for it," said Morris Bird III.

"Oh," said the pretty Red Cross lady.

"I just wanted you to understand that."

"I understand."

"You turn left at the next light. It's Hough Avenue."

"Thank you," said the pretty Red Cross lady. She made the turn on Caution, just missing a streetcar.

It was past twilight, and Hough Avenue was all lit up.

"Morris?" said the pretty Red Cross lady.

"Yes?"

"Mrs. Carleton told me about you. She said you'd told her you'd *walked* all the way over there. And just to see a friend."

"That's right. *I* walked. Sandra rode most of the way in the wagon."

"And why did you do it?"

"Why?"

"Yes."

"Because I wanted to."

"Oh," said the pretty Red Cross lady.

"Lady?"

"Yes?"

"It was more than that."

"Yes. I would imagine so."

Morris Bird III was silent. He looked out the window. They were at East 66th Street. Him and his big yap.

"We're still headed in the right direction?" said the pretty Red Cross lady.

"Yes," said Morris Bird III. "Just keep going straight ahead."

"Thank you."

"Lady?" said Morris Bird III, and he wished he had a cleaver so he could cut out his tongue.

"Yes?"

"It was . . ." He hesitated. He looked out the window. He cleared his throat. Then, after making sure everything was swallowed properly, he opened his big yap and said: "I just wanted to do something on my own. I didn't want anybody to lead me by the hand. I wanted to start a thing and go all the way *through* with it."

"You mean selfrespect?"

"I guess so."

"How old are you?"

"Nine."

"*Nine.* My goodness."

Morris Bird III looked out the window.

"I have two children," said the pretty Red Cross lady. "Karen is four, and Mark is two."

"Mm," said Morris Bird III.

"I love them."

"That's nice."

"Selfrespect is a big thing isn't it?" said the pretty Red Cross lady.

"Yes," said Morris Bird III.

The pretty Red Cross lady made a snorting noise.

He looked at her. So did Sandra.

The pretty Red Cross lady smiled.

Morris Bird III also smiled. So did Sandra. Didn't cost anything.

"Selfrespect," said the pretty Red Cross lady, and she passed a trackless trolley on the right.

THERE WAS A THIRD explosion at 5:10, a fourth at 6:45, a fifth at 7, and a sixth and last at 7:45—but none of them was as severe as the first had been, and gradually the great fire was brought under control. It was the bloodiest disaster in the city's history, but it could have been worse—a lot worse. Two of the four liquefication tanks had been destroyed, but the other two never did go up, and neither did the "holder" tank. The fire burned all night, and well into the next day, but no further serious damage was done. At about midnight, Mayor

Lausche ordered the entire area evacuated—but this was more as a precaution than anything else. The threat of danger had passed. The sky was pink and orange all night, but the wind continued blowing to the north, and the fires did not cross south of St. Clair Avenue. Men—the newspapers called them "rescue workers"—went to work poking through the debris for bodies. They found a great many bodies. They kept finding bodies for three days. The final total was one hundred thirtyfive. In addition, some five hundred persons had been injured. And about two hundred buildings had been damaged or destroyed. (A reporter tried to count the number of private homes that had been destroyed. He came up with eightynine. Actually, he counted holes in the ground. He assumed these holes in the ground represented homes.) Chief Granger's final damage estimate was fifteen million dollars. Nobody believed this. Fire departments show great friendship to insurance companies. Thus, fire department damage estimates always are low. Harry Wrobleski and his Aunt Barbara were, as it turned out, patients in the same hospital—Mount Sinai. The next morning, a nurse wheeled him down to his aunt's ward. He shuddered when he saw all the bandages on his aunt's face, and then he began to cry. He told her all about the football game and everything. She reached to him and patted his hand and told him now for heaven's sake, you had no way of knowing, so now *stop* that. Then she asked the nurse for a pen so she could be the first to sign her nephew's casts. She signed both of them. He smiled, and after a time they got to talking about the insurance money. Mrs. Imogene Brookes arrived home at about 2 in the morning. Her husband Tom got out of bed and came downstairs and made her a cup of coffee. He asked her all sorts of questions about the disaster. She told him yes, it *had* been interesting. Not that she had *seen* very much (all of her time, or practically all of it, had been spent serving coffee and doughnuts in Willson Junior High), but the time had passed quickly enough. Then Tom told her a funny story about their next-door neighbor, G. Henderson LeFevre. It seemed that at about 11 o'clock poor old G. Henderson had come staggering home. And *drunk!* Whoo. Like a boatload of billygoats. Tom had heard him singing something about some bottles of beer on the wall as he lurched up the sidewalk. Then, a couple of minutes later, there was a ringing of the Brookes' front doorbell. As soon as Tom answered it, old G. Henderson fell against him and started to bawl. He mumbled something about his wife having gone away, about how now things never would happen, about how *sorry* he was for having gotten himself involved in such a hopeless situation. Yes sir, Tom old boy old buddy, he said, it's all over. No intestinal fortitude. Fun is fun, but living is different, and I'm sorry, but that's the way things are. So please forgive me. I meant you no harm. It was just something that happened. While delivering himself of all this, G. Henderson LeFevre spoke in sharp clipped syllables, and if it hadn't been for the smell of him a person hardly would have known he was drunk. He stood stiffly, and the words came calmly, and then—as soon as the last one was uttered—he passed out. Grunting, Tom Brookes carried him back home, laid him out on his sofa. Now, telling the story to his wife, Tom frowned at her and said: You got any idea what he was talking about? Imogene Brookes sipped her coffee, looked her husband straight in the eye and said: I think he's had a crush on me. These things happen sometimes. A nod from Tom. A nod and a smile. Yes, he said. It's nothing to worry about, said Imogene. Of course not, said Tom. A little later, Imogene went upstairs to the bathroom. She locked the door, stuffed a towel into her mouth. She didn't want Tom to hear. She sat on the Throne, bent herself double, shook, made fists, chewed on the towel. From time to time little mousy noises got past the towel, but they were the only sounds she made. Her guffaws all were silent, even if they did make her eyes water and her nose run.

He was cold. He missed his jacket.

The pretty Red Cross lady had let them out of the station wagon at the corner of Hough Avenue and East 90th Street. He had asked her not to take them straight to their door. All his family would *need* would be to look outside and see a *red cross*.

The walk was just a little more than a block. He and Sandra walked it every day to and from school. It was good to finish the day with a walk. Sort of helped to get things to come out even.

They walked past an apartment building that said ATLAS. They were holding hands.

He would be glad to get home, if for no other reason than to get rid of his diaper—*loincloth*. He glanced at Sandra. The jacket really hung loosely on her. He noticed that his button that said

ROOSEVELT

was gone. He patted his shirtfront. The little plastic donkeyshaped pin that said

FDR

also was gone. He patted his trousers. The button that said

ROOSEVELT-TRUMAN

also was gone. Three for three. A batting average of 1.000. Well, nothing like being consistent. Frowning, he took inventory of the rest of his possessions. He was out a dollar. He was out one jar of Peter Pan Peanut Butter. He was out one cap. He still had the evil penknife, his Gun, seven cents, the picture of Veronica Lake, the compass, the city map. And oh, he was out one alarmclock. And of course Teddy Karam was out one NOSMIRC KAERTS.

He wondered what had happened to Stanley Chaloupka. He supposed he knew. He supposed the best thing was to look it straight in the eye.

He sighed. He rubbed his arms to keep the circulation going. His baldspots stung. In order to rub his arms, he had to let go of Sandra's hand. She didn't whimper.

He let his mind embrace some names. Stanley Chaloupka. Mrs. Dallas. Hank Moore. Grandma. Veronica Lake. Suzanne Wysocki. Ulysses S. Grant. Then he let his mind embrace some people whose names he didn't know. The tall black lady. The burnt lady. The legless man. The pretty Red Cross lady. He decided he was kind of close to bawling.

They turned off East 90th Street onto Edmunds Avenue. Their house was half a block up the street. The porch light was on.

"Morris?"

"Yes?"

She took his hand. "We going to get it bad?"

He nodded. "But I don't care," he said. "It was worth it."

She held his hand tightly.

He was having trouble with his breath. Greatest thing since sliced bread or no greatest thing since sliced bread, his chest was thick and his hands were damp.

Sandra squeezed.

"Onward, ever onward," said Morris Bird III.

Sandra giggled.